BALLAD OF JASMINE WILLS

By
LEE ROZELLE

MONTAG

First Montag Press E-Book and Paperback Original Edition October 2021

Montag Press ISBN: 978-1-940233-97-0
Design © 2021 Amit Dey

Montag Press Team:

Editor: Charlie Franco
Cover: MaDora Frey
Author Photo: Tonia Eden Mayton

A Montag Press Book
www.montagpress.com
Montag Press
777 Morton Street, Unit B
San Francisco CA 94129 USA

Montag Press, the burning book with the hatchet cover, the skewed word mark and the portrayal of the long-suffering fireman mascot are trademarks of Montag Press.

Printed & Digitally Originated in the United States of America
10 9 8 7 6 5 4 3 2 1

Is not this the fast that I have chosen? To loose the bands of wickedness, to undo the heavy burdens, and to let the oppressed go free, and that ye break every yoke?

Isaiah 58.6

PROLOGUE:
SUMMER 1987

Preston prepared his secret project in the smokehouse while Grandmaw listened with her ear to the wall. Grandmaw didn't understand. All the commotion kept her up walking the floor and sucking down nerve pills with a dipper of water. Grandmaw watched Preston out the window as he walked down the moss rock slope to the bend of the creek where he had a five-gallon bucket and his Zebco 33 hidden next to a rotten log. The lure he used was a purple worm, perfect for this time of year in brackish water. Wearing a Beatles t-shirt over his thin frame, Preston cast next to a bunch of sticks on the far bank of the creek only a couple of times before a bass tapped at his line. On the next cast, he got a hit. The rod looked like a question mark when Preston raised it high and expertly reeled it in as it fought. He gave the fish time, not pulling too hard. Holding the gaping fish by its lower jaw, Preston got the hook out and dropped the bass into the water-filled bucket. He realized that the fish looked like Elvis and before long he had caught three decent bass and a bream.

Perfect for Grandmaw, Preston thought as he opened a plastic freezer bag and poured some white powder into the bucket, then dropped in two white pills. The powder fizzed like an Alka Seltzer and the pills dropped to the bottom and started to disintegrate like the conduits in Preston's adolescent mind.

Preston carried the bucket up the rocky slope and down the long dirt road to Grandmaw's house. By the time he got to her door, the fish were belly-up dead with bug eyes. Behind the smokehouse, Preston cleaned the fish on an old board. He scaled the fish with ease, then gutted them and cut off their heads. Preston took the shallow tin pan full of fish fillets around the house to the water hose and sprayed them clean.

"Lord have mercy," Grandmaw said when she saw the fish. She picked them up appraisingly then got the flour and corn meal out of the cabinet. Pouring some into a brown paper sack, she added salt and pepper.

"I'm gone eat me a bait of these," Grandmaw said as she spooned Crisco into the black frying pan. She put the bass into the bag and shook them and when the pan got hot she laid the fish into the crackling grease.

Preston darted into his room and did 25 shoulder rotation exercises and some deep breathing as he knelt at his bedside, then ran to the smokehouse to check on the device that he had been working on, something he called a "prosthetic entertainment system." The wooden construction had clamps, Velcro belts, and long gray straps. From an angle, it looked sort of like a demented dentist's chair made of brand-new wooden planks. He rolled it around the smokehouse for a second, made a few technical adjustments, then ran back to the house and into his room. Preston pulled the dated blue plastic suitcase from under his bed and opened it. The unmistakable wig was there. The rhinestone jumpsuit. The belt with immense buckle. The boots. The golden sunglasses.

"Preston!" Grandmaw yelled from the kitchen. "Come eat this fish before it gets cold."

"Just a minute, Grandmaw," Preston said loudly over his shoulder.

"Get in here and eat."

"Go ahead, Grandmaw," Preston said, stretching his calf muscles and paying close attention to his breathing. He did this for ten minutes then sat down on his bed next to the suitcase and waited. He had heard the ice rattling around in Grandmaw's iced tea, so he knew that she had started wolfing down the fish. Finally, he heard the delightful body "clunk."

Preston walked into the kitchen and saw Grandmaw face down on the table. He picked her up by her shoulders and dragged her with care to the couch, then removed Grandmaw's shoes, her gray flannel dress, and her white flour-sack bonnet. He did not remove Grandmaw's undergarments, an assemblage of pulleys and harnesses unlike any he had seen before.

It took Preston almost fifteen minutes to get Grandmaw into the white rhinestone jumpsuit and shoes, the gold sunglasses, and the boots. The mutton chop wig was easy to get on, just a little pulling and a few touches with the comb.

Preston then ran back to the smokehouse to roll the platform into the living room. *After you get the head and neck right, the rest is easy. And if you're handy with tools,* Preston considered, *you can get dozens of positions.*

Preston worked as fast as he could to get Grandmaw in the first position: on her toes, knees out, both hands clutching the microphone. He then put her left hand in the air, neck turned in profile. He shot this position with and without the lei.

The only thing throwing him off was Grandmaw's pinched mouth, her lips squinched with great lines going out at all angles like the legs of a spider. It detracted from an otherwise perfect effect, especially if you got the knee turned inward just right.

"Aaaagggh," burbled Grandmaw. A big gob of spittle ran down her pale cheek and the gold sunglasses slipped down to the end of her white nose. Preston thought he had put enough of the special sedative in the bass water to knock out a medium-sized dinosaur, but sure enough, she was eyes aflutter as if she were going to wake. Her elbow knocked over a candy jar of small mints she sucked when she had her teeth out, and when the nippled glass clattered on the wooden floor, Grandmaw's eyes opened.

The aura of the idol broken, Preston dry heaved.

"What you done?" Grandmaw asked as she looked at her sleeves and then at herself in the oval mirror on the wall. "You got me dressed up like Elvis Presley." Then her eyes rolled back and she passed out again. Regaining his composure, Preston got two more quick shots of her doing "Blue Suede Shoes" moves--knee in a little bit more--then removed her from the platform.

The next day Grandmaw was slow to get up. She staggered down the small dark hall to the kitchen where Preston anxiously put her cup of coffee on the table.

"You alright?" asked Preston with a frozen grin. "I think you had another one of those spells last night. I heard you howling in there like a hound dog."

Eyes bloodshot and wide, Grandmaw said nothing. Bent over at the table with her hand on her head, Grandmaw sipped chicory coffee with the hangover of her life. She glanced up at Preston with fear in her eyes. Grandmaw stared at Preston for a long time with a baffled expression until her face faded into white malaise.

PART ONE

THE ABDUCTION

SPRING 2015

1

The Tallapoochee Farmers Bank opens at 8:00 a.m., and every morning Jasmine sits in her car and waits for Kay-Lee to come open the door. At the edge of the Tallapoochee National Forest, the morning air holds traces of ragwort, dogwood, and these vagrant pink flowers that pop up at the edge of the road. Oxeye daisies clinging to gravel lean in the wind as the train clanks by. Alabama is beautiful like that, like flowers clinging to gravel. Like Jasmine.

The slow train passes right behind Jasmine Wills as she sits in the bank parking lot with her foggy windows rolled up. Every morning she parks her brown Toyota at the back of the lot at the edge of the train tracks next to the windowless brick wall of the trophy shop so nobody can see what she's doing. Old painted ads for hair oil, grape drinks, and leather shoes fade across brick walls behind her as she eats. The air in the car is hot and clammy, the smell of old food stark and sour under seats piled high with Styrofoam food containers, potato chip bags, wadded-up napkins, plastic soda tops, and dried up freedom fries. The fogged windows protect her from nosy people.

Jasmine has two bags of sausage biscuits from different drive-thrus so that people won't know how many she is eating. She doesn't want to think about how many she gets either, but let's be honest, she's up to five biscuits now. She inhales the fast-food air and unwraps a grease grenade, damp and gray in wax paper that crackles. The first biscuit goes down fast, her face in the rearview mirror looking flat like a frozen apple pie.

Pig, she thinks as she chews.

She turns back and stares for a long minute at the moving rusty brown of empty boxcars. The long graffiti blur stings Jasmine's gray eyes, makes weak lines of pink and orange that break through before she clamps them shut. The colors fade.

Jasmine eats that first biscuit in a type of frenzy, the second in manic guilt, and third in a state of gobbling nirvana. She washes them down with a Mello Yello as big as a child's plastic pail. When she pulls back the plastic paper of the fourth biscuit, her mouth smacks slowly in anticipation and a babyish "um um" comes from her down-turned mouth. Jasmine glances around the parking lot and hides the fifth biscuit in her purse.

Jasmine peers sluggishly through the oily windshield at the brick bank. At 7:45 Mrs. Salters pulls up in her white Mercedes to the "Reserved for Bank President" parking space and takes out her rhinestone-studded bag with the Eiffel Tower on it. With a swish of her white hair, she hoists the gigantic bag onto her shoulder. Chin raised, she struts across the small-town street and tries the locked door, pulls the door a second time, then glances at her watch. Shaking her upturned head fast with blinking eyes, she looks at her watch again. After digging in her bag to find the key, Mrs. Salters unlocks the first door, slips in, locks it back, and disappears into the bank. Ten seconds later a jacked-up truck clatters up to the bank door and a thin blonde jumps out. She has on a blue security guard suit with shirt untucked, hair pulled up in a hasty rubber band, little hickeys up and down her neck. Obediah's truck peels off and the security chief's shoulders sag when she sees the Mercedes in the parking lot. Security chief Kay-Lee Chandler waves at Jasmine who is having trouble pulling herself from the Toyota.

"Salters beat me to the bank again," Kay-Lee says holstering her sidearm, knowing that she was supposed to be at the bank at 7:30 sharp to program the security system and unlock the doors for early employees.

"You're going to get fired," Jasmine says without feeling.

"Probbly."

Kay-Lee unlocks the first door of the bank and pushes the second door open wide for Jasmine. From behind, Jasmine's legs seem not to bend as she walks, the plastic purse swinging from her corpulent, ivory elbow. Through the shirt, Jasmine's body contains latitudinal cracks between inner tubes that encircle her. When she sits down at her desk, she and the leatherette chair both let out long whistles.

Rumor has it that Tallapoochee Farmers is going to be bought out by some big Hong Kong conglomerate, that there are going to be some "big-time changes" and "cuts." But Jasmine doesn't give a crap. She doesn't think about it much. She has sat in this burnished high-ceilinged room with its mahogany staircase and marble floors for seven years and never wonders about the rooms upstairs. She does not look at the landscape painting with its craggy mountain peaks and the log cabin in the far field. They could cover it all with Chinese writing and Jasmine wouldn't care. She deposits money in the bank like she stuffs food into her mouth, with a deadpan face and nowhere eyes. Jasmine's face becomes a configuration of unmoving slits, cocked upward slightly, as the young woman tries to open a savings account.

"Two forms of ID," Jasmine says, her pudgy knuckles positioned like tanks on the desk.

The young woman digs in her bag, glances at Jasmine with a quizzical smile, and pulls out her Social Security and library cards. She is a thin Hispanic woman wearing a black turtleneck and jeans. Sitting with hands in her lap, she holds a small Gucci purse.

"Proper ID," Jasmine says.

"This is proper ID," the woman says. "It's me. The library is across the street."

"I can't pronounce this name," Jasmine says holding the card away from her with index finger and thumb as if it were a dead rat. "Mon-go-li-to?"

"You don't have to pronounce it," the woman says, "for me to open an account."

"Don't you have an Alabama driver's license?"

"No, I don't drive."

"You *don't* drive?"

"No."

"How do you get to work?"

"What's your problem?" the young woman says. Mrs. Salter's head pops out of her office as she talks on her cell. She stares for a second at Jasmine and her head disappears. With a scowl and exaggerated effort, Jasmine pulls the requisite paperwork out of her desk. She goes through the instructions, pointing the pen at the places the woman is to fill out, her voice becoming suddenly loud.

"And you got to have two hundred dollars." Jasmine repeats loudly with extra movement in her lips, *"two hunnert dollahs."*

The young woman pulls a big roll out of her purse, drops it on the desk with a thud, and crosses her arms.

Jasmine frowns at the money.

"You count it," the woman says. With pursed lips, Jasmine picks up the roll of bills and waddles off to the teller.

It's 9:03 a.m. Jasmine sits on the commode in the bank stall holding the fifth biscuit. She thinks nobody in the office knows, but everybody knows. They are too polite to talk about these things, but they know she goes to the bathroom to sneak comfort food all the time. Jasmine slides the biscuit in its stained wax paper wrapper out of her plastic purse. She can see the biscuit through the wet paper, but still, it crackles when she tries to quietly unwrap it. The white tile bathroom amplifies sound, so she always tries to keep the crackling down.

Dammit, Jasmine thinks as the door opens and she sees the red high heels pass the stall. *That little hussy'll be in here for a half-hour fiddling around with her hairdo.* And indeed, the new girl combs her hair for what feels like an eternity while Jasmine sits frozen holding the sausage biscuit like a safecracker in a spotlight.

Jasmine has a dilemma because if she tries to put the biscuit in her purse it will crackle. She can't eat it, because the wrapper will crackle worse. After a few minutes, Jasmine does the only reasonable thing. She flushes the commode and crams the biscuit down in there. The water in the toilet begins to rise and Jasmine starts freaking out knowing that they are going to have to call the plumber and they'll find the biscuit and everybody will know that Jasmine put the biscuit in the commode. Water fills the bowl like shame, Jasmine's sweaty temples beating out the time as the second-hand on her wristwatch spins. To Jasmine's relief, the commode sucks the biscuit down the pipe with a comforting woosh.

The brand-new teller, Meghan Oswell, glances over her shoulder to see Jasmine wrench herself from the stall. Meghan turns back to the mirror and Jasmine stands at the far sink looking at her own red and sweating grimace in the glass. Jasmine turns on the sink and dabs the sweat from her face with a brown paper towel. She exhales loudly, her mouth making a whistling sound.

"You alright, honey?" Meghan asks as she runs a brush through her hair. Eyes bulging, Jasmine turns her dark face like a slow owl and glares. Meghan tosses her silky hair over her shoulder and keeps brushing.

Back at her desk, Jasmine stares into the void. She looks across the sunlit room at Meghan Oswell and the other tellers making deposits and cashing checks. They're putting money into little white envelopes and giving the customers' children suckers. Jasmine's been stuck back over here for three years between two aging debutantes with big makeup and bigger hair. Jasmine's desk is different from the other two desks. The other desktops are filled with ceramic animals, framed pictures of grinning children, potted plants, finger paintings, Kleenex, lotion, purses, gigantic tote bags, and half-eaten bags of microwave popcorn. There are jars of pens with huge silk flowers attached, and on birthdays these women's desks are filled with roses and balloons. There are quaint cards attached, little notes written by husbands who play golf and hunt Wild Turkey. The women who work from these desks--Lorrie and Mandy--loudly talk all day about their kids' tee-ball games, great recipes for cheese dip, and the reality show *Survivor*, all over the head of a benumbed Jasmine. It's kids kids kids, dips, dips, husbands, and home repairs. They hang out all day rubbing their hands with coconut-scented lotion, eating microwave popcorn, and talking on their cellphones while Jasmine sits there staring into the void.

No balloons ever hover over Jasmine's desk. Nobody talks to her about cheese dip. It's not as if the people at the bank hadn't tried to "bring her around" and "get her up to speed." Lorrie and Mandy have tried to get her to go with them to lunch, but she won't go. Instead, Jasmine totters away with a shake of her head and sneaks off to eat alone. They see her in the back corner of Three Amigos facing the wall, all hunched over trying to hide her jumbo tortilla chicken salad bowl slathered in nacho cheese dip.

"It's just pitiful," Lorrie and Mandy say over their shared chimichanga.

The tellers and even Mrs. Salters have tried to draw her into conversations, to get her to open up, but they just end up standing there blabbering the whole time and all she does is respond with is the occasional grunt. It gets old after a while.

Jasmine's desktop, sticky with lemon furniture polish, holds a computer terminal, a telephone, a digital clock, and a flat paper calendar. Big empty white squares mark the days, and at 5:00 p.m. they get crossed off with a big black "X." The only personal things on the desk are a Pensacola snow globe that when shaken fills with glittering snow over a sunbathing pig in sunglasses on a plastic beach, and a faded little doll in a clear plastic case, the kind that opens its eyes when you stand it up. The doll doesn't work though. She got that doll at the Big Time Pies Christmas party back in 1988. Her father bought the Pensacola souvenir on the way back from her first and only trip to Disney World.

Now that had been a horrible trip, Jasmine thinks as she looks down at the snow globe, *it was just plain sad*. Because sadness is saddest at the theme park, like how a fat lady looking in the funhouse mirror only looks fatter. Jasmine remembers her dad riding the merry-go-round, he was riding a big green turtle, going up and down. He was wearing his short-sleeved button-down shirt and shriveled tie even then. She was watching him perched on the top of the turtle, a cheerless purse-faced little pieman. He looked so blank, beaten, even on vacation. When he and Jasmine sat in the Ferris wheel, they were staring off into flashing yellow amusement lights, silent and morose as their ride rose and fell in sunny arcs.

Jasmine's daddy. The pieman.

He was a man always exhaling, pushing up loose and heavy glasses, a dying distant constellation in his eyes. He had flat brown hair that made his head look like a cube. Then there was daddy's clunky glasses and the way that he would sit eating a pale hamburger slobbered in mustard and ketchup. It was all in the way daddy would hold his plate, looking at a gob of leftover Rice-A-Roni without judgment or remorse. *It's the way you look,* Jasmine thought, *when you're looking at your foreclosure papers.*

Jasmine remembers the time a drunk man drove up beside her father at the red light. He balled up his fist and yelled at daddy, called her daddy a "zigzagging, brake-riding little pork chop lip son of a bitch." Daddy looked down at the steering wheel until the man peeled ahead, swerving between the lanes. *Always shrinking, daddy survived by hiding right in front of you.*

In the air-conditioned hum of their Florida beach motel, Jasmine and her father had sat in silence on the floor and took turns shaking the Pensacola souvenir. Remembering his little rabbit eyes as he watched the snow spiral makes Jasmine's chest pang with regret. He had looked at the souvenir and smiled like a child, shaking it and looking to her for approval. *Snow on the beach. Daddy was too fragile for this world.*

Jasmine clamps her eyes shut for a second, rubs her broad forehead, and stares vacantly for an hour into the open space of the bank.

After an early lunch break, a drive-thru enchilada special with extra cheese, her head begins to bob. Echoes of the tellers' voices lull Jasmine, and her subconscious tugs like the shade of a child. Tiny fingers pull at her, making her want to sleep. Jasmine's breathing gets heavy, eyelids closing, her mouth opening just a crack.

Sit in that bank for seven years and you start to get tired.

Her mind wanders through the little house she bought just last year, a small two-bedroom brick and stucco home in the new subdivision. From the front of the house extends a large, empty garage along a level street of empty garages. Crooked "For Sale" signs lean like tombstones in the browning pre-fab grass. Surely there are inhabitants in some of those homes, people and ideas that move from the white tile of the kitchen to the empty bedroom closet. But there is this feeling that nobody lives there, the narrow sheetrock halls empty with no pictures or maps, no photographs of toothy families at amusement parks, no still life fish on long green platters, no decorative crosses. Ghosts seep like filtered air through the metal ducts but never take shape, and Jasmine's mind stumbles from empty kitchen cabinets to shelves to find the cupboards bare. There is only a little skeleton stacked in the corner, traces of moments that add up to nothing. The only thing worth remembering is Parrish in the pool, the underwater lights marking his pale body with blue and yellow ribbons when they were renting a one-bedroom in East Tallapoochee, the place with the refrigerator that made a constant sound like pouring water on a fire.

"Madam?" the man says, sitting in one of the two brown chairs that face her desk. This weirdo from the street had crept up on her.

"Can I help you?" she scowls and picks up the phone pretending to take a call. Jasmine then looks at the man, stares at him closely, and puts the phone back down on the receiver. The man is sitting in one chair but his head is leaning over the other.

No other way to say it, Jasmine thinks. *He's bent.*

That hair, god-a-mighty.

The hair is the salt-and-pepper mop of a deranged, middle-aged Beatle, cut just like peak Paul McCartney. But his round glasses make him look like some kind of broke-back John Lennon. The milky blue eyes seem to shift from calm to shock, then back to calm. His body does the same thing, spider-like and jittery.

He ain't right. And that grin.

The grin is toothy in a way that makes people want to point and laugh, or look away. And of course, there's the crook. Jasmine thinks the guy's a leaning tower of loony. She purses her lips and waits for him to say something. But he doesn't. He just sits there grinning in his smelly sweatshirt as the changes in his eyes alter his whole appearance. With calm eyes, he looks like you might find him at a facility for special needs cases. *Then they go Manson on you.*

"The bank website doesn't show the interest paid," he finally says as his elbows pop up onto her desk. It sounds like the man is trying to talk through his nose. There is something more than oddly Beatleish about him, and not just the hair and the glasses. But she's not thinking "Let It Be." It's more "Helter Skelter."

"Why, yes sir it--"

"--interest paid monthly for CDs."

"That information is posted quarterly."

"It's supposed to be posted monthly."

"Some CDs post monthly, sir," Jasmine explains as she rolls her eyes. "Some quarterly."

"I would like to know how much interest I have earned."

"When you get your quarterly statement--"

"--I want to know *today*," the man seems to be struggling, his out-of-control hands moving to different parts of the chair.

"Is there any particular reason?" Jasmine asks. "If you break your CD before--"

"--I have a right," he says, reaching for Jasmine's Pensacola snow globe, his voice different from just a second ago.

"Sir, I'm going to have to ask you not to touch that snow globe. Sir?"

The man shakes the water-filled souvenir and watches the snow with an alien gleam. He huffs and puffs as he shakes it some more, looking down at the little pig in silver snow. Out blasts this clownish guffaw and the wrong kind of grin.

There is a button under Jasmine's desk that she can press in case of emergency. This button sends a signal to security chief Kay-Lee's beeper. Jasmine presses it and seconds later she sees Kay-Lee walking slowly to the desk, hand resting on her pistol, elbow extended and head down like a shocked alley cat. Kay-Lee had been out back on a smoke break, so she is still wearing mirrored aviator sunglasses.

"Mister," Kay-Lee says. "Put it down."

The man looks from the security guard to the heavyset woman sitting across from him who has her nose curled and cheeks pulled back like she's sniffing something rotten. He puts the souvenir back down on the desk as Mrs. Salters walks up with a flourish.

"Preston!" Mrs. Salters says with a wide smile. "I didn't know you were back in town."

"I'm here, some," he says, meek all of a sudden.

"Ladies, this is Preston Price. He's a real live celebrity. This man has been on stage with Suzanne Sommers!"

"For real?" Kay-Lee says. "Are you like an actor?"

"Not sometimes," Preston coughs onto the back of his clenched fist.

"Preston used to make exercise videos in Hollywood," Mrs. Salters says.

"Which one was you in?" Kay-Lee says. "I might have seen you."

"My most popular title was *Butt of Iron II*," Preston says between tight lips.

"Dude I used to see that at the video store all the time," Kay-Lee says, her face aglow. "You were on the back of the box!"

"That was before the fall," Preston says.

"Fall?" blurts Kay-Lee.

Preston's eyes flash, his teeth extending from the taut face.

"That's quite enough," Mrs. Salters says.

"No, that's OK," Preston says after a pause. "Let's just say that after I went through that stage in Honolulu, my head was in one bed, my feet in another. Two beds." Preston makes a peace sign. "They had to pull the other bed at an angle so I could sleep."

"Ooh," Kay-Lee says. "That's gotta hurt."

"It did hurt," Preston says nodding. "It did."

"In any event, we're glad you're home," Mrs. Salters says. "It's so nice to see you." Mrs. Salters leans down to hug him. He cringes. "Jasmine, please take care of Mr. Price right away."

Jasmine grunts in exasperation.

For a while, Jasmine and Preston stare at each other, neither displaying any expression. It's high noon. The second hand on the big clock spins. After Preston's fingers start to flutter, Jasmine turns to her computer and begins to push keys on her keyboard. She walks back to the printer in the conference room. As he waits, Preston can see Jasmine through the glass window slurping a yellow fluid and wiping her lips. She does this for a very long time, slowly sipping then gingerly wiping, occasionally glancing at the crooked man with a "Just sit there hippie and wait" smirk on her face that only a battle-worn office manager can make. But just as Preston pulls himself up to find Mrs. Salters, Jasmine totters back to the desk looking at the pages, scowling and shaking her head.

"You said you *think* you are getting interest?" she says and looks back and forth from page to page.

"I *am*," Preston says and tries to catch a glimpse at the sheets.

Jasmine shakes her head again, looking back at the first sheet.

"What do you gain from being this way?" Preston says in monotone.

"Doofus," Jasmine coughs into her hand. She takes a red pen from her desk, stares at it for a long time, and starts to chew on it.

"*Heh heh heh heh heh,*" Preston jeers, his face fills with menace, his mop-top over his eyes.

"Mister?" Jasmine leans backward in her leatherette chair.

"*Heh Heh HEH!*" He bolts up with a flourish, his crooked laugh the grave blast of a vaudeville villain.

"I am going to call security if you don't--"

Preston does a strange thing, the deranged mouth now frozen in a wide sardonic grin. He's a scary clown doing a scary trick. With the air of a magician, he extends his arms toward her, puts the tips of his thumbs together, and points his index fingers at the ceiling. He peeps through the square that he has created with one lunatic eye and bursts forth face to ceiling with a Vincent Price cackle. The effect is pure music hall terror and onlookers across the bank gasp. The impression the gesture gives is that he is capturing Jasmine's image on his imaginary screen.

Bunch of a-holes, Jasmine thinks, driving back to her house as fast food signs loom in the glaring sunset. *It's been one of those days.* Jasmine tells herself that when she gets to the intersection that she will keep driving, she won't turn the wheel. She'll eat the cellophane bag of salad that's waiting for her at home. Another part of her mind tells her that she should have gone the short way through the backwoods and missed the drive-thrus altogether.

No doubt about it, something inside tells her, *you'll turn.*

As she draws nearer, the stark lights of burger heaven eclipse the sun. Jasmine is sweating now, her crowded heart beating faster. The red light catches her at the intersection, and she can see the people sitting there slumped over their plastic trays. Big chicken fried steakburgers and chili cheese fries are being stuffed into big, woeful faces. Pale, bloated children in hooded coats stand near the door. Flattened ketchup packs dot the asphalt as a bony boy with a haywire haircut and long silver chains circles the parking lot, round and round the clock. The place has the aura of glaring sorrow, and Jasmine needs it. She craves it like a vampire needs a neck. The drive-thru window is the threshold of Jasmine's abandoned hope, and when she is feeling low these lifeless teenagers hand her greasy-bottomed paper bags and slide the window closed. The bags are filled with failure. When Jasmine gets the bag she feels the defeat in her heart, but that doesn't stop her from tearing into it like a crazed river horse as she snatches the steering wheel back into traffic. For the few moments, while she gobbles the food, her body hums like a low kazoo and the hurt goes away.

She thinks for a moment about her mama, the large and solemn woman who worked at the daycare across town so that Jasmine could go to the daycare closer to home. Mama also worked a double shift on Wednesdays and Fridays at the factory where her father was the assistant foreman. For a second an image flickers in her mind of her mother on the back docks whirling a forklift one hundred eighty degrees loaded with boxes of pies as her father sat slumped in the tiny corner office. He's staring out at her through the glass window. That's what Big Time Pies was all about back then.

Mama would shrug and roll her eyes when asked to ride the roller coaster or do anything fun. It wasn't that she was scared. Mama just hated being put in a position where she had to feel good. See, Jasmine's mama never danced. Mama covered her jowly face if she even smiled at a funny joke and made a point of saying something awful about every photograph that was ever taken of her. On vacation mama and daddy would stand at the beach with their backs to the water, faking puzzled merriment when other vacationers walked by. Jasmine knows that it's not so much what they did to you, the parents. It's what they did to themselves.

And then it happens, just like that. The memory brings lines of orange onto the horizon and the bottom half of the sky is green. The country music on the radio becomes a yellow swirl. Jasmine's mind clamps down on the images and focuses on the odorless food. The tasteless food. The colorless food. Because the food blocks things out. The food is peace.

Within minutes the feeling is gone, the greasy, pungent double burger and jumbo fries are already in her body building a white wall around her. Jasmine pockets it all up inside her, encased in body layers. Jasmine searches the seat and her shirt for crumbs and sucks at random ketchup packets feeling utterly abandoned. It's a lonely ride home, the radio set on a country station, the windows fogging, Toby Keith fading. Turning on the stark lights of her empty house, the endless channel searching. There are pieces of furniture that everybody seems to own, leatherette couches sticking to sweaty legs all over the nation, flabby backs pressed against fake shower glass, baby blue towels made of Jiangsu polyester. This is how Jasmine ends her days, out of breath as she suffers to roll onto the squeaky bed, the expiration of a country. Her midnight dreams slowly bob to the surface like turtles in a pond. Jasmine doesn't know what she has done, the crooked man dropped from memory in her sleep.

2

But after her showdown with Mr. Price, Jasmine does begin to have the vague sense that she is being watched, by postal workers. Driving to work, Jasmine starts to feel like the men in blue shorts and white Panama hats are staking her out. When a Post Office van pulls beside her one early morning in the Tallapoochee Bank parking lot, Jasmine leans her seat back all the way clutching a biscuit, and waits, frozen until it eases away. Now she often sees Post Office vehicles behind her on her way to work, and yesterday a suspicious white Jeep pulled away from her mailbox. When Jasmine returns to work, she notices that strange man Mr. Price outside the bank staring through the window, the shadow of his crooked body zigzagging the length of the marble floor. He seems to be smiling, even as his bent body twitches. He looks to Jasmine like a roach that just got a squirt of poison. And her Pensacola snow globe is missing.

When Jasmine reports Price to Mrs. Salters for loitering, she tells her to be very nice to the man because he is a "valued customer." When Jasmine pulls up his accounts on the computer, she knows why Mrs. Salters sucks up to him like that. Loony or no, this joker is rich up one side and down the other. Mrs. Salters says that Mr. Price had been at the right place at the right time, twice, that after the lucrative fall on set in Hawaii he had designed entertainment technologies that were later purchased for great sums by Pixar. Mrs. Salters had seen that in the entertainment news column of the *New York Times*, which reported that he was bought out of some web-based digital studio, a group called Liminoid.

"And," Mrs. Salters says in a continual nod, "he *is* the third cousin of *the* Vincent Price!"

"I don't even know who that is."

"So if Mr. Price wants to know his interest," Mrs. Salters says, "tell him his interest. And Jasmine, honey, while you are at it, do try to smile." Mrs. Salters turns and walks back to her office, her expensive heels tip-tapping on her father's marble floor.

Do try to smile. The words slip down Jasmine's throat and she chokes it back up like gristled patty sausage. *Do try to smile.*

Mrs. Salters said it in the same way that Miss Cleecher had said it on the way to Camp Calvary. Jasmine recalled that deflated feeling when she saw the white church van in the driveway, the year Miss Cleecher got the Lyme's Disease.

"This is going to be fun, so do try to smile," Miss Cleecher had said. A school teacher who worked at the camp during her summers off, Miss Cleecher looked like a middle-aged muscular gentleman with a perm, precious curls gracing her forehead and shoulders. A perennial outcast herself, Miss Cleecher prepared the children in her care with the compassion of a combat drill instructor. Eight-year-old Jasmine slugged to the back seat of the van as it lurched forward in the miasma of dirt road dust. In the metal hollow Jasmine turned to look out the back glass at her shrinking home, her father standing in the front yard holding a crimped water hose.

The sun always burned Jasmine good on her first day at Camp because she rarely played outside. By lunch she was a purple toad, entirely without neck, scowling knee-deep in the cold waters of Lake Guin. They had put a big clot of sunscreen onto her nose, too little too late, and gave her a scratchy new Camp Calvary t-shirt with a grinning cartoon Jesus on it. The crucified Jesus had large biceps and hair like Merle Haggard. "For All You Do, This Blood's For You," the t-shirt read.

Jasmine stood knee-deep in the water, stiff as a board, scowling as the rich boys cruised by in their little motorboats. Suddenly she was grabbed around the waist and dunked. Sputtering she looked up at the backs of kids too bored to dunk her again.

"Hey sweet thang, wanna ride?" a rich boy in a boat had said as she stood there feeling like a greased pig.

Jasmine had her first shot of Vodka and her first black eye at Camp Calvary. She remembers the girl who had Chinese throwing stars in her rucksack and the girl with the rebel flag tattoo on her tiny shoulder. Jasmine had never seen stuff like that before. Nights at Camp Calvary were boys sneaking into the girls' cabins with half-bottles of stolen Wild Irish Rose and packs of Pall Malls. One night two kids wriggled together on one of the lower bunks, a wool blanket over them. Jasmine could see what they were doing and instant tears had come to her eyes.

The morning hymns in the retreat center went on in an unending coronach, on and on like a gut-shot animal groaning. After an hour of the music one morning Jasmine's mind got caught up in the rhythm and something inside her started to hum like a low kazoo. She felt her nipples harden and the body part that her mama called her "cooter" tingled. And her brain tingled, like the time she passed out in front of the school water fountain. As the children sang, Jasmine leaned forward and closed her eyes, the tips of her fingers on her temples.

Is this the Lord?

Colors and shapes hovered over Jasmine's eyes as low pink bubbles floated across the retreat center set to pop. The tingling started again and she figured that she was getting what her Maw Maw called "on fire." She could tell that the other flushed girls were feeling this too, or something like it, and her face bloomed.

But this couldn't be evil. It had to be the spirit, the Holy Ghost.

Jasmine had opened her eyes, afraid the spirit would take her in front of Miss Cleecher. She bit her bottom lip and made the tingle die down by blocking the music out of her mind. After the morning singing, she was relieved to jump into cold Lake Guin with the other girls. As they cackled and splashed, Jasmine wrapped her arms around her knees. She became a turtle, held her breath with a gasp, and sank under the brackish water as long as she could.

The cabin girls were wicked, their angular bodies and faces a sharp reproach to chubby Jasmine. They circled her like barracudas, their hands snapping forward from all directions to pinch what the girls called her "jellyfish tits." Jasmine's embarrassing breasts would be mottled blue after a week at Camp Calvary. The girls would cram Jasmine into Miss Cleecher's stand-up locker and beat on it until Jasmine begged to get out. They would kick and lean the locker, the wire coat hangers swinging wildly in the

95-degree heat, and in the hot dark Jasmine would scream until she couldn't breathe, drool running down her mouth onto her shirt. When they did open the door, she would fall on the floor and gasp on her hands and knees, spittle running down her chin onto the floor.

Once she wet her pants in the locker and fell out with purple blood coming out of her mouth and the girls ran out of the cabin to the snack pavilion. Jasmine gagged on her blood, she had bitten a hole on the inside of her cheek, but she didn't tattle to Miss Cleecher. She put a sanitary napkin in her cheek for the day. The next day the girls gave Jasmine a break and put afflicted Bekkah into the locker instead. Jasmine was surprised to find that she was the one beating the locker with a nameless passion. Jasmine beat the locker hardest of all, screaming shrill bad words into the holes in the door. When Bekkah came out of the locker, she just stood there, stared at Jasmine, and said nothing. Jasmine remembers sitting at the muddy edge of Lake Guin and pushing the tongue depressors she had glued together in the shape of a cross into the water and letting it float away.

Images of Camp Calvary sometimes emerge in Jasmine's mind, like staring down at cold fried chicken fingers on a Styrofoam plate, dropping her arrow at the archery range and hearing the bow twang. Year after year, Camp Calvary had strengthened Jasmine's feeling that she was a nobody and a never-would-be. It was there in the blank face of the overaged stable boy with the creepy eyes and beer breath, there in the dehydrated Sunday school teacher in shiny silver high heels, there in the crow squawk of the degenerate Vietnam veteran archery range captain who was always talking about his "hem'royds." Everything seemed to propel her into a life of ill-lighted rooms and processed meals. Everything shriveled in the waters of Camp Calvary, and the sun burned.

Most of all she remembered the day all the girls in the cabin cried. They just started crying together without warning. Girls, looking like young gazelles, standing around a single bunk bed in a circle, all suddenly crying, nobody quite knowing why, with their pubescent tears and open-mouthed lamentation. Even afflicted Bekkah was crying. Feeling the colors inside her, Jasmine did not cry, instead, she shook her toad's head and let the screen door slap behind her. When she looked into the distance, she realized that she was the only one who knew that Lake Guin was awash in pink. Dr. Nahal would later say that Jasmine had a condition known as synesthesia, that her senses were wired together a little bit differently, but Jasmine always knew that this feeling was God.

Jasmine is shaken by Meghan Oswell's red heels clacking toward her across the foyer. Meghan stops at Jasmine's desk, an envelope in her hand.

"What?" Jasmine says.

"A drive off at the window," Meghan says holding out the envelope.

Scrawled in red ink: "JASMINE WILLS."

Jasmine looks at the envelope, frowns, and shakes her head.

"Take it," Meghan says, open-eyed. "It might be from an admirer."

Jasmine's cheeks bulge like half-inflated balloons as her expression turns hard.

"What are you afraid of girl?" Meghan says. "It could be a love letter."

Jasmine looks up at this little pink doll. *She's being serious,* Jasmine thinks, *she believes that someone might be interested in a lemon-filled doughnut like me.* She has never had her valentines returned to her at school, never had a husband leave her. Jasmine thinks that at best this letter is a prank.

"Did you see the car?" Jasmine asks.

"That's the funny part," Meghan says dropping the envelope on Jasmine's

desk.

"It was a Post Office van."

"How is that *funny*?" Jasmine snarls.

"Going postal?"

"That's stupid. Leave me be."

Jasmine puts the envelope inside her desk and leaves it there as the hours slug past. People are opening accounts, getting cash out of their accounts, ordering more checks. As the afternoon blurs, the envelope expands in Jasmine's mind. She thinks about putting the unopened letter into the shredder out of spite. She wants to open it but worries that reading it would give the a-holes power over her.

Am I being stalked by the postman?

Two days later, another envelope comes in the mail. Same handwriting, same red ink. Then Meghan says that she found a third letter in the bathroom stall where Jasmine hides to eat biscuits.

She does not open the letters. To open them would be to get involved in their scheme, whoever the hell *they* are. Jasmine's eyes scan the bank, looking at her co-workers. Some look back at her, some glance away as they talk to each other. Jasmine glowers at them all. When she turns back toward her desk, her Pensacola souvenir has reappeared. Jasmine squints, shakes the globe, and watches the snowflakes swirl around the little sunbathing pig.

Standing at the tinted windows of the second glass door, Jasmine sees a figure inside her car. Jasmine's body snaps upright and she crouches behind a fake banana tree and watches. There's a woman in the driver's seat of her brown Toyota, her shadowy head frozen. Jasmine watches as the woman gets out of the car, closes the door, and walks toward the corner. Jasmine recognizes her. She came into the bank with a roll of bills, a library card, and an attitude. It's that Mexican bitch, *Mongolito*. Jasmine recognizes her even with the dark tortoiseshell sunglasses and trench coat.

Jasmine follows with her eyes as the woman turns at the corner and disappears. Jasmine decides to cut through the side alley and confront her. Running, Jasmine looks as she fast-waddles like so many stern-faced dieters who clog the indoor track on New Year's Day only to disappear from the gym within a week, their gelatinous bodies confused by the sudden motion, their heads snapping side-to-side in seismic lateral movements as they hustle at breakneck speed into a curve. Brand new spandex workout suits several sizes too small cutting into pudgy thighs. Jasmine knows the feeling all too well, her lungs heaving like charred marshmallow pies.

The narrow alleyway is dotted with potholes filled with soapy water as Jasmine becomes a flattened gummy bear to slide her sideways body between the slippery wall and the Golden Flake potato chip truck. She emerges from the dank alley and looks to her right. Two men on the opposite sidewalk point camcorders at her. "Mongolito" stands at the far corner as Jasmine, her face now flushed and sweaty, tries to move in on her. A Post Office van eases in just behind Jasmine. "Mongolito" looks up to see Jasmine closing and makes a break for the train tracks. The Post Office van, unseen, does a slow U-turn into traffic.

"What the hell you been doin'?" Kay-Lee says as Jasmine hobbles back to the front of the bank. Jasmine holds her chest, breathing heavily.

"They said you ran out of here like you was chasin' somebody."

"I was," Jasmine wheezes as she walks toward her car. "I know who left the notes. I saw her." Jasmine opens the driver's side door and snatches the fourth letter taped to her steering wheel. Without hesitation, Jasmine tears open the envelope, reads the page, and looks into Kay-Lee's inquisitive eyes.

The note reads: I WILL KILL HER.

"What's it say?" Kay-Lee cranes her neck to see.

"Let me think, let me think," Jasmine says, her jowls atremble. She goes back to her desk, grabs the other three envelopes, and leaves for lunch. Buying a bag of to-go platters out by Alabama College, she drives with the envelopes to the edge of the Tallapoochee National Forest. It's a stretch for a lunch break, but after what she's been through Jasmine doesn't give a crap if she gets back to work late or not. She eats chips and salsa as her car moves along a logging road lined with tall pines, huckleberry bushes, and Black-Eyed Susans. Her car bounces front-to-back down dusty red roads littered with empty potato chip bags and plastic drink bottles. She turns left, then cuts two miles through a long swath of clear-cut pines. Clumps of twisted little gray trees stand bent and broken in the mangled landscape. Some of the salsa gets on Jasmine's shirt and she says a cuss word. Turning left down a narrow pass, Jasmine drives across a wooden one-lane bridge and stops her car next to an old mill. Tallapoochee Gap Mountain reaches skyward to the east. The sun makes the lake sparkle as sweet gum trees lean in the wind. She and her ex used to come here before he ran off.

Jasmine takes out the letters and tosses them on the hood of her car, then opens a Styrofoam box of enchiladas. Stuffing herself with a white plastic spork, Jasmine puts the letters in order. The first one just has her name on it, the second contains a mailing address, the third letter also has her first and last name in bold print, and finally the one she opened an hour ago. With great trepidation, Jasmine opens the first letter. THE DOLL INSIDE, it reads. Jasmine opens the second envelope. THE PIG INSIDE. The third letter reads, THE CORPSE INSIDE. Jasmine tosses the fourth letter--I WILL KILL HER--on top of the others.

"Don't make no sense," she says and wads the papers up in a big ball. Jasmine tosses the paper into the lake and the white ball floats on the water. A gleam of sun on the moving water stings her eyes.

An image of Parrish drifts into her head, back when they were in high school, his hair hanging over his eyes like a Ramone, pale and pimply, his nose big, those huge eyebrows. He's wearing a black t-shirt, Metallica. His thin, narrow arms and that dumb-looking sweatband on his wrist. Parrish's long face, so close to hers, so still and quiet. Maybe that's why she felt comfortable with him. He would sit on the bleachers in the gym and draw for the whole period, excused from participating with a doctor's note, and she would sit there too, as the other kids ran up and down the high-ceilinged court. The occasional squeak of a tennis shoe carried up into their silent reverie as lines of sunlight glinted through the high gymnasium windows to the burnished wooden floor below them. She never watched him draw. She was just there, close enough to him so that if anybody walked by the bleachers, they'd see Jasmine and Parrish together. So what if they called him "a fuckin' hippy." He could draw anything and make it look right. Mostly he drew the Millennium Falcon and stuff like that, but he would draw her face too, so that it looked like her and was also beautiful.

Jasmine looks at her reflection in the lake, the pinpoint head of a lone turtle, and something in her wants to go under.

3

Dust particles hang in the computer screen haze inside a dark, airless lab. In the glow of multiple monitors, there are wires, cameras, and digital recording devices in boxes and stacks everywhere. Tick and Manuelita sit looking at the same image on different laptops. They watch the subject from two different angles as she gobbles enchiladas and rips open envelopes. One of the monitors displays Jasmine through the dirty windshield of a car, the other from a distant drone. Tick, a blue Post Office cap askew on his head, operates a joystick that keeps the subject in the center of his camera's field of vision. He pushes a button and the camera closes in on the subject's mouth moving slowly as she confusedly reads letter after letter aloud to herself.

"This is golden," Tick whispers.

"Don't make no sense," the lady on the monitor blurts as she turns to throw the ball of paper into the lake.

"He's gonna love this," Tick says.

"Want me to text him?" asks Manuelita.

"Nah, he's getting his Maharishi on." They both smirk, eyes fixed on their respective screens.

"Pan back a little bit. Get that ominous tree limb in the shot."

This conversation between his two colleagues buzzes in Preston's tiny earphone as he stretches in his black kimono before meditation. He moves his free weights in exercise repetitions that only a person who leans at a 45-degree angle to the left can do. Preston switches his satellite radio to ambient space music and sits down on his sloped box. The box sits at an angle that allows him the correct posture for half-lotus position and affords him a view down and across the long valley towards his captive audience of trees. *She's down this mountain somewhere right now,* he thinks. *My rainbow. My star.*

On his sloped box, Preston inhales fully allowing the filtered, uncontaminated air of his private exercise studio into his lungs. He closes his eyes to slits and breathes in through the nose as he envisions the air going inside him being an ice-blue color brimming with purity and goodness. When Preston breathes out through the mouth, he imagines that the air is brown and that all his toxic thoughts and feelings spiral out of his mind in orbits. Breathing out Preston tries to hold only uncomplicated goodness in his head. He pictures a veined leaf. He tells himself that at every moment in life there is a single holy place where a person can fix their eyes, the space that Isaiah Please calls the "love nexus." In this way, if people want to see garbage, they get garbage. If they want to see beauty, they get beauty. Preston learned this from the box set *The Cosmos Calls: Four Steps to Spectral Awareness.* But instead of uncomplicated goodness, the names "Barney Balls" and "Drake McCloud" pop into his head without warning. Both names upset Preston, and his body twitches, the hands come loose and wiggle around the room like frantic beetles. The first name was used by Preston when he was cast for the smut film *Bagtime III* and the second was a name that he used when he was perfecting an online classmate cozenage.

Preston tries to dismiss the thoughts associated with those desperate times. *Nothing's gonna change my world*, he thinks as hard as he can. Cringing, he sees himself pull off his lime-green tie and fling it into the gutter. The image continues to haunt him. He doesn't want to dwell on the lime-green tie or the gutter. Instead, he has asked the image to flow through his consciousness and move on, but here it is again, spinning on Preston's mental carousel circling around and around his brain like a bratty child on the merry-go-round with his tongue out, waving and pointing and jeering at him again and again.

After the accident, the fall, Preston's body festered for the love of a woman like never before, and not just any woman, Preston wanted a doll. Yes, there were women in the valley who would have willingly gone for Preston after the accident due to his wealth and notoriety, but he weaseled at their advances. Preston was instantly repulsed the minute he noticed their interest in him. He felt an indescribable hostility when he realized they would be willing to love him and fondle his bent anatomy. What he wanted instead was to be the envy of his old high school class, to show them all.

To accomplish this, Preston had disguised himself in a wig and prosthetic nose to go to the Francisco Bravo Medical

Magnet High School. There he persuaded the librarian to dig up yearbooks from the mid-1990s. Preston had told the smiling librarian that he was doing a newspaper report on Los Angeles Gen-X fashion. The librarian had let "Alfonse" copy page after page of past Francisco Bravo Medical Magnet students. Then, "Alfonse" had sat in a library reading nook, pouring over the images until he found the guys too good looking for *classconnex.com*. He made a long list of names, then did a web search to determine suitable candidates. Preston had needed a stud, to be sure, with a glimmer in his eye. A person both attractive and lacking in scruples. After narrowing the list to "Ralph Needles" and "Charles Edmondson," Preston had driven to a public library in North LA, set up two accounts on *classconnex.com* for high school lover boys, and let the catfishing begin.

Ralph Needles proved to be a disappointment. It would be a week before he would get even a single hit, and it was from a man named Bruce Tully who wanted to know where "Maggie" moved away to. But for Charles Edmondson, the mail came almost instantly. The messages just poured in immediately from not only Charles' classmates, but from the Junior and Sophomore classes as well:

> From Becky Wiler, Class of 1994: ... I heard that you finished your law degree and moved to Portland and that you got married. Somehow I always thought that we would see each other again. I'm still with Frank... but we both know what that's about. Let's maybe have a drink sometime? And yes, I heard about what happened...

From Susan Escalante, Class of 1995: ... It was great when it lasted, Charlie. Sometimes I think about that cruise so long ago. I have to say that it hasn't felt...

From Nancy George, Class of 1994: ...God it has been a long time! Oh, I heard about your legs and your divorce. Hit me up!...

From Virginia Boone, Class of 1997: ... You don't know how sorry I was when I heard about your injuries. Do you ever think "what if?"...

From Bruce Tully, Class of 1994: ... last time we saw each other it wasn't on such good terms. I distinctly remember punching you in the eye. But that's what happens when you do what you did to somebody's girlfriend in lab. Whatever happened to Maggie anyway? I guess that we should leave that one alone. Charlie, I will always remember that dinner cruise you took me on, and I know that it can't be like that for us, but for what it's worth I still feel the...

Preston patched together a workable characterization of Charles Edmondson: attractive, military background, successful lawyer, promiscuous, and missing both legs. Preston thought about the speech patterns and inflections that "Charlie" might employ. He meditated on page after page of yearbook pictures, circling the desperate online schoolmates who might be vulnerable to Preston's plot. Becky Wiler looked needy enough, but she just wouldn't do because she had a handful of tiny blemishes on her face. Nancy George of the devilish eyes and pouting lips, on the other hand, was quite comely, if not a tad portly. Susan Escalante wore glasses and had a nonexistent nose. And poor Bruce Tully sported a bedraggled hairpiece, surely affixed to Bruce's head by some degenerate friends of his in Lincoln Heights. But these pictures were taken years ago, Preston thought, and these women could have changed quite a bit. It was a tough decision, but he finally settled on Nancy George. The following week Preston drove to a public phone booth and called Nancy at home.

"Hello?" Nancy said.

"Hey girl," Preston responds as he fights the jib-jabs, his knees locking and unlocking in the phone booth.

"Who is this?"

"It's me, Charlie. Charlie Edmondson."

"Oh god! Charlie! I was so excited when I got your message!"

"I've been thinking about you."

"You sound so different, Charlie."

"I am."

"You mean, after the accident?"

"That, and a lot of things," Preston glanced at the studio across the street. "I've been doing a lot of soul searching. Baby."

"We're just glad you're OK. We all heard about what happened."

"What, actually, did you hear about what happened?"

"That you, you know, ran over a cow outside Camp Pendleton and went through the windshield into traffic."

Preston covered the receiver as his face exploded in nervous giggles.

"We know each other inside and out, don't we, babe?" Nancy said.

"We certainly do," Preston said, his hands trembling, not knowing what he was doing.

"God, you sound so different. So like all professional or something."

"Growing up changes things."

"I hope it didn't change everything..."

"No, I'm ready and able, if you know what I'm trying to get at."

"Yeah, I do," Nancy whispered.

"Nancy, do you *really* want to help me out?"

"Honey, let me."

"You want to make it better?"

"Mmmm. Yes, please," Nancy said, her voice breathy.

"Then *please* go out with this Army buddy of mine. Show *him* a good time."

"I thought you were in the Marines."

"Uhm, you know, joint operations, special ops..."

"I don't know, Charlie. It's been so long."

"I just want you to take my close friend to dinner. Talk to him, like you did with me all those years ago."

"Is he OK? Why can't he get a date by himself?"

"His name is Drake McCloud. He's a Captain that was shot down behind enemy lines. He's a true American hero, a sniper. But I must warn you, he is slightly disfigured."

"Disfigured, like how?"

"Well, heh heh, he is...how should I say it...crooked."

"He's crooked?"

"Yes, he is in fact kind of crooked."

Nancy exhaled, "Charlie, my patriotism does have its limits."

"He just needs to get out a little bit. Prime the pump, so to speak, heh heh heh. He is a great guy. Great guy, actually very attractive when you get beyond the fact that he's, you know, bent. He was parachuting into Baghdad holding a machine gun and..."

The following afternoon, Preston was sitting in the hotel lobby bar, stirring his club soda. He stared down at a thin wedge of lime speared with a toothpick. His hair was gelled in a fashion that made hairdo and head distinct in an unsettling way.

"Charlie" had said that "Drake" would be wearing a lime-green tie, but Nancy certainly could have identified him without it. "Drake" tried to appear relaxed as he watched the windows facing the street. A woman in a yellow dress popped in from the revolving door. Preston thought she was an attractive little shawty indeed, but when he gave her a special grin, she turned to the concierge. *Not Nancy.* And from the look on her face, she was horrified. Another woman came in and Preston thought that if this woman were to be Nancy George he would have to think fast. She wore a most unfortunate lime-green sweater and her mouth seemed to slant as if she had suffered a minor stroke. Preston, of course, always noticed the asymmetries of others and judged them harshly for it. *Worst of all, she was fat. Wider than tall kind of fat,* thought Preston. *Pig in a goddamn blanket kind of fat.* Preston felt the salty water hot in his throat and his head filled with memories of his mother stuffed into a shiny casket shaped like a Gemini Four space capsule.

Mommy play dress-up? Preston's brain went echo chamber. *Mommy dress-up like Bionic Woman—Bionic Woman—Bionic Woman*....

Seeing him, Nancy bit her bottom lip and sat down at the next barstool.

"Are you Captain McCloud?" she said, wide-eyed.

"Excuse me?" Preston said and shrugged at the bartender.

"You're Drake, right?"

"Who?" Preston frowned in the direction of the bartender again.

Nancy appraised Preston's lime-green tie and spinal column with a furrowed brow.

"OK...?" she said with a frown and ordered herself a margarita. She sipped her drink as Preston pretended to watch the baseball highlights on the bar TV. A commercial for a reality program called *Studs and Duds* came on and Nancy George's eyes lit up in a smile.

"Oooh, you watching *Studs and Duds* tonight?" Nancy said putting her palm on Preston's forearm.

"No," Preston exhaled into his free armpit. "I've never seen it."

"I just love it."

Preston retracted his arm.

"I watch it every week."

His fingers jittered.

"I know nothing about this."

"See, they send these 20 women to this 'stud' ranch in the middle of Texas. And they all try to get a date with this cowboy, 'Johnny Stud.' The women have to walk through cacti, rope cattle, eat bugs off cow manure, ride a bucking bronco, take mud baths with the pigs, all kinds of *extreme* stuff."

"Wild," Preston said, his voice muffled.

"And at the end of every show, Johnny Stud sends one of the girls packing."

"And at season's end," Preston said, his eyes rolling back exasperated, "Johnny mounts the winner."

"Oh yeah," Nancy beamed, nodding.

Preston knocked back his club soda and bolted through the rotating door. When the warm wind of the street hit him, Preston felt rage cascade through his bent frame. Preston snatched off the stupid lime-green tie and flung it at the gutter, but a breeze whirled it flapping around his ankle. His body began to shimmy as a peal of confused laughter erupted from his wide-open mouth. Preston covered his face with both hands like a mischievous child, his sinister eyes glancing back and forth at the shocked passersby. He bent over to snatch the tie, people on the sidewalk stopping to stare, and his forehead thudded against the bumper of a parked sedan. With a refined gesture, Preston put the tie back on, tightened it while looking into the car's side-view mirror, and turned to swagger in the other direction down the sidewalk.

Feeling cameras upon him, Preston stopped and happened to glance at a corner bookstore. The books that lined the marquee were white with the image of a blue-eyed man in a white robe meditating on a wooden pier, the white snow-capped peaks of Mt. Rainier, and brilliant turquoise sky behind him. The eyes beckoned Preston. The book was called *The Dharma of Success* and the author was Isaiah Please. As if drawn by a magnetic field,

Preston went to the book. On a back avenue rooftop, he read the book into the sunset, making notations and reading important passages aloud as he paced on the ledge, blimps black in orange smog emerging from the sunset palms below.

The cosmos calls dammit, Preston thought. *Frontal lobe epilepsy my butt.* He stood on the roof with his lime-green tie flapping as the blimps hovered over the Figueroa at Wilshire Building. Preston would later say in both the *Entertainment Tonight* interviews and police interrogations that this was the most important moment in his life.

Looking out at the forest, Preston's face was now all fist and shakes, all tears and saliva. He cries for a while, then gets back into a half-lotus position and begins to breathe from the beginning again. This time the names "Barney Balls" and "Drake McCloud" do not enter his consciousness. He does not think of Nancy George. He doesn't think of anything but the way that his body might wobble and spin if he were floating across the universe.

4

It's a moonless midnight and Jasmine can't sleep. She snatches at her tangled sheets and rolls over in her narrow bed. A small crack in her curtain allows a beam of light to disturb her clamped eyes. Dogs behind her house start making a racket and she can tell that there's an intruder out there. Neighborhood spaniels make threatening snaps with throaty snarls and promises of teeth. A struck chain length fence rings out as a trash can lid clatters to the asphalt. Jasmine rolls out of bed in her filmy nightgown and peers out the window. There is a shadow of a man standing at her back door. Jasmine goes to her bedroom closet and grabs her .22 pistol. She then rummages around under the sink in the bathroom for the flashlight. In a huff, she shines the flashlight through the window adjacent to the door and illuminates the side of her ex-husband's head. He covers his heavy-lidded eyes with a slow, open hand and just kind of stands there.

"Parrish? Get your ass off my yard!"

"I gotta talk to you."

"It's called a damned phone! You scared me to death messing around out there!"

"Let me in," Parrish says as he pulls at the screen door.

"No, Parrish. You've been gone too long to just walk up in the middle of the night and get the royal treatment. Now you get off my property! I ain't kidding! Just get your ass out of here."

Parrish lets the screen door shut and turns to leave.

"Parrish! Parrish!" Jasmine says.

"What?"

"I'll meet you at the pancake house."

"In the morning?"

"No. If you want to see me so bad, make it Wednesday. Wednesday morning at seven o'clock. But if you are just here for dope money don't bother showing up at all."

"Wednesday," he says as he disappears into the dark.

Jasmine turns to the refrigerator and pulls out the gallon can of nacho cheese dip with the tin foil on top, her hands trembling. She spoons the orange goop into a bowl and puts it in the microwave. Her mind spins along with the gob of cheese, softening and bubbling. She looks down at the pile of greasy dishes in the sink, stringy hair hanging over her round face. Jasmine hears something crack in her throat as she lets out a tight-lipped moan. The light of the microwave flashes off and she looks up to see her wide face in the rectangle of glass, bewildered.

He left me, Jasmine thought, *after I told him about the miscarriage*. But Parrish didn't run off because of that or even because she pushed him away and attacked him like a bulldog the night she almost had her first orgasm. It was because of her weight and nobody could tell her different. After they got married, Parrish worked as a bus driver for the blind school and Jasmine worked in the lunchroom. Parrish's grandaddy had some pull at the blind school, so for being eighteen and just out of school themselves, they felt like they had it made with state jobs like that. But after Parrish worked on the bus for a couple of months, he started in on the drugs. He would just stand out on the deck of the second-story apartment all the time and smoke the best crack he could get. For months, the refrigerator made the sizzling sound, with Parrish looking out at the cow pasture behind their apartment complex, stoned out of his mind. *But sometimes,* Jasmine thought, *sometimes he cradled her sore little heart, didn't he? Sometimes they'd kissed in the pool's underwater lights.*

Jasmine was sad whenever Parrish would bring Ezekiel to the apartment to play video games. The two of them would sit up all night drinking beer and pushing buttons while Jasmine laid in the bedroom with her legs open listening to them talk. After playing Super Mario, Ezekiel and Parrish would kneel on the floor together and pray to Jesus. Then he would stagger back to the bed with bad breath, where she would lay there waiting for him to roll over and give her a hug and a kiss, but he never did that after playing video games with Ezekiel. Jasmine knew that she embarrassed him because she'd heard Ezekiel call her a BBW, even though he'd meant it as a compliment.

A lot of nights after watching TV, Parrish would come into the bedroom with a big, goofy smile and make her squeeze her breasts together with her elbows. He would then slide his penis back and forth between them with a big hayseed grin like he was having the time of his life, but it never felt right to Jasmine. It made her feel like a big, fat cow and she wanted to go on a diet, but she couldn't stop bingeing. Jasmine couldn't help dipping the chicken fingers she'd swiped into vats of chocolate pudding when she went into the walk-in cooler at the blind school lunch-room. She thought because they were blind no one could see her do it, but everybody knew who was eating the cheese off the faculty salads.

Their sex life for the first few months of marriage contained these puzzling silences, both of them looking at each other's anatomies in mute confusion. Jasmine would make Parrish turn the light off before she took off her clothes, and then it was over before it ever got going. Hopping atop Jasmine as if she were a pool inflatable, Parrish would hasten to insert himself, clamp onto her bulbous breasts, and with a dozen thrusts collapse with a high-pitched wheezing whistle in Jasmine's thick arms. When he was like this, Jasmine would hold him tight, stroke his body, and whisper baby talk to him. This was the only time that she felt comfortable enough to do that. It was great for a while, but then he had to go and mess it up. One winter night after a hasty tousle, Parrish didn't lie there in her arms. He pulled himself off of her and sat on the edge of the bed looking all serious.

"What is it?" she said.

"I don't know what you are getting out of it," he said. "You never get off."

"It's fine," she said with a trace of hostility. "It's nice."

"Nice. Nice is taking your demented ass aunt to the botani-cal gardens."

"Aunt Clottie ain't got nothing to do with it."

Parrish kept sitting there on the bed, his face grim. Then he turned to her with a look of determination in his eye. For the next hour, Parrish worked his back, his tongue, and every avail-able appendage using tricks learned from a cousin's dog-eared

Hustler. He bumped away at Jasmine and stared red-faced at the wall behind her. Their bodies came together in repeated flat claps. Jasmine at first seemed flummoxed, but then all of a sudden she began to feel something she barely could recognize. It was the way her body had felt at Camp Calvary. Something in her began to hum like a low kazoo. It began to tingle and she could smell her own body. As her fingernails dug into Parrish's back, he pumped even harder in a single-minded, slack-faced fugue.

As she smelled herself and felt the kazoo get louder, colors began to seep into Jasmine's vision, and the room suddenly filled with bright yellows, whites, and golds, spinning and blinding her as she felt her body about to burst.

"Get off me!" Jasmine had screeched and pushed at Parrish's face. When he didn't stop, she slapped and then slugged him in the chest. She hit him with her open palm then her fists, finally connecting with his nose. Parrish doggedly snapped his hips until her final punch rang true.

"Christ!" Parrish had screamed as he held his bleeding nose with both hands.

"Get off me!" Jasmine pushed up, clawing at Parrish like an animal, fists and fingernails tearing into him until he retreated to the bathroom. Then she sat at the edge of the bed speed eating doughnut holes as the tingling feeling faded.

"What the hell is the matter with you?" Parrish had yelled from the locked bathroom.

"There were colors," Jasmine had said. "It ain't right."

Later that night, when there was nothing left to say, Jasmine lay stretched out on the bed, faking sleep. She heard Parrish sneak out of the bathroom, unlock the front door, and steal away to sleep in the car out back. After that, it got bad for Parrish and Jasmine. Night after night, they argued. Weeks went by as she shamed him, chewed him out until his face began to take on the swollen, defeated look of her daddy. She pushed him away until he just stood there blankly at the door, his eyes gray, distant and empty. She found out that she was pregnant when she had the miscarriage and then waited for just the right moment to rub Parrish's face in it. When she told him about it, saying that she didn't love him and to get his ass out of there, he shrugged and walked out the door. It had been close to ten years since.

And now he shows up, she thinks, fluffing her pillow, rolling over, her mind spiraling into troubled sleep. Round and round she goes.

5

The turtle is the only relic from psychotherapy that Preston's subconscious will not let him hold up to the light. Everything else he thinks about, but not the turtle. And the turtle is still down there hiding with its eyes closed in a tangled underwater crevice of Preston's mind. It's not that Preston caused his first and only pet to die by suffocation. That he did do. It's that for three years, the boy talked for hours with the turtle, responding to his own questions in a high-pitched turtle voice. He would swing the turtle on the baby swing in the park for thirty minutes at a time. And for two of the years that Preston had "Shauna" for a pet, it was dead. Preston had suffocated the turtle one day when he had it duct-taped to his stomach. After that, he did not allow himself to believe that Shauna was gone. For two years he sprayed it with disinfectant and room deodorant. When a doctor came to the school to examine the third-grade students for scoliosis, she was shocked to find a thin boy with gray tape wrapped around his torso, a dead turtle nestled there like a prosthetic fetus. Preston distinctly remembers that his social speech condition and nervous twitches started the moment the doctor asked him about his turtle.

Preston couldn't hold the turtle in his mind because it was still attached to his dead parents. He wanted to remember them in a nice way, to place them on some high shelf in his memory and think of them fondly.

Spiritual advisor and self-help guru Isaiah Please says in his YouTube seminars that dwelling on the mistakes of our parents is a crutch. He says that if we take responsibility for the past then, and only then, do we have the potential to find our love-self. Preston has tried very hard to accomplish this. He doesn't fixate on the fact that his mother and father didn't notice the dead turtle taped to his body, or that when he was in the third grade Shauna was the only friend he had.

Preston's parents were busy, his mother larger than life. But, as Preston was to find, she was not larger than death. When he thought about her, he clamped his eyes shut and tried not to recall her loud, affected Southern drawl, the clinking of ice in her highball glasses, the way the big-boned woman would stuff herself into a crowded hotel reception suite and blabber on until the last of the chardonnay was sucked dry. She had trained to be a civil liberties reformer in the Deep South but had instead moved to California to try divorces and draw up deeds. In their study at home, she had enshrined herself in high walls of dank files, her cheeks flushed pouches hanging loose as she'd stand staring down at stacks of yellow legal pads. Despite their later financial success, the decision to leave Alabama was a source of constant shame for Preston's mother. Every night she'd sit at the edge of her chair in the study thumbing through files holding a lipstick-blotted glass wrapped with a white paper towel. She always had a case to try. Later when she came to tuck Preston in, he could smell the walnut smell of Bourbon on her breath as she staggered around his room talking long strings of non-sense. Sometimes at night, they played long, elaborate games of dress-up, his mother costumed as the bionic woman or an astronaut. Preston's father had said that "regional guilt," what-ever that meant, made her drink too much. On many evenings Preston stood at the edge of some reception or another wearing his father's bow tie where he'd stare at her aura in the middle of the crowd in a halo of light.

For a year after the car crash, Preston would wake in the mid-dle of the nights, in sweats and terrifying memories. If he was honest with himself on this point, the dreams made him relieved that his mother had been found dead that night in 1981. In the dreams, his mother stands at Preston's bedside staring at him as he sleeps. Preston knows that she is there and he is comforted until he feels her large stomach and breasts on his chest, and he can't breathe. The breasts and stomach push the air out of his lungs and he screams but she doesn't notice, she is talking loudly to him about some probate judge as Preston chokes. She isn't looking at him at all and it's like he's in quicksand. He pushes at the bionic fat and it keeps flopping down on him. "Do try to smile," his mother would say in the dreams as her body engulfed and suffocated him.

Preston's mother often took him to the parties as a substi-tution for his father, a thin psychologist marathon runner who communicated to the world with a nettled exhalation through the nose. It was well known that the relationship of Dr. and Mrs.

Ackerman Price, Jr., was based on vehement political oratories that lasted all night. They would watch the evening news, talk themselves into a frenzy, and drunkenly take turns attacking Ronald Reagan and the *National Review* in flowing kimonos until sunrise. Other than that, they had little to do with each other. *At least*, Preston had thought, *my father's patients at his institution near San Luis Obispo let me play a game they called "fart poker."* Most of the patients at Megargel State Hospital were more like mentors to him than the father who would make him sit alone in the MG during group sessions with the fretful addicts.

Preston's mother had simply gotten drunk and flipped her Mercedes off a curvy hillside road between San Luis Obispo and Monterey. She was dead, just like that. One result of mother's untimely demise was that for many years Preston summered with Grandmaw, a very old lady who lived on a big patch of woodland at the edge of the Tallapoochee National Forest in Alabama. Dr. Ackerman Price Jr. seemed to always need to leave abruptly on research trips, or to work on a book about Jung and addiction that he had been writing since before Preston was born. Preston, who never quite adjusted to either California or Alabama, began to see himself as a misunderstood intellectual. He frequented anti-apartheid protests and "save the whale" meetings and bought his first pair of round steel-rimmed John Lennon glasses. These changes in Preston's demeanor displeased Grandmaw, as did his disdain for Christianity.

"You've got to kneel to Jesus," she would say as she sat knitting, her lips wrinkled with age, "if you want to be washed in the blood of the lamb."

"It's a fairy-tale, Grandmaw."

"What's wrong with you, boy? That's Jesus you're talking about. If all you gone do is hurt Jehovah's feelings, why don't you go fishin' and catch us some bass?"

"I don't want to go fishing," Preston would say, perplexed by this old person, this "Grandmaw."

"Get that Zebco and catch us some bass."

"Grandmaw, you don't seem to understand that what you call the moral majority just makes people docile…don't you see? Don't conform to the system, Grandmaw."

"You don't know jack squat, boy. Get down to that creek and I'll make some cornbread. Look at you, you need to eat."

That day Preston left the kitchen humming, "Blue Suede Shoes."

6

Somebody's trying to mess me up, Jasmine thinks. She drives to work from lunch, her mouth making a slow chewing motion. She considers the weird letters and the Pensacola souvenir. *Who put it back on my desk? Who's messing with me?*

She sits up when she sees a Post Office Jeep stopped at a mailbox on its rural route, the driver's head low, leaning out toward the box. She has a vivid flash of memory from elementary school and the horrors of riding the bus. She feels the same way now as she did then when somebody slapped the back of her head and when she turned around there would be a dozen smiling faces looking back at her from the rows of seats. *Which one did it?* If she hit the wrong kid, they would take it as an excuse to beat her up, but if she turned back around, they would do it again and again. Jasmine remembers that she just sat there as they hit the back of her head over and over. *Slap slap slap slap*, all the way to school. She went on with her life, coloring, watching cows out the window, and finishing her homework as they struck the back of her head over and over again. Everybody at the bank must be in on it, just like all the kids on the bus.

When Jasmine opens the door of the bank, everybody stops and stares up at her, their faces grave, some of them whispering to each other. After she sits down Mrs. Salters meets Jasmine at her desk looking solemn.

"May I sit down?" Mrs. Salters says.

"It's your daddy's desk."

"I have some terrible news, Jasmine."

Jasmine furrows her brow.

"It's your mother," Mrs. Salters says.

"What about her?"

"I'm afraid she's passed away."

"Who told you that?" Jasmine says.

"I received a phone call."

"From who?"

"I didn't get the name. She sounded upset."

"News flash, my mother has been dead for years."

Mrs. Salters gives a quizzical look.

"Can we trace the call?" Jasmine says.

"Ask Kay-Lee, if you think it's important." They walk to the side-office at the front of the bank to see Kay-Lee on the computer looking at pictures of muscular dudes with tats on Facebook, angry men who look to Jasmine remarkably like Miss Cleecher at Camp Calvary. Above Kay-Lee's desk is a large panel with eight surveillance screens. When Kay-Lee sees Mrs. Salters, she stands up in front of the computer.

"Can you trace a call that was made to my office phone today?"

"Probbly," Kay-Lee says as she digs at her teeth with a toothpick. Jasmine looks up to see her own desk alongside the others on one of the surveillance screens.

"And somebody put something on my desk this morning around 11:00," she says. "Rewind the tape of my desk and find out who it is."

"What was left on your desk?" Mrs. Salters says.

"Nothing," Jasmine says. "Just look at the tape."

"What do you mean?" Mrs. Salters says with a frown. "You just said--"

"--It was a souvenir, just some stupid souvenir from my daddy, if you got to know. But that ain't the issue. The issue is somebody is messing around with my stuff."

"I'll check it out," Kay-Lee says. "Come back in an hour."

Jasmine is dizzy as she sits waiting at her desk. She needs a candy bar, a bag of cheese curls, a bag of biscuits. She sits at her desk staring at the Pensacola Beach souvenir and then picks it up. It feels different, heavier. Jasmine hears the computerized double ding that lets her know she has an email.

It's from Kay-Lee with the subject line "lookit this."

The email reads:

That call came from inside the bank

Jasmine clicks the link and sees the surveillance download of the three desks. The image is muted and grainy. Lorrie and Mandy appear to be rubbing their hands with lotion and waving their arms talking. Jasmine's desk is empty between them. A woman walks up-a woman wearing a miniskirt--and leans against Jasmine's desk. Jasmine can't see her face but can tell from her rear end she's got to be Meghan Oswell. As she makes conversation with Lorrie and Mandy, Meghan slips the Pensacola snow globe back on Jasmine's desk. She takes time to turn it just so. A few seconds later Meghan walks out of the range of the camera. Lorrie and Mandy continue to rub their hands with lotion.

Kay-Lee and Jasmine stand facing each other in the conference room. Jasmine is holding up the souvenir and looking at it. "Do you have a knife?" she asks. Kay-Lee pulls her Swiss Army knife from her pocket and Jasmine uses it to pry a tiny metal object from the side of the souvenir. Jasmine hands the device to Kay-Lee, who scrutinizes it closely.

"Lordy, it's a camera." Kay-Lee looks through the glass door of the conference room at the tellers, hands on her hips. "It might be a bank job."

"It ain't no bank nothing," Jasmine says. She looks up at the ceiling and blows out a mournful whistle.

"We've got at least one clue," Kay-Lee offers. "Meghan Oswell's butt. I'm thinkin' all we gotta do is stake out Meghan's butt and see why she's messin' with you."

"Yeah, let's follow the little hussy and find out what she and the postman are up to."

"Now, don't go and get all paranoid," Kay-Lee says. "Don't tell nobody nothing. And regardless of what happens, there ain't no way a butt will hold up in court. A lot of butts look like that."

"I think you would be more paranoid than I am being, Kay-Lee. They're leaving notes, stealing stuff, calling about my dead mother. Ain't no doubt about it, somebody's out to get me."

On Wednesday morning, Jasmine sits motionless at a booth at the roadside pancake house with puffy eyes half-closed. The line of steam from the coffee cup in front of her breaks when she exhales. She listens to the young couple in the booth behind her, coddling and cooing, *the little shits*. She recognizes the weirdo sitting alone at a corner table, the crooked one who had acted the fool at the bank. He is turned the other way wearing headphones. Lorrie and Mandy, her co-workers at the bank, are there as well but are too caught up in conversation to notice her. A blonde man in a postal employee uniform sits up at the bar reading the newspaper and sipping coffee. The silence of the place grows as the cook tosses pink patty sausages onto the hot grill. Jasmine's body feels like sizzling pork.

Parrish slides into the booth across from her and looks hard at Jasmine. He's wearing jeans and a black t-shirt, his hair hanging over his eyes like back in high school. She doesn't return the look but remains as motionless and morose as possible.

"Thanks for coming," he says lighting a cigarette.

"What are you doing here? I thought you moved to Mobile."

"I did."

"Still unemployed? Living with your granddaddy?"

"No, I uh manage a video store."

"You look just the same," she says not looking at him. Parrish knows better than to take the bait and say anything about her appearance.

"Let's get some pancakes," he says and waves over the waitress.

"I don't want nothing," she says.

"Well then gimme--"

"--I'll take a three-egg breakfast, scrambled," Jasmine blurts. "Bacon, hash browns, and gravy biscuits. And a sausage biscuit."

The waitress smiles and positions the honey jar just so in front of Jasmine.

"So what are you doing here?" Jasmine says.

"Well," Parrish crouches in nervously. "Something funny happened last week. I was in the back office at the video store and these two women came in all quiet-like. They had on these trench coats and sunglasses like that chick in *The Matrix*. I thought they were gonna rob the place."

"What you looking at?" Jasmine grunts at the blonde Mr. Postman without taking her eyes off her coffee. With a cock of the head he swivels around in his stool and returns to his newspaper.

"Then," Parrish says, "they took me out of the shop and put me in the back of this old car and start asking me questions, uh, questions about you. I tell them that I haven't seen you in years. They wanted to know if you had any any any interest in the entertainment industry, stuff like that."

"Entertainment?" Jasmine says. "Why?"

"I don't know," Parrish says. "They said they wanted me to get back into your life."

"What the hell for?"

"It sounded like they wanted to like put you on a show."

"That is the stupidest thing I've ever heard."

"I'm just telling you what they told me," Parrish says.

"What did the girls look like?"

"One was blonde, the other Hispanic. Skinny."

Jasmine's eyes widen.

"I told them that I wanted to come to talk to you first. Listen, Jasmine, they've got big money."

"How do you know?" Jasmine says.

"That's what they told me." Parrish puts out his cigarette.

"They told you or gave you?" Jasmine sneers. "I thought that was a fancy-looking watch."

Parrish lights another cigarette and slides his arms under the table.

"You've already taken their money, haven't you?" Jasmine snarls.

"J-j-just enough to get me down here, and, you know, the watch."

"You liar. You goddamned liar. You're working with them already ain'tcha? Do you know what they've been doing to me?"

"But maybe we can do this together," Parrish says, his voice pleading as the waitress puts the food on the table. "Then we could both be on TV or something."

"I just have one question," Jasmine says. "Did you tape us talking last night? Did you film it?"

"I'll be honest with you. There was a woman. She had a camera behind the car."

"They are filming us right now, aren't they?" Jasmine whispers. "You're acting."

"Wait a minute," Parrish says. "This could be good for us."

"Ain't no us." Jasmine stands up, grabs her purse from the table, and snatches up the sausage biscuit. "I always knew you were crazy," Jasmine grumbles, "come down here talking about TV shows...."

"Jasmine, please."

"And all you creeps can stay away from me too," she snaps over her shoulder to everyone as she flounces out of the restaurant.

7

Perfect shapes exist, Preston thinks, *but only in our heads. And only when we're thinking about what we've seen on screens.* He leans into his stick and extends his right leg onto the jutting rock. Pieces of flat stone drop from the cliff as he strains to push his bent body onto the ledge. Oak and hickory trees stand cliffside at angles curving from the trunk turning upward to the stark white of sky. It takes a long time to pull himself onto the ledge, many tries, as Preston's breathing gets jagged. He's been wandering for days, dehydrated, hands trembling for lack of food. Sweat and dust have made his clothes a scaly second skin that he will shed when he finds another pool of mountain water. Preston stinks, his body exhausted, but his mind has been alert and alive all morning. Ideas burst in every direction faster than he can record them in conscious thought. In the extremities he feels his creative mind rise and fall, his self-image redeemed by a combination of positive self-concepts and visualizations. *These extremes are a means to self-realization*, Preston thinks. He pictures himself achieving his goals. He creates a mental movie of a favorable outcome in his mind–himself on a fabulous stage

accepting an Emmy, for example–as the failures and embarrass-
ments of the past disappear from his subconscious. Hours pass
as Preston hobbles alongside the ridge. On the steep incline, he
can stand upright.

In the valley, he sees old Grandmaw's house, the place
where he has so often came back from his rambles. This was the
place where Preston returned after he imploded in California.
He spent most of 1999 wandering around the West Coast in a
stained Members Only jacket over two sweatshirts, his sunburned face and faded eyes resembling hopped-up derelicts who
do electric dances in the streets. He forgot about things in San
Francisco sitting under their bridge in a fog, his mind lost, his
fingernails black with dirt and second-hand chicken grease. He
ate dumpster pizza with an old man in a tarp, every once in a
while. There, as he found hustling, free cups of coffee in Silicon
Valley don't come easy.

While he was living in the Mission, people would see him
crying as he held onto the backs of garbage trucks working part-
time. Hopping off to grab long, wet bags of rank garbage while
staring at the sky with a dirty face and long-lost eyes. He felt like
a movie actor clinging to the side of a cliff, fingers slipping one
by one, about to fall to his death, but who somehow gathers the
strength to pull himself back to the ledge to look out at the endless Frisco peaks, of garbage.

Somehow, after Preston had staggered around California
in a fog for a year, he was finally able to get a clean set of clothes
from the Fish and Loaves Catholics and the Capitol City gave
him a bus ticket back to Alabama. Preston was 27 then, but on
the long bus ride from Sacramento he made up his mind to

go back to college. After shaving in Tulsa, Preston realized he needed a base, an anchor, something to keep him from wandering again. Something to keep his mind and karma right. He had walked the long miles from the Tallapoochee bus station to Grandmaw's house wringing his hands and talking to himself the whole way.

On that day in late 1999, Preston had pushed open the wooden door and stood in the black-walled pantry of what had been his mother's family home for generations. Rusty lidded jars of pickles and green beans lined the sidewall, and the door of the deep freeze was open like a casket. Unmoving spiders, their legs clenched, dared him to pass. Preston picked up a stick from the sunlit yard of knee-high grass and turned it as he rolled up the webs. The spiders crawled off their webs and hid in dark corners. A pile of rotten clothes and an overturned television were the only things left in the living room, except for Aunt Bessie's kewpie doll in a World War II sailor suit nailed to moldy wallpaper. The floor creaked when Preston shifted his worn-out legs in front of the white stove. The frying pan sat on one of the stove's sunken eyes. He stared at it, into it. The dark skillet had cooked countless pones of cornbread, fried lakes of fish. That frying pan had been in his family since the 1880s when Grandmaw's grandfather William had made a clearing near the creek and worked a long, narrow field that was now scabby with pine and sweet gum. In Preston's cockeyed imagination, William had worked in swamp sun and beech shade, spent summers in the clean fast-moving creek water with its dark, flat rocks, laughing and splashing with the son who survived. At least that's the way Preston liked to envision the deceased bootlegger as he stared down into the hard blackness of the pan. Preston picked up the frying pan by its handle and looked into it like a mirror, seeing only dark crust.

Preston lived alone in that old house until the Fall of 2000, and during that time he got the place in working order, found the orchard, and cut back brush around the aged pear and apple trees. He bought a used tiller, sharpened Grandmaw's garden tools, and planted peas and tomatoes. Preston also tried to cut the wisteria away from his house, but the wisteria always came back. He would cut at it until lunch and when he got back to it later in the afternoon, it seemed to have returned in clusters like a brain tumor. The stuff ran in long lines across the yard then popped up to choke the life out of whatever it could clutch in its million slithering fingers. Preston woke in the middle of the night in cold sweats picturing tulip trees and houses strangled by the wisteria. He could never get rid of the stuff. It worked at him day-by-day, creeping, coming up from holes in the ground like hairs from a dead man's ears. Once a year it bloomed this purple grape-like lattice, but he didn't let the momentary beauty fool him, it was always winding, climbing, knuckled vines like sickness engulfing the waning face easing its tendril tongues into every cranny.

Preston stood in front of the house holding the family machete in his shaking hands, Christmas songs and to-do lists jingling up and down his nervous system. He slashed away in the front yard, his eyes frantic and tempestuous. Since his return, he had wanted to clean it, to clear out a space that could be pristine. He chopped at the monstrous vegetation again and again swinging the dull machete in all directions. He hung like a chimpanzee on a thick vine that drooped under Grandmaw's porch awnings, his knees up against his chest and feet kicking out in all directions. Preston looked up thinking that it must have grown up into the house and wrapped around the beams in the attic. Preston swung like a contorted trapeze artist, back and forth holding onto the wisteria bough, back and forth until he was thinking more about the swinging than the pulling, his face relaxed, his mind uncoiled.

In this moment of swinging, he finally felt his long-sought love-self emerging from consciousness, echoes of "Lucy in the Sky with Diamonds" in his head and water drops in concentric halos pulsing out of his mind. He got to swinging so high that the heels of his medical shoes thudded against the ceiling of the porch when he swept backward and the toe of his shoe could almost kick the lightbulb dangling from the porch ceiling. When his heels struck the well-hidden wasp nest, a dozen black stingers struck deep into Preston's ankle and a constellation of the demonic raiders burst from the nest spiraling around Preston looking for a soft place to strike. Still swinging Preston let go in midair and did a flailing flip off the porch landing onto his back in the thick grass thrashing his arms and legs wildly, which only made the circling wasps crazier in the heat. He rolled back and forth across the yard screaming as they orbited and struck. The last wasp took its turn at Preston's red neck as he sat in the middle of the yard hitching like a babe with hot tears running down his pink cheeks. But the look on Preston's face was that of exaltation as he smelled his very bones, saw the family attic caked with wisteria and giant wasp nests blooming. Preston at this moment was sure that he felt the presence of some higher being. And when he did, he looked over his shoulder to see Venus shining.

When Preston went to the post office to collect Grandmaw's mail, he found a letter from the law office of Lionel Fredericks. The letter explained that Grandmaw had eleven thousand dollars in the bank, a small insurance policy, and a 70-acre plot of land adjoining the Tallapoochee National Forest. A simple will bequeathed all of her assets to Preston. This money afforded Preston, who had been working part-time feeding chickens, the chance to get back into college. This time Preston would study computers.

To complete his college studies, Preston drove back and forth from the mountain to the University of Alabama in a used Post Office Jeep he had bought at an auction in Montgomery for $200. After the first semester, he was known by his professors as a student with great potential. His meteoric success would shock them all.

Private properties at the edges of national forests mean clear cuts, wide scabs in the tortured, naked earth. Preston loves them, the twisted and mangled piles of dead trees that make his slow treks even more painful and tiresome in the hot sun. As he climbs over vast mounds of limbs and tree trunks rotting like teeth in the blank sky, he feels that every place is always being born, that the razed earth is at this moment coming to life, gestating to emerge anew from horror. Preston's head reels and he feels sunlight on his face

and everywhere and every person is
in between here and there and
possibilities arise from fixating our minds on
the moment
not yesterday but now and
tomorrow and
chances emerge in the
affirmations and blessings of
what remains in
our collective dreams.
Think positive.
Think positive.
Think positive.

In his dead forest delirium, Preston feels the urge to dance, to perform a cockeyed off-Broadway extravaganza among rotting limbs that extend like dancers' hands. Emotions burst forth as he spins in the dust.

As Preston pirouettes in the sun, he hears a truck coming in the distance, the rattle of designer tailpipes. His body snatches itself down the path. For the first time since he wandered away from the compound, he feels a tingle of dread and annoyance. He cringes. His meditative state has been violated and the stress that changes his speech and behavior begins to creep up on him. It's like a snake moving up his esophagus in serpentine coils between his lips so he can't talk right. Preston hears the truck move in behind him but doesn't turn around, his ankle almost twisting as he staggers into the dry gravel gully on the roadside.

To the driver of the jacked-up red monster truck, Preston looks like a hobbit with special needs.

"Mister?" shouts the young man in a crisp white shirt as the truck's window slides down with an electric hum. From the window, Preston feels the air-conditioning and smells heavy cologne. Preston looks up at him, his eyes glazed and mouth open.

"You feeling alright?" the young man asks as Preston stands there like a boozed-up circus clown. The young man gets out of the truck holding a bottle of water and looks at Preston's pupils. Face slack, Preston spins once more, hands on hips.

"Dude, I'm going to call the rescue squad," the man says. "You've had a seizure or something old school."

"I can get a ride, home school." Preston touches his right cheek multiple times. He raises his hand and in it is a tiny cell-phone. They sit together on the truck's tailgate and wait a few minutes, and the young man wonders why he had to go and stop for this deranged bum, this stinking crook-back who now glares at him with anger and condescension. The young man in the crisp white shirt has got a honey over in Horn's Valley waiting for him, and he knows that if he doesn't go get her soon, she'll be gone.

"Sorry to spoil your, you know, vision quest or whatever," the young man says. "But you look like you're about to keel over."

"I've never been more alive, Cletus."

"The name isn't Cletus. It's Jimmy."

Preston hears the thwack-thwack-thwack of a helicopter as it echoes across the valley, then he sees the dot to the north flying treetop high. Jimmy points as the helicopter moves in and lands at the edge of the clearing. Its engines wind down as two figures jump out and trudge toward the truck through the dust. The blonde man in vest and tie who looks like a tan David Bowie hangs back balancing a GPS on his finger. The Latinx woman in a halter top walks up and without much ado hoists Preston onto her shoulders like a soldier wounded in the field. It's easy to carry Mr. Price, Manuelita remembers, if you get the crook just right on the back of your neck and hang the two sides of the body over your shoulders. Not looking at slack-jawed Jimmy, Manuelita hoists Preston into the helicopter and straps him in. Tick nods and smiles dimpled-cheeked at Jimmy, his index and middle fingers raised in a peace sign.

"Where you been, nowhere man?" Tick yells in the helicopter, tapping Preston on the head with a clipboard.

Preston offers a warm smirk and Tick hugs him with one arm. Preston responds by elbowing Tick in the ribs.

"Dude, you need a bath," Tick coughs. "Let's get some breeze going in this thing."

"Good to see you Mr. Price," Manuelita says after helping Preston with his headphones. The chopper banks as she passes him a moist towelette. She has learned that talking to Mr. Price takes a bit of finesse as she watches him look at the blur of trees below. Mr. Price is especially troublesome after he's been out wandering. He is now grinning widely and staring at the curves of the mountain range before him, tears dropping off the end of his nose. Tick looks at Manuelita, rotating an index finger at his ear. Preston puts his head in his open hands as his shoulders shake. He mutters something about catching a fish. Manuelita recalls the time she found him in Memphis sitting in the tall gutter grass facing the trains like a deranged child. His face had been so open as he stared at the boxcars, but when he saw her standing there, Mr. Price's face had instantly squinted with paranoia.

"Mr. Price?" Manuelita says through the tiny mike attached to the headphones. He glares like a wolf and turns back to the window.

"We're making our move today," she says.

His eyes sharpen.

"Today?" Preston says. "To the holding suite?"

"As instructed."

The helicopter descends to a rectangular patch in the middle of a vast, green forest. Almost undetectable from the air, Preston's compound is on an oddly-shaped two hundred-acre longleaf plantation bordered on all sides by federal lands. A twisting, turning patchwork of logging trails is the only way in or out, unless you know how to fly the chopper. There is a sprawling out-of-place faux plantation house, a line of simple cabins, numerous storage buildings, a barn, an orchard, and a series of gardens. And there's the egg.

Sitting fifty feet high on its cylindrical shaft, the gigantic egg would be out of place anywhere, except maybe the Vegas strip or some B science fiction movie. It appears to have no doors or windows, no way in or out. Manuelita knows only bits and pieces of the philosophy behind the egg, the part about the self-help guru Isaiah Please. A German firm built the installation and has maintained it with a high level of secrecy. She has only a vague sense of what will happen in there, but with the extravagant pay and extreme confidentiality of this production, she doesn't ask questions. Up until now, the job has been pretty simple: find, follow, and film Jasmine Wills.

But now it's time for the intervention.

8

The Alabama asphalt breathes wavy lines and blurs vision. It's a scorcher. Jasmine and Kay-Lee crouch in the brown Toyota with the windows rolled down. They chew gum and keep their peepers peeled. The street scene is suddenly mysterious to these two improbable spies as they stake out their only link to the cryptic notes and disappearing Pensacola Beach souvenir, the new teller named Meghan. A mangy white dog on the sidewalk gnaws at a paper burger bag. A real estate agent wearing a tan suit crosses the street with a sub sandwich. Everything slows, every moment filled with implications. Popping gum in her wrinkled security uniform, Kay-Lee uses binoculars to follow Meghan around the bank, in case she goes out the side entrance. Meghan has been the subject of this investigation for 48 hours, but the surveillance has resulted in no leads.

Yesterday they trailed Meghan to the nail salon where she met an unidentified Vietnamese woman wearing a surgical mask. The two leaned in close and spoke in hushed tones as the woman polished Meghan's fingernails. Positioned in the shadows outside the nail salon with the binoculars, Kay-Lee could not read the woman's lips because of the mask.

They did find that Meghan Oswell likes banana smoothies, does Pilates, takes shiatsu massages, and worships Satan. They were surprised to find that she lives in a brick townhouse all the way up in Mountain Brook. Both women were shocked to see how many men positioned themselves along Meghan's path, casually drifting towards her, all the time, every day, full of smiles with twinkles in their eyes. Young and old, snappy-dressed hipsters and leering grandpas alike, they'd make small talk and smile, smile and talk, their trajectories changing to stand as close as possible to Meghan with her tight business suit and fluttering eyes.

"He's passing her a note!" Jasmine said.

"It's just his digits," Kay-Lee said.

"His digit?"

"His digits, idjit. His phone number. He's trying to get a date."

"Oh."

Jasmine glances into her rearview mirror and notices a Post Office Jeep parked at the edge of a side alley.

"I think we've got ourselves a tail," Jasmine says. Kay-Lee turns in her seat and focuses her binoculars on the Post Office Jeep.

"It's empty," Kay-Lee lies. Her cell rings, a digital "Giddy Up a Oom Papa Oom Papa Mow Mow."

"It's Obediah," she says and opens the car door. "Gotta take this."

Jasmine wonders why Kay-Lee is getting out of the car to talk to her fiancée. Kay-Lee and Obediah have had every imaginable kind of conversation right in front of Jasmine. They've talked about everything from Obediah's faith healing to the right way to tongue Kay-Lee's clitoral piercings. Kay-Lee has never had a secretive bone in her body and Jasmine finds it strange that she keeps glancing into the car. Picking up the binoculars, Jasmine notices that Meghan is also talking on her cellphone. And she's looking out the bank window.

"What was that about?" Jasmine asks when Kay-Lee gets back into the car.

"Nothing," she says. "He wants pork chops tonight."

"Oh crap," Jasmine says, cranking the car. "She's coming out."

Meghan Oswell steps across the street and hops into her silver Lexus.

"Let's do this," Kay-Lee whispers. "Get in behind her, but not too close. Stay two cars back like they do on TV." They speed behind Meghan's car toward the strip mall as Jasmine watches the passing fast-food restaurants fly by. Talking on her cellphone, Meghan suddenly turns, careening into a burger joint parking lot.

"She's going for the drive-thru," Kay-Lee says. Jasmine falls in behind and watches Meghan talk into the speaker to make her order. Then Meghan pulls around the side of the restaurant to pick up her smoothie.

"What are you doing?" Kay-Lee says as Jasmine pulls up to the speaker and hits the brake. "You can't wait for food. We'll lose her."

Breathing heavily, Jasmine stares at the metal speaker.

"*Can I take your order?*" the voice box says.

Jasmine's thick knuckles squeeze the steering wheel as she peels around the restaurant past Meghan and into traffic.

A concerned mother snatches her flabby child from a stroller and a pickup truck in the street slams on its brakes and slides sideways. An entire family of shocked rednecks gives Jasmine the double bird.

"Oh crap," Jasmine says as the car fishtails.

Kay-Lee's cell goes off again.

"Pull over before you kill us!" Kay-Lee yells, looking down at the number of the caller and frowning. "Calm down. Maybe she will come this way and we can tail her again."

"OK, OK," Jasmine says, her hands shaking as she fumbles to parallel park.

Meghan pulls by in traffic then makes a sudden U-turn to go back the other way.

"Now what?" Jasmine says.

"Get on her," Kay-Lee says and they follow. Meghan takes Highway 14 out of town toward the Tallapoochee National Forest.

"But she lives in Mountain Brook," Jasmine says. "That's the wrong way."

"Just keep following."

"Good god-a-mighty," Jasmine says, seeing two Post Office Jeeps at a red light.

"Don't freak out, girl. We'll be there soon."

"Be *where*?" Jasmine says and glares at Kay-Lee.

"Keep going."

Once they get out of town, the two-lane road narrows to become a corridor of high trees, the Tallapoochee Gap Mountain rising in the distance like a thumb. A few isolated houses dot the forest for the first mile, then it becomes a vast and endless wood. Everything gets quiet as Jasmine speeds to keep up with the silver car in front of them. Buzzards circle in the stark mountain sky, a cluster of the grave and ominous birds on the side of the road digging inside the rib cage of a dead deer. They fly into the branches of a high pine tree when Meghan's car passes. *Bad sign*, Jasmine thinks, her breath short, strands of light purple now seeping into her vision.

"Mama didn't want me to see no colors," Jasmine blurts out of nowhere. "She told me that if I was strong and believed in God that it would go away."

"What you talking about?" Kay-Lee says.

"I smelled myself," Jasmine says blankly. "Right when Parrish started to make me feel it, all I could think about was the shapes. The shapes was telling me the good feeling was just for God."

"Girl, stop with the talking, you're freaking me out," Kay-Lee says. "Oh look she's turning onto a dirt road. Slow down and pull in behind her."

"I don't know."

"*Do it.*"

Jasmine bellows as a white van slams into her pushing her car into Meghan's rear end. She looks back just in time to see a black bag flash over her head and feel the rope going around and around her neck. Jasmine's foot hits the gas and she can feel the car accelerating.

"Cliff!" Kay-Lee screeches as the car flips off a steep embankment. Jasmine feels herself flung about as she's if inside a clothes dryer, broken flipping car glass spattering her exposed arms. The airbag pops out of the steering wheel like a poked pig bladder. As the overturned automobile slides down into the gorge, Jasmine claws like an animal at Kay-Lee who is still holding both ends of the rope tight around Jasmine's throat. Shock drains from Jasmine's purple inflated face as her hands drop from the rope. Jasmine then feels the syringe push into her side, bubbles and the bright colors rising to the top of her skull. Voices yell from the road. Hands grasp at her body.

"Angelique?!"

Sliding into unconsciousness, Jasmine can still hear the voices through the bag.

"I'm going to be so famous."

Everything goes buzzard black.

PART TWO

THE EGG

9

Back in the '80s, Preston and Tick spent their summers tooling around Lake Guin in Tick's little Boston Whaler. Brown lake houses with screened-in porches dotted the eastern shore as red-faced men with melon bellies mowed their lawns at the water's edge. They frowned as they watched the boys on the boat playing air guitars to hair metal as they buzzed the shore leaving chicken bones and beer cans in their wake. On the west end of the lake, Camp Calvary and the paper mill bordered one another, separated by a thin wall of pine. If the wind was good on the lake you only got a little of the fetid creosote smell, but if the wind was bad you got it all the way down to the marina. Circling the lake in sunglasses larger than their adolescent heads, Tick and Preston loved to speed over floating trash, milk jugs, and ominous black logs below the water's yellow surface trying to broadside the occasional blue heron or duck. But never a turtle. Once, when Tick dared to veer the boat toward a turtle, Preston struck wild with sudden punches, fists swinging out of nowhere and flying in all directions.

"Clown," Tick had said dodging the blows. "Fool." Glancing Tick's ear with a misguided uppercut, Preston had deflated like a hot air balloon struck by lightning. He then curled up on the boat's bottom, one eye clenched, his face buried in his hands. Laughing, Tick had poured a bottle of Thunderbird all over Preston's limp body. Enraged, Preston stood up and began swinging a second barrage of crazed punches. This time he slipped on a boat paddle hitting his head on the outboard motor. Tick kicked Preston in the stomach and dove into the water with Preston leaping in right behind him. Splashing in the lake they grabbed at each other's throats as the boat floated toward the dam. Seeing that the boat was perilously close to the dam, the boys started screaming and swinging their arms for help. They were picked up by the first boat that came by, which happened to be a patrolling Alabama Marine Police vessel. First aid was administered to both inebriated parties by the Marine Police officers, and all the alcohol found on Tick's Boston Whaler was poured into the lake.

"You just cost us a six-pack and a bottle of T-Bird," Tick had said shaking his head at Preston after the police left them with a warning. "Now we gotta go back to Bobby Cleecher's."

South Gulch back then was a swampy patch where two narrow creeks came together. On its bamboo-choked peninsula, there were a dozen rusty house trailers, abandoned RVs, and wood-floor fish camps with blue tarpaulin roofs where sunburned country folk came to get down. Gunfire sometimes erupted from South Gulch and the occasional Sasquatch sighted.

Bobby Cleecher lived back there somewhere in a silver RV from whence emanated hour-upon-hour outdated tunes such as "Calypso Breakdown" and "Night on Disco Mountain." But despite his fanatical love of disco, his thin belts and tight polyester shirts, nobody messed with Bobby Cleecher. It is rumored that once when a man in a Halloween mask came in to rob the marina, Cleecher shot him in the guts, tied him up with a rope, stole the robber's clown mask, then wore the mask the whole time the Tallapoochee County Sheriff investigated. Bobby Cleecher's tiny cinderblock marina sold mainly bologna sandwiches and beer, but one entire wall of the little store was devoted to fishing lures, spinners, three-pronged hooks, bobbers, and plastic worms. Tick was the only underage kid Preston knew who could get beer at Bobby's. When they went in the marina to get a six-pack, Preston stood mouth agape looking at the colorful fishing tackle.

"What's wrong with your boy?" Bobby Cleecher asked Tick at the cash register.

"He's just wrong," Tick said with a shrug.

"Let's go in back for a minute." Bobby opened a small door and let Tick in behind the cash register. They walked back through to the storage room.

"Preston," Tick said. "Go around behind the store and I'll pass you the beer." Before Preston could protest, Bobby closed and locked the storage room door. Preston kicked at soda bottles and oil cans as he shambled around the marina. The place was junky out back, piles of burned garbage and rusted-out boats scattered around a dried-up melon patch filled with thistle and cattails out to a pair of tall boat houses. Preston stood next to the back door of Bobby Cleecher's in the midday sun, spots of sweat growing like gunshot wounds on his faded blue shirt. As he waited by the door, he started to feel a knotting in his stomach, his mind filling with dread. *What*, Preston thought, *is Tick doing locked up in there with that disco dancing madman?*

Preston knocked on the back door, leaned in close, and heard only the *tat-tat-tat* of the attic fan. The figure of a woman had been sprayed across the concrete wall with obscene features and no head. Preston banged on the back door a few more times and tried to look through the keyhole. Nobody came to the door. A single dark cloud came and went as Preston laid down flat in the powder-dry dirt to peer through the door crack. Sweat from his face made drops like bloodstains in the dust. In the middle of the storage room was a dried little hair sack that used to be a dead mouse and Preston caught a whiff of mothball and paint. When Preston exhaled he blew the fine, powdery dust back up into his eyes. Tick wasn't in there. Coughing and rubbing his face, Preston noticed in the center of the stark room two tables covered in clear plastic. On both goo-spattered tables were bowls, measuring cups, and strips of white cloth. Except for a wall full of canned food and chips off to the side, it didn't look like a storage room in there. It looked to Preston like a place where you might find a stack of murder victims. Behind the table, Preston spied this intricately crafted macrame vest worn by a full-size plaster cast of Bobby Cleecher. Preston couldn't see hide nor hair of Tick and assumed that he was being strangled in the walk-in cooler. The large attic fan above the door blocked out sound as Preston yelled through the crack until he was out of breath. Looking through the crack again, Preston noticed something else that shocked him. On a high shelf, Preston saw a long line of solid white heads. Each ceramic bust on the shelf was a perfect replica of a boy Preston had seen out on the lake, and three of the heads looked like Tick's. Preston heard the door unlock and jumping back saw a six-pack of Pabst Blue Ribbon dangling out of the crack.

"Put it in the cooler," Tick said and the door slammed. When Tick ran back to the boat, he was smirking and flushed.

"What were you doing in there?" Preston said.

"Wouldn't you like to know?"

Out on Lake Guin, Tick and Preston roasted in a land of metal bass boats, rods and reels, tackle boxes, pontoon party barges, boogie boards, Nerf footballs, merciless horseflies, and the thunderstorm's daily reckoning. It was summertime in the Heart of Dixie, and Tick Godwin free-wheeled in the lake's deep center. He turned the boat with his chin raised and golden hair bouncing in the breeze. He sported a copper tan, white Izod shirt, and khaki shorts. Preston stared into the teenage horizon, biting his nails, sporting bedhead, and wearing an orange life preserver. The beer hidden in the bow of the boat was for what Tick called the "willing bubbettes" across the lake at Camp Calvary. Whenever they were going to cruise by Camp Calvary, Tick would replace his Duran Duran or Depeche Mode tapes for something he thought the Camp Calvary girls just wouldn't be able to resist: Ozzy. He would crank up songs like "Bark at the Moon" and "Crazy Train" because he thought it excited them. It didn't excite them.

"Ozzy baby," Tick would say pulling his Ray-Bans down so that everyone could see the whites of his eyes, "The Madman.

The Wizard of Ozz." He would putter by girls swimming or paddling around in canoes with the Prince of Darkness blaring just to watch their reactions. Some stared with absent grins, others just stared. But Preston's mind was jolted by this one girl, a sunburned little toad who scowled at them and shook her head in disgust. That look in her dead, flat eyes contained less feeling than Preston had ever seen in a kid, and it fascinated him.

"Hey sweet thang, wanna ride?" Tick had yelled in a falsetto Southern accent to the round chick roasting in the summer heat. When the sun came out from behind clouds, the aluminum canoes glared like dull mirrors in flat water. And in their midst, the girl with the awful stare continued to stare, and stare, until even Tick got the creeps. She was a bullfrog in the pitiless sun with a face that appeared to repel all sense of feeling. It was the face of the captive, the summer camp prisoner, the fat kid doing time. Preston always carried that face around within him, that frozen, defiant face petrified like Alabama deadwood.

"See ya later sweet potater," Tick said in a Kermit the Frog voice as the Boston Whaler motor whined to life. Water splashed on Preston's hairless sunburned legs in the front of the boat as it bounced toward a stark hill of pine. After they sped to a small inlet at the other end of the lake, Tick shut down the motor and let the boat float without course. He then grabbed a beer from the cooler and stretched out on the bough next to Preston.

"I'm away all next week," Tick said spinning the unopened beer in his palm. "The parents are taking me to New Orleans for a few days."

"Awesome," Preston said.

"Awesome, if you like to follow a pair of gaunt alcoholics in thousand-dollar duds to the bottom of a case of vodka."

"You have to admit, your parents are kinda radical."

"Radical? Oh, they're *radical* all right," Tick murmured sitting up. "There's this club on the causeway they used to take me to when I was like four or five. Daddy was, as you know, this big shot because he's a senator with a lot of pull, so I'm allowed to go in the club because he's Mister VIP, you know, bull goose loony. You should have seen it, the whole nine yards, fancy dinners, music, women juking it up... *radical*, right?"

"Rad," Preston said.

"Have you ever had to curl up in a restaurant booth with your jacket as a pillow and sleep all night, some crappy horns section playing in your ear? For hours and hours and hours I would lie there with my head on the table until it was filled with glasses and ashtrays. Welcome to a seedy underworld filled with smoke and halitosis, Preston. Woo frickin' hoo. Did your parents ever do that to you?"

"No," Preston said noticing that the boat was floating toward the bank.

"No. It sucks. I was just a little kid."

"That sucks brah," Preston said absently. He pushed the boat away from an overhanging tree branch with his paddle.

"My mother told me that because I was four I wasn't supposed to be in there and if anybody asked, I was to say that I was a midget, OK?"

"A midget?" Preston, suddenly interested, turned to look at Tick. "You mean a dwarf?"

"Yeah, dude. I didn't stutter. A mid-get," Tick said as he shook the beer a little and then cracked it open. Some of the foam got in Preston's hair.

"Suck my big one," Preston said wiping his hair. Then he punched Tick in the shoulder.

"Quit it, man. You suck mine. I'm not joking."

"I mean, was she laughing when she said it like a joke or was she serious?"

"That doesn't matter," Tick said. "I was four. I *thought* she was serious."

"So, you thought you were supposed to act like a midget, or, uh, you know, did you think you *were* a midget?"

"The point is," Tick said cocking his head with a sad smile, "I'm nothing to them but a troll."

"So you feel like a leprechaun," Preston offered, "and stuff."

The boat, now under the sunless shadow of overhanging limbs, rocked and lightly bumped against the shore.

"So what happened?"

"So I'm curled up with my coat one night, remember I'm four, and this longheaded Black waiter in a stupid purple cummerbund comes over and pulls on my foot. So I wake up and see this guy's face and start crying. The guy frowns and looks over at my dancing parents. And I scream--"

"--and you scream, 'I'm a midget! I'm a midget!'"

"Shut up dude, this is my pity party. But yes, I am yelling 'I'm a midget' to this guy and everybody's laughing at me. I'm looking around at this drunken circle of old faces and start holding my tongue all loose and stuff, you know, contorting my face, staggering around like I had a touch of the palsy, clapping my arms like a penguin, looking up at the lights and gargling at the top of my lungs. I then poured a highball down the front of my slacks to make it look like I pissed my pants. Finally, when I had embarrassed my drunk parents enough, they took me home."

"That would make a good Norman Rockwell painting."

"Do you want to know why the witch calls me that name?"

"What name?"

"Tick, dude. My nickname. *She* came up with that. She says I'm a leech, like a parasite, you know, that attaches itself to a host and sucks it dry."

"You are kind of a mooch."

"But don't you think it's kind of messed up for the person who says that be the one you supposedly, you know, suckled?"

"That's messed up."

"And she didn't even breastfeed my ass," Tick said. "I had a wet nurse."

"A wet *what*? What you talkin' 'bout Gary Coleman?"

"A wet nurse. A lady who lived in the basement. I fed off her so mother could keep her boobs from sagging before mommy dearest got the augmentation surgeries."

"Who?" Preston said coughing beer from his nose as he cackled. "You are saying you sucked on some other old lady's titties when you were a baby?"

"Yeah, dude," Tick said with a single eyebrow raised. "And she was a *Black* lady, too."

"Why should *that* matter?" Preston said, suddenly defensive.

"My mom said that she wanted to be *progressive* or something."

Tick had told a version of this lie before, but that time it was his grandfather who had suckled at the breast of a Black wet nurse.

"Oh you got it bad, man," Preston said wagging his head. "I feel sorry for *you*." He adds in a high-pitched whiny voice, "Poor little troll gotta go to New Orleans with parents who like to party hearty."

"Quit being a dick."

"My mother's dead, dude, my deadbeat dad takes care of dope fiends, and my Grandmaw eats poke salad."

They sat for a long minute as the sun hid behind a lakeside hill, the sky a hard blue.

"Let's cruise Camp Calvary again," Tick said tossing his empty beer can into the lake.

"Word," Preston said looking down into the water, spitting into his own reflection.

Two decades later, Preston and Tick stand over this Alabama bullfrog of a woman whose round, unconscious face is frozen in a scowl. The room in the plantation house is fashioned to look like a suite in a historic hotel complete with high ceilings, chandeliers, and walls of eggshell white. Preston talks on the phone and paces back and forth across the mahogany floor with a large suitcase in his hand. Tick stands at a rear window sending texts and edits to the lab in Colorado. Talking on his cell with Bill Dew at TBS, Preston examines Jasmine's body for injuries, rolling her side-to-side with effort in the four-post bed. A small scratch here, a tiny bruise there, possible drug overdose, nothing serious.

Preston digs through the woman's purse finding nothing of personal value but a single photograph. It is a picture of a girl and a boy at the beach, both holding up small fish with big smiles on their faces. The skinny children are red from the sun and both have long hair. The back of the card reads, "Jasmine and Don-Don." He puts it into his pocket, pushes a button on a wall fixture behind an ornate bedside lamp, and opens the suitcase. It contains a white plus-sized jumpsuit, socks, white headband, and sneakers.

"Just finishing up a little pre-production," Preston says on the phone, cringing as he rubs his crooked back. With trembling fingers, he takes the jumpsuit out of the case and holds it up to the light of the antique lamp.

"And you got the girl?" Bill Dew asks over the phone. "Are we talking a flabalanche?"

"She's a gigantic woman. Just *gigantic*. She works at the bank, full of all these repressed energies, every eating disorder you can imagine, and this condition that makes her see colors. I mean, she has this big gallon of nacho cheese dip in her refrigerator. Great back story. Take my word, she is the one."

"Congratulations," Bill says. "In a week?"

"We'll send you something."

"Keep me posted," Bill says with a click.

"Put this on her," Preston says to Manuelita. "Let's move that rug aside." As Preston paces around the suite, Tick rolls up the rug to reveal a round platform in the floor. Preston pushes a series of buttons on the wall fixture and stands upon the platform. With a mechanical buzz, the platform descends down the shaft with Preston on it. Manuelita looks down into the hole seeing only blackness and the top of Preston's shaggy head. As Tick helps Manuelita pull the polyester outfit over Jasmine's ivory buttocks, straining and grunting as they try to roll the large woman's body, the floor panel reappears with Preston on it, leaning against a doublewide wheelchair.

"Put her in the wheelchair," Preston says, rolling it around toward the bed. The dead weight is almost more than they can together lift. "Let's roll her onto the platform." This time they all ride down the subterranean shaft with Jasmine slumped over in the wheelchair. When they reach the bottom, they see the motion-sensor fluorescent lights of the narrow white hallway pop into half-life. Tossing his mop-top out of his frantic eyes, Preston scampers ahead down the spherical corridor of the bunker as Tick pushes the wheelchair and its unconscious occupant. At the end of the hallway, twenty feet underground, they come into a round room with concrete walls. In the center of the room is another platform in the floor, like that of the holding suite. They step onto the elevator and move upward into the egg.

The oval room inside the dome shines because the walls are made of curved mirrors. A blue bed, couch, bathroom, and exercise equipment line the circumference of the white room like furnishings in an Airstream trailer. Preston stares awestruck at the interior's Venusian gleam.

"Put her on the bed," Preston mutters and walks to the mirrored wall brandishing a key card. Swiping the key card over a seam in the mirrors, a hatch pops open and Preston walks through a slot in the glass wall. There is a narrow space between the two-way mirror and the outer surface of the egg where multiple mounted motion-sensor cameras record movement inside. The trio pulls and pushes, their faces sweating, as they try to get the woman onto the bed.

"Wow, it's like concentric circles, a concentric dome," Manuelita says, breathing heavily. She tucks Jasmine under the sheets and glances around, trying to decipher the space.

"Yeah, the aesthetic works," Preston says as he smiles for a second. "My apartment is under the floor over on this side."

"I feel like I'm in a spaceship," Manuelita says glancing around inside the egg-shaped set. "It's like some Gemini capsule or something."

"The lighting was difficult because it's both a set, you know, but also a prolonged habitat. We had to--"

"--Oh I just *love* this," Tick interrupts, pointing at the disk-shaped silver lampshade. "How much did *that* cost us?"

"Look," Preston says poking his head through the door. "Food and laundry will be brought through this dumbwaiter. The elevator will be offlined as soon as you leave. Don't forget to seal both hatches from the outside when you go."

"By your command," Tick says as he double clicks his heels together.

"He's just pissed because he thinks I shut him out of set design," Preston says to Manuelita.

"Now that you mention it, Preston, you did shut me out," Tick says. "You've been so territorial with this."

"I thought you would be pleased, partner. Next show, Tick, *you* can design all of the sets and *I* will spend the two weeks in Fiji."

"Don't get sensitive," Tick says. "I like the set. The set's great. I'm pumped."

"Glad to finally hear it."

"Egg man, let's do this!" Tick bellows as he slaps the backboard of Jasmine's bed. "*Diet Extreme* baby!"

"Aren't you coming out with us?" Manuelita asks.

"No," Preston says, handing Tick a key ring with five jump drives attached, each with a name scribbled with magic marker, except one. "I will remain in the outer corridor of the egg operating the hand-held as well as the central mainframe. Your directions are all on here. The guests should be waiting for you at the Tallapoochee airport. Airlift them over and take them to the plantation house."

"Who gets the fifth jump drive?"

"The fifth jump drive is for Bill Dew's cousin," he says with a hint of impatience. "Jaekel Sneade. Grounds crew."

"Don't do anything I wouldn't do," Tick says as Preston shuts the hatch with an airtight clink.

"What *do* you think Preston's going to do with her in there?" Manuelita says as they ride up the house elevator.

"Probably play dress up," Tick says. "He's into that."

"Let's look at our instructions," Manuelita says as they return to their basement lab in the plantation house. When they get to the murky room they see that the monitors are already recording sleeping Jasmine from twenty angles. The set is full of stark light. They slip the jump drives into laptops and what looks to be a simple word document pops up on both monitors.

"Mine's time-delayed," Tick says. "Little asshole."

Manuelita looks up at the monitors to see twenty pictures of looming Preston Price standing at a 45-degree angle over the sleeping Jasmine. "He shouldn't be inside there. What if she wakes up? She's not supposed to see him."

"Relax, with the drugs we gave her she won't wake up for hours."

"Preston's scaring me," Manuelita says. "Look at his face."

"Brace yourself because it's going to get scarier."

"Who are these people?" Manuelita asks. "Preston's *guests*?"

"He hired them through the agency. Cast and crew."

"Let's go. If they are waiting at the rinky-dink Tallapoochee airstrip, you know they're already pissed."

"Besides we need to get back 'cause I want to roast a couple of Cornish hens, just you and me, and a nice bottle of Beaujolais."

"No really, what's Mr. Price gonna do in there?" Manuelita repeats as they get into the golf cart and drive toward the small heliport. "They're both completely locked in there together, right? Mr. Price has the only key?"

"He's got a shower and some clothes, a mini-fridge, and some space food down in that capsule. He's in it for the duration, you know. He's as happy as a monkey in deep space. Don't worry, Preston thrives on this stuff."

"How's he going to live inside the wall of an egg for a whole season?"

"The guy's a vermin," Tick says. "He'll be fine. It's Jasmine you should worry about."

10

Between the concrete and glass eggs, there's a dark crevice where Preston crawls and schemes. After all the planning and work, he's finally sealed up tight with his new star. The inner egg is made of seamless glass and shiny steel, and Jasmine is his sleeping turtle in her terrarium. The glass egg is a two-way mirror, so unless he's down in the apartment beneath the floor Preston can see her at all times. Below Jasmine's room, there is a low-ceilinged compartment just large enough for Preston to sleep, shower, and watch a dozen monitors fixed above his computer terminal. There are, of course, cameras attached to the glass egg with motion sensors to follow Jasmine when she does begin to move around in her cell, but Preston can also use the hand-held. She is sleeping now, her chest rising and falling. In the morning she will wake and *Diet Extreme* will begin.

Preston climbs a rope ladder down the curved looking-glass and sits at the small table in his soundproof apartment under the floor. His quarters are not much larger than an airliner cockpit. There are three books on the table, the three books that have meant the most to him in his life. The three books he would take on a desert island or into the dark heart of the Tallapoochee. There's the worn two-volume set, *Facing the Hate-Self* and *Finding the Love-Self* by Isaiah Please M.D., Ph.D. The third book, also threadbare, is *The Real Mother Goose*, copyright 1916. He reads "Jack Sprat" aloud, then skips forward a little to look at a drawing of himself clad in a green suit and red leggings. He's hiking to a valley in the distance between two mountains. Preston reads:

> There was a crooked man, and he
> went a crooked mile
> He found a crooked sixpence be-
> side a crooked stile;
> He bought a crooked cat, which
> caught a crooked mouse,
> And they all lived together in a
> little crooked house.

Preston thumbs through the book staring at the haunting, agone drawings of foppish children and well-dressed animals. Something in him uncoils as he stares at the pictures. A terrified Humpty Dumpty in bow tie and gray suit, a young Robin Hood kneeling in the woods, a boy and girl returning from market with a pig on a rope, and a grinning lad behind a wall over his pouting hostage in white bonnet:

> Peter, Peter, pumpkin-eater,
> Had a wife and couldn't keep her;
> He put her in a pumpkin shell,
> And there he kept her very well.

On the monitor, Jasmine rolls in her bed. *Possibly troubled,* Preston thinks, *by some momentary synaptic event. Perhaps she is finding her hate-self in those narcotic dreams.* Preston tries to enjoy the moment and keep reading the children's rhymes, but the stinger of memory pokes at him again. Just as he was starting to calm down, Preston finds himself thinking of Maddy, feeling that old black magic, the jib-jabs coming back.

I-I guess I shouldn't have done that to Maddy, his hate-self whispers as he watches Jasmine breathe.

But this is different, a second voice whispers back. *I'm a different person now.* But Preston doesn't feel like a different person now. He doesn't feel any real remorse over what happened to Maddy, the one he called his sleeping beauty. He just wishes he hadn't destroyed the photos.

Maddy had rosacea and this habit of extending the stud in her tongue and flicking it against her large white teeth back and forth, back and forth. It was a reflex, but Preston didn't know the young woman and thought she was trying to turn him on. On the night that he did what he did, Preston tried not to keep looking at the white borderline her shirt made along her bust, her tangled red hair covering her freckled face, and her hands toying with the silver rings on her fingers and thumb.

Preston had seen Maddy working at a coffee shop near the studio when he was doing a five-box set. He had called her for weeks leaving long befuddling messages, but when he had her alone in the car Preston couldn't think of a single thing to say. As they lurched and stopped along the freeway, she sat turned away from him staring out at the traffic jam. *She had seemed livelier in the coffee shop,* Preston thought, *more maternal when she brought him his bagels.* He had gotten her number because she had seemed interested in this coalition trying to free the animals at the zoo. He had nervously talked to her about a sad-eyed hippo named Cecil, wildebeests with self-esteem needs, and manic-depressive hyenas until she put her name and number on his clipboard. Then he called and called, inviting her to one of the meetings when finally, one Tuesday, she came. After the meeting, Preston invited Maddy to his producer's condo where he told her he partied with dudes like Yakov Smirnoff and Garry Shandling. To his surprise, she said yes, but just to "hang out." After some small talk at the condo, Preston was disappointed to learn that while she wanted to spend the night, she would sleep in the small bedroom without the beach view leaving him all alone in the master bedroom with the beach view. She had tossed her Czech army surplus backpack onto a bed in the narrow bedroom, sat down, and shrugged.

"What are we going to do?" she finally said with a loose smile, her tongue ring flicking back and forth across her teeth. Preston had leaned in for the kiss and she had let him. But when his fingers touched the cleft between her breasts, she twisted away.

"I didn't mean *that*," she said.

Preston shrugged darkly and went out onto the deck. *Lame,* he thought, *Loser.* He brooded feeling that the overwhelming pink sunset was far too profound, too rich, to watch alone. He had hoped that Maddy would come out to the deck too, but she didn't. After twenty minutes he walked back into the bedroom where she was sitting on the edge of the bed watching *Candid Camera* reruns on VHS, a sketch with Fannie Flagg as a firefighter. TV lights flickered across her face as Preston stood in the doorway watching.

"What?" she had said, looking up at his shadow.

"Want to get some dinner?"

"Whatever," she said. "Sure."

"I want to do what you want."

"Dinner's fine," she had said with a strained smile.

They walked silently down the neon seaside corridor as a rangy guy with a pompadour juggled bowling pins and a lady with longish feet played "My Bonnie Lies Over the Ocean" on an old synthesizer. Potato chip bags and dirty red straws choked the long gutter between the grass and the concrete. Couples snuggled on blankets in the sand as they stared out at the ocean, dwindling lines of purple sunset turning them into shadows. Preston had put his arm around Maddy where it just hanged there like a plank, her shoulder stiffening as she walked. He held onto her for one delusional second longer, then lifted his arm.

"Next weekend Dennis and I are going to see Chili Peppers," she finally said.

"Dennis?"

"Yeah, you know, I told you about him at the shop. I told you about him many times. He's the guy I'm seeing."

"You mean are you two an item?"

"I don't know, he's so..." He saw her face brighten, her mind elsewhere.

"He's so what?"

"He's so different than any of the guys I've been with before."

"Like how?" Preston snapped, his body turning into lead.

"You know, he's really..."

"Really what?" Preston's arms flailed in desperation. "*Really what?*"

Maddy looked over at him, no longer trying to smile.

"What's eating you?" she said.

"Nothing. Nobody." Preston frowned as he rotated his neck a few times.

"What?" she said.

"Here you are on a date with me and you can't shut up about some other jerk?"

"This isn't a date, Preston. You said we were just hanging out."

"It's just that I can tell that you understand me. You get it," Preston continued. "You *understand*. These people--"

"--Let's stop in here," she said flicking her hair out of her eyes. "I've been here before." The bar's neon sign read "Hammerhead's." Preston exhaled as they walked into the dank bar, the jukebox death metal repugnant to his hypersensitive ears. Maddy smirked, her head banging a little to a screeching guitar solo. She couldn't help staring over her shoulder at the muscular bikers at the bar as Preston tried to talk over the music, gesturing wildly. Preston reluctantly bought Maddy two beers, but when she asked him to buy her a Mai Tai he shook his head no. He covered his ears, signaling that he was ready to go.

After walking silently on the promenade, they ate a quiet meal at an empty Thai restaurant out by the dock. The waitress kept staring from their plates to their faces. Preston felt the cooks looking at him from the steamy kitchen.

"How is everything?" the waitress asked as they slumped over noodle dishes.

"Perfect," Preston lied as Maddy managed a polite face. But it wasn't good. Nothing about the food was right. Preston's dumplings drooped loose from his chopsticks, overcooked vegetables languished in a turgid brown sauce, and his fortune cookie read, "Your Dreams Will Not Come True – Find New Ones." Preston felt unexpected anger course through his body, and a sudden cold spasm shot through his back. When they got back to the condo, Maddy said she wanted to go out to make a phone call.

"You can make the call here," Preston said, holding up a phone.

"Nah." She raised her shoulders and turned away, her hand already twisting the doorknob. "That's alright man."

She didn't come back for hours. All the while, Preston sat on the couch, his hands scuttling like bugs across the imitation leather. He went to the bedroom closet and fingered the costume ball dress he had hidden there the day before. It glittered at his fingertips. After doing that for an hour, he sat back down on the couch and moped. When Maddy finally got back at 2:00 in the morning, she was blotto. She staggered around the condo looking at the signed pictures of celebrities like George Goebel and Milton Berle on the walls. The comedians seemed to stare down at Preston with their wacky smiles, all in on the joke, waiting for the punch line. Preston's back straightened when she edged close to him.

"I am so messed up," Maddy had said. She leaned back into his lap and looked up at him with dazed eyes. She was breathing hard, their faces close, her tongue stud sliding back and forth against her teeth. Preston stood up abruptly and walked out of the room.

"Now what?" she slurred. "Your timing is just the worst--" she said shaking her head.

"I just wanted to make you one more drink," he said coming back into the room with a big grin.

"I don't think so. I'm bombed."

"Try this," he said, his smile still taut. He gave her a glass of bubbling liquid and turned on his favorite Kinks mix. "Grandmaw used to love it."

After a few sips, Maddy became a peacock, all smiles and exaggerated dance moves around the room as Preston watched stunned. Sadly, the peacock dance would be short-lived. She stood in front of him unbuttoning her blouse, her red hair draped over her face.

"…leave the sun behind me…" she crooned, "…watch the clouds as they sadly pass me by…"

To Preston's stupefaction, Maddy unfastened her black bra with a cocked head. She leaned in close to his pursed lips. Preston froze in paralysis.

"I've gotta tell you…I tried to get with an old guy before," she said, her voice syrupy. "But I didn't have the feelings."

Her body collapsed to the floor with a clunk.

When Maddy saw Preston next, a week had passed. She figured she'd never see the creep again, but there he was sitting at the coffee shop wearing a blue spandex exercise suit. She walked by him stiffly without saying a word, glanced at him for a second, and then blinked to look away. They hadn't spoken since she hightailed it out of the condo while he was out getting them Eggs Benedict breakfasts.

"Hiya Maddy!" he said in an overly loud, strained voice.

Customers turned to stare.

"Sit down," he said.

"I have an order up." She turned to the kitchen. Faint bruises could still be seen on her neck.

"Sit down," he said, pulling a phone from his fanny pack. "Heh heh, I just wanted to show you the pics I made of us at the condo after you crashed."

"Fine, freak," she said, sitting down, not looking down at the phone.

"Just look," Preston said as he started to flip through the images.

When Maddy stared at the first image, her look of irritated resignation was replaced with puzzlement, then alarm. She had expected to see pics of hostile sex, her tied up in some demeaning posture, but this was far weirder. It took her almost a full minute to comprehend what she was seeing.

"Sleeping Beauty," Preston whispered as she glared down at the images.

Maddy inhaled like waking when she saw herself in the peasant's dress wearing a blonde wig pulled back long and flowing like the princess in the Disney film. She seemed to be dancing like Sleeping Beauty danced in the forest with whirling cartoon birds. Maddy looked closer to see the straps and belts that held her into position, her stoned face that of some besotted royal. The second shot was of Maddy touching the magic spinning wheel that was to put her asleep until Prince Phillip woke her with a kiss. *Where*, Maddy thought, *could this crazy person have gotten a real live spindle?* Then Maddy was positioned in a photoshopped gilded bed, her hands clasped together and waiting for her kiss. And in the last photograph, Maddy wore the princess dress and crown, her face raised in a halo of golden light. Propped up just so, she stood glowing and magnanimous as her gown flowed all around her.

"This is how I see you," Preston said.

"I felt sorry for you," she said as she recoiled, pulling at the phone and choking back confused anger. Preston snatched her wrist and plucked the device from her fingers.

"I want to talk about my feelings," Preston said, grabbing for her free hand.

"Dennis!" Maddy yelled. People sitting in the coffee shop turned to stare, their eyes wide. A squat college kid in a goatee and black shirt came out of the kitchen waving a long squeegee handle and connected once with the top of Preston's head. The wood made a sharp snapping sound as Preston extended his tongue and screamed. A dominance hierarchy was instantly established. Coffee cups crashed to the floor as Preston stumbled back against a table filled with disgruntled children.

"I'll break it," Preston said, grabbing an unused teapot and holding it over his head.

"Just get out of here," Dennis said lowering the squeegee and pointing it at the coffee shop door.

"Hey, Dennis I got the pictures!" Preston laughed crazily as he leaped around like his father during the fire, his eyes gleaming with tears. "I got the shots!"

"Go," Dennis said, snatching at the phone and pointing at the door.

"You don't understand her, man," Preston said still holding the teapot, "You never will." He looked longingly one more time at Maddy then bolted out the door into the stark sunlight.

"We're back," Tick says into the microphone, startling Preston out of a daze. "Some of our guests have concerns."

"Fantastic. Teleconference in five," Preston says turning himself sideways, his right elbow up, to get through the small door. There he swivels around to his desk and turns on his computer monitor. Clicking his mouse a few times, he sees onscreen the empty oval table in the main house conference room. Practicing deep breathing for a few moments, he pulls a suitcase from under his bed. White dinner jacket and black bow tie. No pants. *Magic time*, he tells himself. *Magic time. Magic time. Magic time.*

A few minutes later, in the ornate conference room of the plantation house, Tick wanders in wearing a gabardine jacket and Manuelita follows in a pilot's gray jumpsuit. A short goateed Black man wearing an elegant suit follows. It's Chef Annon Martiz of Food Network fame. At the oval table, he sits down with a flourish. Behind him walks in a blonde woman in her early forties, a full six feet of wiry muscle, her body copper with large white teeth and a determined grin. Then a thin man in a tall toupee, very solemn, tiptoes in behind her wearing a chef's smock. A gaggle of geeky young UCLA production assistants and camera-operating hipsters come in and take their places along the back wall. Finally, a bandy-legged bald man in a black turtleneck, earpiece, and dark sunglasses sits down in the last available seat.

Quite the photogenic assemblage, Preston thinks, *straight from Central Casting. Picture perfect.* He turns on the monitor and everyone looks up at his giant image on the conference room screen.

"Greetings!" Preston says in his commanding podcast voice. "Annon, nice to see you again. Long time no see, Suzie. I want to thank you both for having the imagination, the *vision,* to take part in this production. This show, people, is going to be huge. Why? Edge. This is the edgiest thing to hit the air since *Fear Factor. Diet Extreme* is going to make TV history. I can feel it."

The geeky UCLA crew members standing around the table clap and whistle.

"As indicated in your contracts," Preston continues, "you have agreed to be remanded on this compound in the middle of the Alabama woods for several months. Little to no communication with the outside world will be afforded you, and for this sacrifice, you will be paid amply. I regret the fact that you will only leave the compound on occasion to pick up supplies that pertain to your tasks. I do have a suite at the Atlanta Hyatt reserved for the occasional day off, but it's an understatement to say you won't be getting out much. Understand that at times the work will be intense and quite often trying, and the inherent secrecy of this project might prove to be a bit much, especially as you are now essentially lost in an endless forest so far from civilization that you would have to walk three weeks to find a decent pumpkin latte. Please understand that the Tallapoochee is vast, with a labyrinth of logging roads so elaborate that if you don't know the terrain it's virtually impossible to leave on foot. It's mountainous, craggy, with cliffs, mountain lions, and, of course, the coyotes. And the forest goes on for miles. I ask that you give your personal cellphones and computers to Tick or Manuelita. Please say goodbye to your loved ones for a while and remember that we're in information blackout mode. Your phone and wireless privileges will cease at the end of the hour. Cast and crew will be able to talk to each other but will not be able to communicate with the outside."

Chef Martiz's green eyes flutter. Blonde Suzie Baxter flexes a bicep. Morris purses his lips. Tick grins. The nerds and hipsters smirk. Manuelita rolls her eyes. And the man in black touches his ear.

"Now for the introductions. First, let me introduce Mr. Annon Martiz, the head chef of the celebrated four-star restaurant franchise in New York, Tokyo, Amsterdam, and the new Annon's in Beijing where we met last winter and established an immediate rapport. Surely you've seen him on the *Today* show and, of course, as a master chef on the Food Network. Chef Martiz's single purpose for the season here is to prepare the dishes for Jasmine, our star. His kitchen is also set up with cameras and we will splice in the preparation of her meals into the program. I dare say that after our little venture, Annon will be more famous than Paula Deen after her plantation wedding. His sous-chef, Morris, as you can see, dressed in his chef garb, is ready to dazzle us with his gustatory expertise."

With closed eyes, both Chef Martiz and Morris tilt their heads upward slightly with taut lips to accept the praises.

"Ms. Suzie Baxter," Preston continues, "has worked with me on numerous workout videos and is, in my opinion, one of the best at her trade. Her short-lived cable program *Crunk-'N-Jive* was as good an exercise show as I've seen. Suzie will serve as Jasmine's exercise coach and work with her via teleconference according to a pre-set schedule. Your workout studio is the fourth floor, and our assistant producers will help to operate the cameras and offer tech support as needed."

"Hooah!" Suzie shouts trying to give Morris a fist bump. "I'm ready to get extreme BABY!"

"Suzie you'll get your chance. Next, let me please introduce Tick and Manuelita. I've collaborated with Tim 'Tick' Godwin, our executive producer, for many years. Though he is probably most notorious for his directorial debut, the first-ever X-rated feature using Claymation technologies. You'll recall from the *LA Times* review--"

"--Ha ha Preston," Tick smiles widely. "You gotta bring that up, again?"

"Why not, Tick? I mean, I paid for that turd. I should be able to get something for it."

"Then we can also talk about Barney Balls, can't we, bud?"

"Barney? Who?" Preston laughs and tugs at his bow tie. "I'm just ribbing you."

"You kidder." Tick grins and swats at the large screen with the back of his hand.

"Jokes aside," Preston continues, "Tick is a known quantity in this business and he's been involved with dozens of feature films and television programs, as well as commercials. And, as you all know, Tick and I collaborated to create Liminoid, a company that advances computer animation through a process that enables dated footage such as historical figures to be spliced into a single scene with actors and animation. Remember in *Forrest Gump* when Forrest talks to JFK? Nobody? Does nobody remember that? Just you, Tick? Well, Tick Godwin was instrumental in making that happen. Tick hopes to use this technique in adult entertainment, right Tick? Like a movie with Stormy Daniels and FDR in a wheelchair? Heh heh heh, ain't that right chief. Tick will be around to oversee things outside the dome. Tick?"

"Thanks for that intro, Preston," Tick says standing up, running a tan hand through his golden hair, his face just beaming. "As executive producer, I'll be spending a lot of time in the computer lab as well as the field trying to make sense of the multiple feeds we're receiving. We have cameras everywhere inside the egg, in the kitchen, and anywhere on the compound that might give audiences that *Diet Extreme* experience. We'll be streaming to our studio in Boulder, where the pilot is being edited as we speak. We're talking TBS, people. BBC 4. We have 120 days to transform this woman, change her body and spirit, and capture it for the American viewing audience. Jasmine needs us. The public needs us. *Diet Extreme* is going to shock, and heal, this weighty world!"

More cheers and hoots from the lackeys.

"Indeed," Preston says. "Manuelita is our assistant producer and will help with day-to-day concerns, as will our production assistants. Manuelita and I have been working on v-various projects for f-five years and she has p-proven to be a g-great ass-ass-asset. She has a d-double maj-major in mil-military science and broad-broadcasting from UC-UCLA..."

Preston feels his throat close up, hands now icy and trembling. *Please, please, no jib-jabs no jib…*

"…and…and…she's just back from a tour…in the Middle East…so…so…so…"

"--so after this meeting," Tick continues with a tilt of the head, "Manuelita will distribute iPods, laptops, and jump drives to help with logistics and scheduling issues. You will receive your daily instructions via text. Let's plan on a video conference at 3:00 p.m. tomorrow to work out any bugs. If there are no questions or problems, we will--"

"But as I have mentioned," Chef Martiz says in Jamaican patois, "there are problems."

"OK…" Preston chokes. He fumbles at his tie for a second then abruptly leans sideways in his pod chair, hand on chin.

"The kitchen facility is overall first-rate, as I designed it," Annon says, "but as I told you I needed tongue if I am to get through the week. How does one cook *fonds d' artichauts farcis* without it? Where are the frog's legs, the Dover soles, Preston? I need red currant jelly and the Bibb lettuce. *Bibb* lettuce."

"What do you suggest we do, Annon?" Preston says.

"We fly to Atlanta this afternoon, Preston," Chef Martiz says. "I hand-pick the things we need for the week, spend the night, and come back in the morning."

"Then go," Preston says. "Everybody go. Have a good time. Tick will arrange for there to be a car waiting for you at the Atlanta airport. But enjoy tonight, Annon, because you won't be in an international city again for at least a month. And don't go too heavy on the hotel bubbly you little fucker because Jasmine's five-star breakfast will need to be prepared and in the dumbwaiter tomorrow morning at 7:00 a.m. sharp. Do you understand? Yes? Thank you all very much. Let's reconvene tomorrow morning."

"Wait a minute," Tick says. "I have a question."

"Yes?" Preston says.

"Who's *that* guy?" Tick points down the table at the man in dark glasses and black turtleneck. "Who invited the mole?" The "mole" appears not to notice the term of disrespect.

"Ah, of course," Preston says with a folksy chuckle. "That's Mr. Jaekel Sneade, our new head of the grounds crew. You'll see Mr. Sneade and his team around from time to time. They will be mowing the lawns, doing surveillance, whatnot. I've hired Mr. Sneade and his team to provide perimeter security and firearm training for the compound and just to, heh heh, help out around the place."

"Ah," Tick says, frowning at Sneade. "Manuelita and I can get up to four in the chopper. Jaekel, you coming? No? Angelique, chef suit, let's go."

Preston feels relief wash over him as he watches his handpicked production company and guest stars as they leave the mansion. Motion-sensor surveillance monitors capture every step they take. There's a little trouble with the sound when they ride the golf carts from the main house to the tiny heliport, but he can have the camera crew fix that. *The snobby and flamboyant Annon Martiz*, Preston thinks, *is a perfect choice*. His presence adds immediate tension and the human conflict that audiences crave. The best part is that they don't fully realize that they are already part of the show, *his* show, even though he choked during the teleconference and Tick had to take over. *But it was only for a minute. Only for a minute.*

Preston crouches at the apex of the glass egg looking like a human boomerang, then slowly slips apelike down the side of the curved glass on a rappelling rope as he films the sleeping Jasmine with his hand-held camera. *This isn't about the ratings*, Preston muses. *It's not even about the audience's obsession with losing weight.* If Jasmine can grapple with her hate-self and embrace her love-self in his celluloid egg, then emerge triumphant on prime-time TV, then there is hope for a spiritual awakening for everyone watching. Then the cosmos will undoubtedly feel the karmic reverberations of one soul set free. When Jasmine embraces her synesthesia on television and opens the colors in her heart, he will have given birth to a rainbow. *Jasmine will be the symbol for a new age*, Preston thinks, running his hands through his mop-top, his body adangle.

11

Jasmine is still unconscious the next morning at 7:00 a.m., her nose whistling in a slow cadence. At times the breathing stops altogether, and when her open mouth finally sucks in air it sounds like a deep-sea diver with sleep apnea. In the deepest levels of her consciousness, there is a steady hum, like the sound of a kazoo. The gulf of her mind is empty, the seafloor flat. Jasmine drifts to the surface like a jellyfish, floating upward, her gelatinous body undulating in many directions at once. Jasmine's mind doesn't struggle to get to the surface, she doesn't stretch and curl into the fetal position to awaken. She just hangs there in the water as some unseen force propels her aloft.

The first thing that comes to Jasmine's mind as she begins to awaken is that she's got to get to the bank, but with a jolt, she remembers the notes, the mysterious Post Office employees, and the stolen snow globe. Her blood pressure rockets as the car crash, the syringe, and the kidnapping domino across her psyche. Suddenly wide awake, Jasmine is filled with terror, but she doesn't dare move. *These aren't my bedsheets*, she thinks, *they feel too slicky.*

Freeze, something in her mind tells her. *They won't fool with you if they think you're still asleep.* Jasmine clamps her eyes shut and lays there for another hour even though her foot and nose begin to itch and she's gotta pee. It feels like there is a bug crawling on her leg. Her stomach growls.

It's killers, she thinks. *Killers.* Breathing faster she recalls every true crime show she has ever seen, scruffy-looking creeps in mug shots with zany eyes who grill their girlfriends' hearts, grab school-bound children and hide them in the attic for sex slaves, stab babies in devil worship rituals. Dudes who hear people on their electronic devices telling them to cut some old lady's arms off and hide them in the freezer. She wonders what they have already done to her.

They must have done something, she thinks, *and it usually involves the privates. They probably messed around with my privates.* After a quick inventory, Jasmine realizes that her privates feel pretty regular. Then she starts thinking about every horror movie she had ever seen on cable in the middle of the night when she couldn't go to sleep. *People who get a big butcher knife and kill you. People who squeeze your head and your eyeballs pop out. Then you got to take a saw and cut your own leg off.* Movies like that made her too scared to walk down her empty hallway and lock the back door.

All I got to do is act like I got Ebola, she thinks. *If they think I'm sick as a dog and contagious they'll be scared to kill me.*

Kick them, she thinks. *If I kick them in the guts I can run off.*

Beg for mercy, she thinks. *Talk them out of killing me by begging.*

Jasmine's mind flits like this for another hour, her eyes squinched and her pink hands clutching the soft blue sheets.

Then she spends another half-hour listening, just listening, to hear somebody else in the room. She detects not a soul, only the air conditioner kicking on with a low mechanical hum.

She decides to open an eye. The white light is stark but not blinding. She opens the other eye for a second, then shuts it. Opens it again and scowls. Glancing straight up at herself, she thinks, *the whole ceiling is like one of them funny mirrors at the carnival.* The entire wall is a looking-glass that makes her appear three times as big as she is. She's up there on the ceiling of some round mirror room looking like that 900-pound social worker in Idaho they had to bury in a storage shed.

What the hell am I wearing? Jasmine thinks, peeping down at her cleavage.

Oh God, it's sex freaks.

Eyes closed, Jasmine runs her fingers down the white spandex of her workout suit.

They gone make me do perverted stuff in a funhouse mirror.

Jasmine remains frozen in the bed for another thirty minutes feeling like livestock in a crate. When she has to pee so bad she can't stand it, she sits up and looks around the room. To Jasmine, the space looks like the inside of the silver trailer Uncle Patrick had, except this one is all new and fancy. Everything looks compact and shiny. To the right, there's a restaurant booth sticking out of the wall, a bookshelf that runs nearly around the room, a big TV, and a square-looking couch. To the left of the couch, there are workout weights, cardio machines, and a small monitor in the wall. Above the wall monitor, there's a big scoreboard.

What sport? Jasmine wonders.

No refrigerator, no stove, no food?

Right next to the bed, there is a clear, plastic curtain. Jasmine sits up and pulls it back to see the blue commode and shower. She dives from the bed into the bathroom, her drugged head pounding. As she wrangles to pull down the jumpsuit, the spandex snaps and flaps like a wet flag. Jasmine rubs cold water on her face and looks up at the mirror to see two shocked eyes bugging out of a pale face, globular. A small cup and two Aspirin tablets sit on the sink. Without thinking she swallows them and flops back on the bed.

"What do you want?" Jasmine says out loud lying flat on the bed looking up at her monstrous reflection in the egg mirror. There is no answer, but Jasmine hears a different mechanical hum and sees a green light pulsing above the booth. Moving to the booth, she realizes that there's a sliding door there, and after waiting a long minute, she opens it. Inside the dumbwaiter is a tray with food and Jasmine slides it onto the table. She looks down at the breakfast and frowns. It looks like something you would find on the cover of *Better Homes and Gardens*, a bunch of fruit in a doughnut-looking thing with some dried seeds sprinkled on top. A little bowl of plain yogurt and some oatmeal in the shape of a heart. *No eggs, no bacon, no pancakes...no biscuits?* She is glad to see the coffee urn and shakes her head at all of the vitamins she finds in the saucer when she turns over her cup. She has the sense that somebody's watching her, eyes peering at her body from every direction. More importantly, it doesn't look like there is any door out of this strange room, except the little sliding door where the food came from.

Do what they want, she thinks and makes a show of swallowing all the pills in one gulp. She then picks up her fork and stabs the doughnut, lifting the entire breakfast to her mouth and taking big bites. Raspberries and pastry flakes fall to the table as she chews, her cheeks stuck way out like an incensed child.

Crappy, Jasmine thinks.

She sips the organic fair-trade French Roast, and it stinks too. *It kind of tastes burnt,* Jasmine thinks, *like maybe somebody took half a can of Luzianne and put it in the filter with only one cup of water.* Jasmine is still hungry when she slides the tray back into the dumbwaiter and shuts the door, but she knows better than to say a word. The dumbwaiter makes another sound and Jasmine tries to open the sliding door to look down the shaft to see if she could see somebody. It's bolted shut. Jasmine stands up and looks around the room for a cubbyhole, a secret panel, a window, anything. She pulls some of the books off the bookshelf looking for a rotating door, then tries under the bed.

No way out.

"I've gotta go to work at the bank!" Jasmine yells. She doesn't start crying and throwing things around, even though she wants to. She just plops down on the couch and stares straight ahead feeling like a pig in a poke. The large plasma TV comes on and Jasmine sees what looks to her like some homo Kenny Rogers in a white vest talking on a microphone on some big stage. He's working the room in white boots and silver trousers. The man sits down on the stage and starts flapping his arms and talking a bunch of crazy stuff into the microphone. Jasmine can't make heads nor tails of him but sits there on the couch watching him anyway because there's nothing else to do. Every once in a while, a name flashes at the bottom of the screen--*Isaiah Please: Renowned Psychologist and Self-Help Expert.* He's saying all of this stuff about how you picture yourself in your head, how he hates himself all the time. *This show sucks,* Jasmine thinks. *Just some guy sitting in a room with his legs crossed talking to a bunch of blubbering wusses.* Jasmine gets up and tries to turn the channel then looks around for the remote wishing she could watch a little bit of her favorite shows.

I could watch me some Survivor *right now,* Jasmine thinks. *And I'm about to starve.*

"Give me something to eat!" Jasmine yells as she stretches out on the space-age couch. She hears the dumbwaiter again and sees that the light above it turn green. Jasmine stands up and lumbers to the dumbwaiter to find a blue cylindrical glass and a blue cylindrical pitcher filled with water and lemon.

"Water?" Jasmine snorts. "What are you trying to do to me? Gimme some Mello Yello at least!"

No response.

"Sausage biscuits!" Jasmine bangs on the dumbwaiter. "Mello Yello!"

No response.

Jasmine sucks down the water then sticks the pitcher and the glass back into the dumbwaiter. It closes with a mechanical hum.

I know three things, Jasmine thinks with dread ...

1. *they're watching me from the other side of the mirror*
2. *they are going to feed me but it don't taste good*
3. *they ain't got cable*

"Get me some good shows!" Jasmine yells at the dumbwaiter, but the self-help program stays on for what feels like a long, long time. After it finally goes off, the lights in the egg studio go down and Jasmine hears some weird computer music with nobody singing. It's like that New Age puke Lorrie used to listen to after her trial separation.

"Let me out of here!" Jasmine screams after a few minutes of the ambient Brian Eno soundscapes. She goes hysterical, grabbing book after inspirational book off the circular bookshelf and throwing each one wildly at the mirror. The books bounce off with a thud and she flings herself onto the couch clutching her head.

"Hey, you!" Jasmine leaps up. "Creepy pervert! I know you're looking at me. You want some?" She yells at the mirror. "You trying to get some?" With some effort, Jasmine pulls down the front of her white workout suit to expose her breasts and starts to gyrate her body to make them swing around and around in circles, Ferris-wheel style.

"You like that? You think this scares me?" sweating Jasmine wheezes as she begins to wobble her large buttocks, bumping and grinding to mimic striptease twerking moves, bouncing up and down on her knees and then rolling over on her back with her legs up, turning, bending, then licking her finger and touching a buttock while making a sizzling sound.

No response.

After lying there frozen with a stern face for a few moments, she sits up and pushes her body back into the workout suit, the ambient gongs and ocean waves persistent in the background. Another hour passes, and Jasmine busies herself by tidying her room. She sits on the couch looking at the black monitor screen until she sees the green light and hears the dumbwaiter.

Lunch, Jasmine thinks. *Let's hope it doesn't taste like crap.*

When she slides the door open and pulls out the tray, she feels a little bit better. The plate has grilled fish with some lumpy stuff under it, some sticky-looking yellow rice with nuts, and a naked salad without dressing. There's some granola stuff sprinkled on top. There is also more fruit in a little bowl but no doughnut. There is water, a glass of white wine, and more vitamins. Jasmine doesn't usually drink alcohol but figures the Lord would forgive her for having a little snoot full now that she's abducted and probably about to get mangled. Jasmine turns up the wine glass and chugs.

"Phew-wee!" Jasmine twists her face, staring at the glass of exorbitant Pinot Gris as if she just found a roach in it. "At least gimme some Boone's Farm!" Jasmine yells at the mirror and puts the wine glass back into the dumbwaiter. She thinks that the fish isn't so bad and the stuff under it tastes like the stuffed crab she got on a seafood platter in Atlanta when she went to the bank conference. *But why do they want to put nuts and stuff in rice? What about some brown gravy? If they are going to give you a dessert, why not something that tastes worth a flip? And I ain't even going to touch this salad,* she thinks, sliding the dry, fresh greens to the side. After gobbling down everything else, Jasmine pushes the tray back into the dumbwaiter and goes back to the couch. Just as she sits down, a computer-enhanced voice shocks the air. It sounds to Jasmine like the robot who gives the weather reports for the Emergency Broadcast System.

"Jasmine," the voice says.

Startled, Jasmine looks around the room.

"Hello, Jasmine."

"What."

"Do you see that scale at the workout center?"

"What you talking about?"

"I'm talking about the place in your room that has the work-out equipment and the scale."

"What about it?"

"I would like for you to get on the scale."

"For what?"

"To weigh yourself."

"Not no, buddy, but hell no."

No response.

"What are you trying to do to me?"

"I'm asking you to get on the scale."

"How come?"

"To see how much you weigh."

"It ain't none-ya damn business. What are you trying to prove?"

"We have a lot to discuss, Jasmine, in due time. But for now, please just get on the scale."

"I ain't doing a damn thing until I see a lawyer."

"There are consequences in life, Jasmine, for not having a 'yes' attitude."

"What are you talking about?" Jasmine stands up. "What you gone do to me?"

"Please just get on the scale."

"I want to see a judge." Jasmine steps onto the scale and looks down at the digital readout in horror.

248 pounds.

The lights flicker in the egg room and Jasmine hears the sound of boos in surround sound. She stares at the scoreboard above her head.

248

The number hovers like some hog of bad omen.

248

Didn't know I'd gained that many pounds, Jasmine thinks, now seeing herself from every angle. *This funhouse mirror ain't no fun at all.*

"Turn that thing off," Jasmine says pointing at the scoreboard but not looking at it.

"I'm sorry," the voice says. "But it won't be turned off, not ever again. Not until you leave."

"Leave me alone."

"You've been alone all your life."

"Me and eight billion other people, chicken shit. Now let me out of here."

"You will release yourself."

"How? Are you going to hurt me?"

No response.

"You're going to do an advanced interrogation?"

"Of course not, Jasmine. This process may prove uncomfortable, I guess, perhaps a bit extreme, but the pain is meant to heal."

"What's that supposed to mean? I'm gone saw my leg off for my own good?"

"No, but I do have a painful question for you. We might as well get started. When did you first see yourself as an *obese* person?"

"I don't know," Jasmine says staring at the floor.

"You know you're overweight."

"Yeah, and you're ugly as a dried-up old dog turd."

"What makes you say something like that?"

"If you looked good, you wouldn't be hiding behind some mirror."

"I-I-I," the voice stutters. "I'm not so bad."

"But that speech impediment don't help things. Is that why you are too chicken to talk to women and have to kidnap them without their permission?"

"This isn't about m-me, Jasmine, this--"

"Riiiiight, mih-mih-mihster," Jasmine articulates while making robotic motions with her hands. "You've got me dressed up as a 200-pound trapeze artist to help *me*."

"You mean a 248-pound trapeze artist."

"Whatever."

"Please, answer the question."

"If it's any of your damn business I got 'obese' in the third grade."

"Did anything spark the weight gain?"

"Yeah, doofus. Food did."

"What did your family cook for you?"

"The usual, you know. Food."

"What did you eat?"

"What do people eat? I don't know. Meals."

"Give me an example of what you used to eat. You are getting home from school. Supper's ready. What is it?"

"We didn't eat until daddy got back home."

"OK, daddy's back home. You're sitting at the table..."

"A lot of the time we didn't sit at the table. We ate in front of the TV."

"OK. OK, good. You're skulking in front of the TV. What are you eating?"

"I don't know, pizza, tater tots, chicken pot pie, TV dinner--you know, food."

"Out of a box?"

"Well, yeah, out of a box. What you think?"

"I don't know, you live in a very fertile part of the Deep South. Maybe fresh vegetables?"

"I don't eat hillbilly food."

"I see. And your family was fat?"

"Daddy was real skinny if you want to know. What's it to you?"

"And you lived in a trailer?"

"A double-wide and then later a brick house. What's that got to do with it?"

"Doublewide indeed. Daddy was poor?"

"He did the best he could."

"Which is code for he was too ignorant to adequately provide for you."

"You shut your damn mouth talking about my daddy like that you slew-footed son of a bitch!"

"Uh, what did you just call me?"

"You heard me," Jasmine yells, pointing in all directions from the center of the room, "you gimp-ass bastard."

"Stop saying that."

"Must be something bad wrong with you, mister," Jasmine says with a sudden grin.

"As I said before, my situation is not in question here."

"Your *situation*? What kind of situation you talking about?"

"We are talking about you."

"For your information I was talking about you."

"This process will help you find your hate-self."

"I sure as hell don't know what you're talking about, but it sounds to me like you got some serious afflictions, and you're a gimp to boot."

"Your mother looked like Petunia Pig."

"You shut your damn mouth about mama. She had a glandular disorder."

"Like you?"

"No, ain't nothing wrong with me."

"Ha ha! Heh heh heh."

"Is that supposed to be a put-down or something? Ha ha heh? Fool you need to get you some better put-downs."

"You've said to yourself over and over again that you would do anything, just anything, to keep from being like your mother. And then you turned out just as fat as she was."

"I was real skinny until the third grade."

"And then?"

"And then, what?"

"And then what happened to make you realize you were fat?"

"Kids called me moo-cow and said I had a big...chest."

"You weren't pleased?"

"I was in the third grade, jackass. People ain't supposed to pooch out like that in the third grade."

"Did you talk to your parents?"

"Daddy said to mama to go buy me a bra and cover 'em up."

"What did your mother say?"

"She took me to K-Mart and got me some bras and said don't ever let cousin Don-Don squeeze them." Jasmine's face suddenly becomes a pale blank.

"You mean Don Wills? The car salesman?"

"So what."

"Don't you understand what this means?"

"I don't give a crap!"

12

At midnight, Preston stoops over his computer terminal watching twenty feeds from around the compound at once, twenty squares in columns playing videos from multiple fixed positions. There are hidden cameras everywhere and Preston watches them all. He's getting a handle on the behavior patterns of his guests, the camera crew, and the increasingly militant grounds crew, which makes it easier for him to eliminate inactive feeds. The barn, for example, has proven a complete waste. Preston has eleven thousand dollars of surveillance equipment in that barn and not a single person has entered its useless stiles. The walking trail, on the other hand, has given Preston several nice tidbits, but only early in the morning. The kitchen is a hotbed of chatter and intrigue, while nobody steps foot into the high-tech conference room. Most of Preston's charge at this point has been deleting recordings that will have no use, finding what might be spliced into the program, and forwarding the best segments to a young assistant producer and staff in Boulder who archive and compile them for upcoming episodes.

Already Preston is exhausted, but he knew what he was in for when he locked himself into the egg. Three hours of sleep per night for months of shooting with occasional catnaps while trying to cut thousands of hours down to twenty-four shows, including a two-hour season finale. The constant editing is maddening, his inbox growing at more than one hundred emails every half hour. He knew from the onset that sleep and sensory deprivation on this production might become a fast ride to temporary psychosis and the jib-jabs, but he hoped that the extreme nature of the project would also help jumpstart his creativity.

Preston is glad he forwarded maps of the logging trail that circles the compound because everybody is using it for exercise. Everybody, that is, except for Chef Annon Martiz, who acts like a little monster whenever he's not cooking and a big monster when he is. Cameras attached to rocks and trees along the two-mile perimeter have been very helpful as Preston has gotten numerous shots of Suzie Baxter jogging on the ridges and through rough terrain. *Her bronze form is very stirring*, Preston thinks, as he watches the exercise instructor leap from one jutting rock to another. She's in touch with her body, and seeing her mount a boulder at high velocity fills Preston with complex sensations. But he thinks that there's something off with her, some aspect of her personality is simply missing.

Somehow she's dangerous, he thinks. *Suzie's dangerous.*

Preston remembers that once when they were shooting a hip-hop video Suzie began taking on the attributes and dress of a gangster rapper, but then a year later with Jane Fonda she cut her hair and began espousing leftist politics. It had scared Preston to see the woman transform herself so completely. He watches Suzie Baxter's powerful legs as she scrambles upward toward a dark draw in the rock worn by rainwater. There is a steady stream that pours down the face of the rock and Suzie cups her hands in its shadow and splashes water on her face. Preston feels his back starting to freeze and spasm.

"What's *he* doing there?" Preston sputters. He watches as Tick moves shirtless into the field of vision and leans his head of dirty blonde hair into the waterfall, all of a sudden very close to Suzie Baxter with a boiled egg jutting from his mouth. Tick is so buff, so tan, and he seems to know that there's a camera there because he positions his fit physique for maximum effect. Tick leans in with the boiled egg between his teeth just touching Suzie's lips. She bites it like a wolf. Preston closes the feed and forwards the file to the team in Boulder. Preston is sure the scene will be great for the show, but he doesn't want to watch Tick and Suzie Baxter at play, not just now.

Sometimes Preston wants to fire Tick, to get rid of him once and for all. He is sure that Tick has been bugging him for years, listening in, and he has always known that there's a sick and diseased beast behind the capped teeth and tanned Botox. But Tick knows Preston's darkest secrets, things that if ever leaked would be disastrous. Their lives and fortunes have been intertwined for so long that there's no easy way to get rid of him. They were inseparable every summer in the mid-1980s when Preston lived with Grandmaw and Tick's family summered at their vacation house on Lake Guin. Tick's family on his father's side was full of lawyers, and they were fellow University of Alabama alums as well as political allies of Preston's deceased mother. The paths of Tick and Preston had crossed and re-crossed ever since the Godwins gave young Preston an open invitation to hang out at the lake, swim in their pool, and ride jet skis. Tick had shown up in California and tagged along with Preston during the heyday of his exercise video career, and then, by sheer coincidence, when Tick was taking criminal justice classes at UA, Preston showed up with his decommissioned Post Office Jeep and damaged spine. From there, their lives kept winding and knotting together like wisteria vines. Preston remembers the exact moment that would seal their deadly, preposterous fate, the moment that jump-started Liminoid and made *Diet Extreme* more than a demented American dream. Preston asked a question and it snowballed, growing out of control down the slippery slope of his imagination. The two of them had been sitting under a bridge just outside of Tuscaloosa years ago eating Dreamland ribs when their partnership took shape.

"Why the hell," Preston had said as they sat under the bridge gnawing meat off the bone, "are you majoring in criminal justice?"

"Two reasons," Tick said. "You know my family looks kindly upon any overture to starting a career in law, so there's that. The second reason is that I secretly yearn to be in the CIA or Hollywood, but I can't make up my mind. I could go either way if I learn about high-tech surveillance, digital multiplexing, CCTV technologies, stuff like that, know what I mean?"

"No, I don't know," Preston said, turning back an Old Milwaukee and tossing it into the Black Warrior River.

"You are saying that you don't see the potential connection between filmmaking and investigation? New spy cameras, concealed mikes, digital video recording...you don't see how they might be useful?" Tick finished his sentence with a condescending belch. "Your Grandmaw may be right about you," he said as he made a pinched face and did a pretty good Grandmaw impression, "Boy, you dumb as a 'possum." Preston cocked his head and stared at the sun reflected off the river, his mind spinning like an off-kilter gyroscope.

That night they sat in Tick's townhouse playing Castlevania on PlayStation and drinking beer, their faces fading in the blue light and computerized voices. Around midnight they began to hear a woman moaning through the thin walls and not just the occasional "yes" or obligatory "oh god" but a combination of high-pitch keening with a masculine "aaargh...aaargh" that had them both sitting instantly upright.

"Clockwork," Tick said. "You should see her, dude. Senior theater major. Silky, well-brushed, long red hair. Refined, comes from 'good people,' you know? Fairhope type. And she regularly exploits this half-witted buck-toothed hulking caveman of a pizza driver with tattoos up his arms for hours. I mean, this guy is a real Viking."

"Damn," Preston said.

"Want me to make it worse?"

"How can it get any worse? I'm in here searching for hidden orbs on this stupid game with you while the Viking with death breath does the wild thing with the hot theater major."

"Look at this," Tick said pushing a couple of buttons on a remote control. Preston is shocked to see on the television screen the theater major and the Viking on her leather couch. The quality isn't that great, but it's easy enough to identify the Viking's buttocks bouncing in sync with the sounds through the wall.

"How?" Preston shook his head startled. "How did you *do* this?"

"It's just a little camera. I had a few glasses of wine with her one night, you know, and when she went to the bathroom, I just stuck it to the corner of the Ansel Adams print on the wall across from the couch. There's another one in the bedroom."

"Wow," Preston said watching how the theater major's raised knees and feet bounced to the sound of her moans.

"Now think about the implications for espionage, as well as moviemaking," Tick had said with a sick grin. "This gentleman, the Viking, is not her boyfriend. Her boyfriend is a second-year med student at Tulane. Eight hours away and definitely *not* a Viking. Elmer Fudd-looking drip shows up every couple of weekends and it never quite sounds like *this* next door. It sounds like," Tick says in a whiny voice, "'Why don't you care about my feelings?' and 'I have so much studying to do.'"

"Poor Elmer," Preston says.

"Poor Elmer has a bloated trust fund and a renovated mansion in the New Orleans garden district. *Old* money, son. So if this woman's acting career doesn't work, you know, Mrs. Fudd here can be the belle of the Krewe of Comus ball."

"That strumpet," Preston said.

"Stop moralizing, man. Don't judge. She just needs some-body to hold. It's just that right now, look at that, she wants to hold the Viking's cudgel like *that*."

"I must say, I've never seen such a thing," Preston said staring over his shoulder at the screen.

"So two weeks ago, I went over there with a nice bottle of wine and a VHS tape, asked her if she wanted to watch a video. She popped the cork as I popped in the tape. Just friends hang-ing out. And you should have seen her face when she saw herself in the limelight. Her face went from pink to purple to white in about three seconds."

"What did she say?" Preston said.

"Nothing, especially when I showed her the manila enve-lopes with Fudd's address, Fudd's mother's address, her Catho-lic high school's address, the Dean of the Theater Department's address. I mean, she looked ready to pass out."

"You sent them the tape?"

"No, doofus, I didn't send them 'the tape.' I would never do something like that. I simply told her that I would like to, you know, occasionally call upon her, to talk, maybe have a drink, maybe when the Viking and the boyfriend were out of town..."

"I can't believe this," Preston said. "What did she say?"

"She didn't say anything. She just opened her kimono."

"You're exploiting that girl," Preston said, "you creep bastard."

"Don't lie to yourself," Tick licked his lips. "I just take the chances you wish you could, living your dream life, baby."

Preston was perplexed by the fact that Tick had the type of charisma that enabled him to leave a flashy bar with a party girl on his arm any night of the week if he so desired, but most of the time he had darker cravings. *It wasn't good enough,* Preston thought becoming flustered, *for him to get the girl. Tick had to lie to her, do something degradin*g. Preston told himself that he found it sick as he fumbled with a camera. *But that's the way it always was, wasn't it? Tick lied, he played vulnerable women like bagpipes just to hear them cry. He charmed the people around him so he could ease in the polished ivory fangs.*

And now, Preston thought, *Tick, who had been bleeding his talent for years, was now making his move, taking over the show, creeping in for this ultimate cable network grab. Tick had already gotten to Suzie Baxter, hadn't he?* Stuck in the dome, Preston was cut off from the camera crew and all the gossip and moral support that they afforded him. He had reason to believe that Tick was already holding secret teleconferences with disenchanted members of the camera crew and Morris, the sous-chef. *But what were they scheming?* Preston knew he shouldn't start thinking too much again. *But hadn't Tick always pounced, gleefully, when Preston found himself on the ropes? Always.*

"Live and let die," Preston says, his chin just touching the screen.

13

Day after day, Jasmine sits on the couch watching the TV man in the white vest and silver trousers prattle on. He just goes on and on strutting around in a big room that looks to her like some space-age tent revival. She pays enough attention to know that he's trying to sell a six-box-set about hating yourself for $49.95. The man in the white vest reminds her of the preacher at the Tabernacle of Baptismal Flame who got caught with one hand in the collection plate and the other in a missionary's girdle. Because she's lived in Alabama all her life, Jasmine knows all too well about this sort of rascal. She knows all the preachy tears and the blah blah blah. They just want your money and to mess with your head, or worse.

Jasmine feels her body go numb when the camera pans down to one man's face in the audience. He's all boo hoo hoo right there with the rest of them, all nervous like, but Jasmine feels a moment of shock because she thinks she recognizes him. He's got round little glasses, all hunched over, and is as bald as Samuel L. Jackson. Jasmine tries to place him, to recall where she might have seen him. *Didn't she maybe see him on TV?* She can't quite remember. She waits to get another glimpse, but his face never again appears.

The food gets crappier and crappier in this place, Jasmine thinks during lunch. This despite the calligraphy names in French on little cards and the gilded platters. Flat-looking ducks, animals stuffed inside other animals, bird's nests, snails, charred organ meats, and frightening green soups are all pushed back into the dumbwaiter uneaten.

On the other hand, Jasmine admits that the ambient music is starting to grow on her, but she protects herself by humming "I'm proud to be an American where at least I know I'm free" over and over. *They are trying to brainwash me with this stuff,* Jasmine thinks, *and it's probably to make me rob the bank.* Jasmine has decided that the only reason somebody would want to abduct her would be so that they could get into the bank and steal some money. Controlling her food and TV is just part of the brainwashing. *It's one of those Patty Hearst deals,* she thinks. Jasmine has no idea how to get into the vault, but she isn't about to tell them that she doesn't know diddley about the vault and that most everything is on the computer anyway. She reasons that if the kidnappers find out she can't help them rob the bank, they'll murder her for sure. Jasmine plans to play along and then make a break for it during the robbery. The bank security cameras will record the truth. She'll turn her pistols on her fellow robbers and fire at will.

Play along, Jasmine thinks, *until you get your chance.*

Jasmine knows they abducted her at the edge of the Tallapoochee National Forest. She knows that Kay-Lee Chandler was in on it and figures they couldn't have taken her too far. Regardless of what kind of egg-shaped sealed-off building they got her in, they can't filter out the smell of pine resin and huckleberries from the outdoors. They can't filter out the mountain air, so Jasmine knows she's still got to be somewhere in those woods. The problem is that those are some big woods, so the authorities could search for months and never find her. The terrain is also rocky, craggy, with sharp inclines and cliffs, wildcats, and rattlesnakes. "Them there woods have Bears," Paw Paw used to say, "with teeth like ten-penny nails."

Music interrupts Jasmine's train of thought, but it's not the kind of music that she's heard in the egg. It's not ambient but techno, bass-heavy, and fast. The television monitor comes on and Jasmine sees an athletic blonde in her mid-forties doing stretching exercises.

Oh no, Jasmine thinks, *more of this help-you stuff.*

"Jasmine!" the lady on TV chirps. Jasmine bolts upright when she hears her name. It's not just another tape. There's an actual person on the other side of that screen.

"Jasmine!" the woman says with her hands on her hips. "Hey girl! It's time to start your stretching exercises! I want to begin with your neck and back, then move down to the hips, OK? Now stand up and--"

"Lady!" Jasmine cries. "Help! Help! I've been kidnapped!" She runs to the monitor and puts her hands on the screen. "Lady, please call the Sheriff!"

The woman on the screen rotates her shoulders with a big smile.

"Lady!" Jasmine screams. "Help me!"

"I am helping you," Suzie says with a stretch of the hamstrings. "I'm helping you reclaim yourself, Jasmine, to give you the body you deserve."

"Help me out of here!" Jasmine yells.

"There is only one way out of here," Suzie says. "Now stand on the blue mat and face the monitor."

"Why are you doing this to me?"

"Jasmine," she says. "I am your personal trainer--"

"Dogs have trainers, lady, you ain't--"

"--and I know you don't want to look like *that*. Think about your health, Jasmine. It is your time to recover the beautiful body that's in there somewhere."

"That's not for you to say, Granny Barbie," Jasmine says backing away from the screen.

"Oh, come on," Suzie says with a beckoning hand motion. "Let's just do a few stretches. The hardest part is unrolling the mat! And girl I know sitting in that bank for eight hours a day has gotta be hard on the neck and back. Come on! What do you have to lose except pounds? You don't want us to have to do lipo, do you? *COME ON!*" Suzie screams and claps her hands. Terrified, Jasmine stands to face the monitor, her heavy head forward. She feels bad about the loose skin around her neck, her small chin engulfed by its monstrous double, her flabby arms crossed over bulbous abdominal rolls, and the insides of her legs that bulge like big balloons. In their matching exercise suits, Jasmine thinks she looks like a distorted reflection of the thin woman on the other side of the screen.

"Now let's start by rotating the shoulders, like this," Suzie says. "Great, now the other way. Two, three four. Good, now forward. Two, three, four. Now raise both hands and stretch to the ceiling...goooood."

As she starts the exercise, Jasmine's neck and shoulders burn, the sweat beading on her face.

"Now let's try to touch our toes," Suzie says then shakes her head at the result. "Hmm...gonna need a bit of work there."

"Hmm," Jasmine says not looking up. "I thought they were going to send somebody a whole lot younger."

"Really?" Suzie says, her capped smile fading just a bit. "How about some deep knee bends." Jasmine bends and stands up surprisingly well.

"Great!" Suzie says. "Now touch your knees, toes, and then back up. Knees, toes, right back up. Good! Knees, toes, up. OK, let's tap it out. That's pretty good!"

"I guess you can't have plastic surgery all over," Jasmine says, "when you get old there ain't nothing much you can do about them flappers on the backs of your arms. Is there?"

"Flappers?" Suzie says, her eyes glimmering.

"Whatever you call them, on the back of your arms, that wobble. And them two creases that go up the middle of your forehead," Jasmine put her finger between Suzie's eyes on the screen. "Like old people. That goozle you got on your neck, like a turkey, that's what old people get." Jasmine puts her thumb on Suzie's TV neck.

"Let's get back to it," Suzie says. "How about let's try some sit-ups. Down on your back, Jasmine. It's taking a while, but that's OK honey, go at your own pace."

Jasmine grunts as she gets down on the floor.

"Let's sit up on one, down on two. OK? Let's go! One...let's try that again. *One...* The abdominal region seems to be another problem area, but I guess you already knew that."

"What's your name, 'personal trainer?'" Jasmine looks up wearing a craven grimace.

"I'm Suzie."

"What do you put on your face for wrinkles, Suzie? Cause honey I gotta tell you it ain't working. And all the big old fake-looking plastic teeth in the world can't help your face from sinking in like it is. Men don't look at you like they used to, I guess. Do they say you're all dried up?"

"And you smell like bacon when you're clean," Suzie utters moving forward so that only her face can be seen on the monitor.

"Get this through your pea brain," Jasmine growls back, "I don't want to be you. You people think you know every damned thing, but you don't know me. You just see a fat dummy with a hillbilly accent. You don't even think I'm a person."

"Time for cool down," Suzie says, smiling again. "We can talk about your feelings tomorrow."

After the session, Preston uses various monitors to follow Suzie down the stairs to her room. Suzie says nothing to Angelique, the young camerawoman. Locking her bedroom door behind her, Suzie stands still in front of her full-length mirror, the space reflecting on her body every crease, every crater. She stands in sunlight silence with her veined hands over her eyes.

In the dome, Jasmine stands looking into her bathroom mirror, frowning at her jowly red goose egg of a face. It doesn't matter what her body looks like, her face will always be a big zero – a big round nothing. *It's just how the past shaped me*, she thinks. *Where the past shaped me. Where heavy fingers chastened the very clay.*

"Good afternoon, Jasmine," the automaton voice says at 3:30 p.m. sharp.

"What do you want?"

"Enrichment time! Interested in seeing another PowerPoint?"

"No, I ain't."

"Don't be that way, Jasmine."

"I'm going to lose my job if you don't let me out of here."

"That's all been sorted. No need to worry. All of the incidentals have been seen to on your behalf. Right now, you are on leave at the bank. We even turned off your hot water heater, Jasmine. After this life-changing experience, you will be able to slip back into your life without a hitch, if you should choose to do so."

"You didn't touch that pilot light."

"I don't--"

"Do you know how hard it is to relight that pilot light? Why did you have to go messing around with that hot water heater?"

"Please, Jasmine. The hot water heater is not the issue."

"That's easy for you to say. I'll be the one trying to get it back on."

"Jasmine, please, I will relight the pilot light myself if you'll just listen for a minute."

"It was Kay-Lee and that bitch Meghan Oswell who back-stabbed me. They set me up."

"We all want to help you. Consider this an intervention."

"Whatever you say," Jasmine mutters, "you stuttering hunchback."

"Charming as always, let's do go ahead and look at the first slide." The large monitor comes on, and Jasmine sees a black-and-white photograph of what appears to be a stone sculpture of a woman. Instead of a face, her entire head is covered with what looks to Jasmine like studs. The stomach and breasts bulge over a hairless pudenda.

"What do you think of this piece?"

"What do you mean, what do I *think*?"

"What comes to mind when you see this?"

"Not a damned thing."

"What do you notice?"

"I don't 'notice' nothing."

"Could you at least describe what you see?"

"I see somebody who ain't got nothing better to do than to sit around looking at pictures of a rock with jugs."

"Jasmine, this sculpture is the famed prehistoric piece 'Venus' of Willendorf. It is housed in Vienna."

"La-Dee-Da. Looks like Uncle Patrick's man boobs."

"Uncle Patrick? The one who died of heart disease?"

"What's that got to do with anything?"

"Why do you think the piece has no arms?"

"I guess cause they broke off."

"But what if they didn't break off? What if the artist intended for the woman to have no arms?"

"How do you think somebody could stick arms on a rock back then? It don't have no arms because it don't have no arms. Quit trying to make something out of nothing."

"Perhaps, just maybe, the armless woman is a metaphor?"

Jasmine yawns and looks up at the ceiling.

"Jasmine, at least admit that something is going on with the head."

"Oh, something is going on with the head alright."

"The woman is lacking a face. The face is covered by a veil."

"What about that Mello Yello?"

"We aren't even talking about the Mello Yello until you are morally present for discussion. This work is significant because its egg-shape makes it a symbol of fertility, like an ancient fertility goddess."

"So if I talk about the picture I get a Mello Yello?"

"I didn't say that, but you will without a doubt not see a Mello Yello if you don't at least make some effort to cooperate."

"I get you, buddy. No picture, no Mello Yello."

"Just tell me what you see."

"OK mister," Jasmine smacks her lips, "the sculpture ain't got a face. This means something to you because you can't show yours. You got something wrong with you. We know that for a fact. And now you're trying to get me to feel like crap about myself because I'm fat."

"No, Jasmine, that's not quite it. To face your hate-self, you have to stare back at the naked truth."

"Because you're the one trying to fix the trailer trash. As long as there's Alabama to kick around you can feel good about yourself, you smug snob."

"That's an oversimplification. How many times do I have to tell you that this isn't about me? Let's take a look at this next slide, Titian's *Pastoral Concert*..."

"Bo-ring," Jasmine says.

"OK, what about this one? Cézanne's *A Modern Olympia*."

"That's a little better."

"Why so?"

"I don't know. Can't I just like it better?"

"Sure, you can appreciate the Cézanne more than the Titian, but I am hoping that we can look deeper."

"What's with you?"

"We are not only talking about your weight problem, we are talking about seeing the patterns that make you consume, you know?"

"You can keep that liberal mess to yourself, buddy. I ain't saying another word until I get that Mello Yello."

"Jasmine, I swear to all that's holy, I promise, I will get you a Mello Yello if you just make some effort."

"Now you're talking, red snapper. You scratch my back and I'll scratch yours."

"Tell me what you see."

"I see a woman with a big butt, that's what I see."

"And..."

"And she's laid up on a fancy bed. She's trying to cover herself up."

"Is she?"

"She's trying to pull the covers down so he can't see."

"Why Jasmine? Why is she trying to cover herself up?"

"Cause she's a lard ass!" Jasmine wails and covers her face with an oval pillow.

"Good, Jasmine. Good. She hates her body, doesn't she?"

"She sure as shit does!" Jasmine weeps from behind the pillow.

"It's OK to cry," the voice says. "Let's hit rock bottom together. Sharing is important for this process."

"Waaaah!" Jasmine wails, still hiding her face.

"Tell me about when your mother called you ham legs in the third grade after Don-Don left for military school. How did that make you feel?"

"She told me--" Jasmine whimpers, "she told me--"

"What? She told you what?"

"She told me," Jasmine pops her head up with a grin. "'Go get me a Mello Yello,' you doofus."

"Good grief."

"Ha! Ha!"

"Jasmine, please."

"Doofus, your slip is showing."

"What?"

"That's a metaphor, stupid."

"This just signals that you are too frightened, emotionally, to face your true feelings. These artworks--"

"--OK OK mister kidnapper, don't get sensitive." Jasmine cocks her round face and scowls. "You want to know what I see in this picture? I see little pee wee hiding in the dark and a woman sticking her butt in his face. He's staring at her, but he don't know his ass from a hole in the ground. She ain't no masterpiece, and he ain't nothing but a fool."

"Three cheers, Jasmine. Congratulations, this session has been a resounding triumph for defeatism and denial. But do me one favor before this session ends."

"What?"

"Get on the scale."

"Whatever." Jasmine flounces over to the workout center and steps on the scale. Waiting for the surround-sound boos, she cringes and looks up with one eye at the scoreboard.

227

Jasmine looks again.

227

"You've already lost twenty-one pounds, Jasmine."

Jasmine looks up yet again at the scale in surprise, and then feels an intense desire to eat.

"Ta-ta."

He's messing with my head, Jasmine thinks after the session. *He probably has got that scale rigged so it will say whatever he wants it to say.* Jasmine wonders how somebody would put together something like this round room with the slide show and the bad food and more importantly why they picked her of all people. *And even though the guy doing all this is not that bright,* Jasmine thinks, *she is going to have to think for her life.* For the next hour, Jasmine mentally constructs the events leading up to her abduction. She closes her eyes and dredges her memory for clues. She traces her steps from the sausage biscuits to Meghan Oswell, from chasing "Mongolito" down the street to the rope around her neck. As she does, two puzzling questions emerge:

> *Why did they call to say my mother was dead?*
> *What did those letters mean?*

It's simple, she thinks, now that she has a decent grasp of her kidnapper. *The dead mother means what's done is done, that she doesn't have to do all the things her mama did anymore like wolf down Big Time Pies and be miserable all the time. But that is such bull because the bad things you see your parents do they never die. They cling to you like when you walk through a spider's web in the woods and you can't pull off the strands. You didn't get caught by the spider, but stuff sticks to you. And to say everything will just fall away when your parents die is stupid.* She remembers the message that the letters made when she put them together:

THE DOLL INSIDE
THE PIG INSIDE
THE CORPSE INSIDE
I WILL KILL HER

She now understands the message. *It's easy. The doll inside is the plastic shape that your mind makes so you're able to deal with the world. The pig inside is the hunger that can't be filled no matter how much you eat. The corpse inside is the deadness your heart feels every day. And "I will kill her" just means that this guy thinks he is going to make it right. Fix it. Fix her.*

Fat chance.

14

Preston burns through half the summer staring at computer images, cutting scenes, and emailing the good stuff to the lab in Boulder. On multiple screens Jasmine exercises, Jasmine eats, Jasmine drives the cast and crew to the brink of collapse. He knows this is going to be a Reality TV hit if he can keep the compound from falling apart. Guiding Jasmine to her love-self has proven a bit more difficult than he thought, and with every failed session the anxiety builds. Most of the last two sessions will have to be scrapped, but damn if she isn't losing the weight. *And she's smart,* he thinks. *Really smart.* She has this ability to offer sharp comebacks, her titanic wit borne of what must have been years of schoolyard misery. She has this hard shell that prevents her from facing her true feelings, and the shell keeps her from confronting her own image. And it is this uncomfortable tension, Preston knows, that creates great TV.

He's a little hurt by Jasmine's constant jabs about his body, even though she has no idea who is behind the glass. Or does she? She seems to readily pick up on his inherent weaknesses and sometimes calls him "slew-footed" and "gimp." But how could she know he's both?

Preston comes to the realization that he needs a different approach. He prepares by listening to an abridged audio version of *Facing the Hate-Self* by author and inspirational speaker Isaiah Please. Preston has seen Dr. Please many times in rented convention halls, community college classrooms, and at the Academy of Comparative Visualizations in San Luis Obispo. Dr. Please always wears a white vest, his piercing eyes and sharp voice able to cut into Preston's deepest levels of consciousness. In his books and workshops, Dr. Please guides Preston to a transcendental state akin to nirvana. The New Age guru shepherds Preston to the bottom of his psychic underground. Preston leans back in his desk chair, closes his eyes, and listens to Dr. Please:

> ...when, you know, you can face it. Face it. Face the hate underground. It's there that you realize that memories never die. Memory doesn't die, sir, you in the back. What's your name? Bill? Bill with the pale face and the sad eyes back there. You have to kill it, Bill. I once knew a man who sold cars in Portland. He was very successful, but a persistent memory of his father calling him a nonstarter kept him from self-actualization. He lost his wife to bone cancer, he lost his business, and he started thinking about suicide. I told him, don't kill yourself, kill "it." Kill the memory. And the only way to kill a memory is to run it to death. So under suggestion, I had him relive the memory. What kind of shirt was your dad wearing when he shamed you? Where were you in your home? All

that. And then I had him make a mental movie of the event, script, lighting, angles, all in his mind, right? And then he had to play the movie of his dad in his mind two hundred times a day using the comparative visualization techniques I describe in my first book, Seeing Yourself Achieve. *After the three days of intense visualizations, he came to me and I said, "Now, O.K., write the movie a new ending. Now you tell him what you're feeling. Tell him how much he hurt you. Start from the beginning of your script, as before, but now respond. Rewrite the memory. Rewire the memory." See, if you agree to lose, they'll take you underground every time. But you have to agree, right? Why do I lose? Because I agree with them. The hate-self always wins and I agree to lose...*

Preston clamps his eyes shut, both fists in front of his face, and then he breathes slowly out of his nose and mouth, his fluid hands and wrists circling one another upward like a belly dancer. He does this odd mudra for a while and then submerges, feeling highly relaxed. In Preston's mental movie he sits straight and comfy under the sea, near a cave. Dr. Please says:

> *... and it always appears to us that there's somebody better, right, so use the comparison as a challenge to break from it. Break out of the hate cycle. But here's the paradox. You must embrace the ghouls and psychic grave diggers, those poisonous people who try to infuse themselves into your karmic flow. What do those people teach us? They teach us about our undergrounds, don't they? Delve, people,*

wallow. Wallow with me at the bottom. You are facing it. Can you feel it? Can we feel it underground together? Some of us here at the bottom today are feeling the need to cry. That's OK, everybody, cry. Close your eyes, breathe the pure oxygen from your oxygen tubes, and let it out. Your hate-self is right outside the threshold, the fragile egg of emotion and consciousness called ego. Break it. Break through it in one clean stroke. You have been trapped in a psychic egg stage and it's time to be reborn. Now open your eyes. Stare up at the eyes of the past and see how feelings run like pigs from a gun--

Preston startles awake on the cubicle floor, crazed. It's after 8:00 a.m. and he's had another whiteout, a trance, like when Manuelita found him staggering down Hyde Street in San Francisco near an open space on Russian Hill wearing gloves but no shoes. Luckily this lapse was a short one. The feeds are still running and there's a hum in his ears. He knows that whatever he didn't catch will be lost in the data stream, yesterday's files forgotten as a new day's shooting begins. *Everything is moving too fast,* Preston thinks, *in too many directions.* Preston's back tingles as he crawls back to the control center to survey his compound in real-time. Preston scrolls down the endless feeds until he finds the interior of the barn. Rubbing his exhausted face he enlarges the images to see Manuelita and Tick sitting together on a hay bale. Both attractive and hearty, they do look as if the elements might be taking a toll.

Manuelita scratches at the swollen redbug bites on her ankles, a scowl on her lips. Sunburned, Tick yawns and sips coffee, his thin legs crossed.

"Martiz is such an ass," Manuelita says. "Every day lying in wait."

"So much flaccid rage," Tick says. "All these sad little men. You do know that's what drives Preston there in the dome."

"You're suggesting that Preston is a little light in the medical shoes."

"Aren't we all? Seriously, don't you get the feeling that he's kind of losing it in there?"

"He's always kind of losing it," Manuelita says. "That's his genius."

"I don't know. He seems to be slipping more than usual. And not letting us access the central mainframe makes our situation here very precarious."

"You should have a heart to heart," Manuelita says. "Zumba?"

"I think I'll skip today, but do enjoy."

Preston clicks on an outdoor screen. Two members of the grounds crew sit on four-wheelers at the compound perimeter. They sport buzz cuts, black sunglasses, and navy tactical trousers.

"Is she in the exercise studio?" One holds his earpiece and speaks.

"That's a roger. Manuelita and Tick now leaving the barn."

"Keep your eyes open."

"Copy that."

Later in the exercise studio, Manuelita and Angelique stand beside each other in white spandex suits taking turns doing elaborate dance moves to the Lionel Richie song, "Say You, Say Me."

Preston watches and quivers. As the young camerawoman spins, Preston cannot help but admire her silky hair, polished nails, and trim physique. *Maybe I should get Angelique back in front of the camera*, Preston thinks.

On another monitor, Tick is now in the conference room working feverishly on his laptop. He has the screen tilted at just the right angle so that for the life of him Preston cannot make out what his business partner is doing. Tick seems to glance at the hidden surveillance camera and smirk as he works. *Was that a wink?* All the while, on all the screens, Jasmine stares into the vortex like an alabaster bust of Venus.

Doubt worms its way through Preston's thin shell of self-esteem. He turns away from the terminals and staggers to the bathroom in his cubicle where he opens a brown bottle of pills. Things are getting away from him, and it's much too early for that. He drops several pills into his mouth, one by one, and looks into the mirror at the highest point of his body, which happens to be his right ear. One eye hovers at an angle over the other, the ear pointed upward like a satellite dish. The calculus of his body bedevils him. For two hours, Preston paces in tight circuits around the front of his computer and the monitors, swinging his arms, spinning on one foot, over and over his mind going, *Say You Say Me Say You Say Me Say You Say Me*. Wobbling his head, Preston sings aloud with soul, "I had a dream, I had an awesome dream," then he says, "shut up shut up shut up."

Preston opens his eyes to both his footage and memory running like rainbow trout upstream and he is losing them all. The trout are moving so fast and he's on his knees in the digital pool and he can't grab a single one. It's like the fish are slipping and swirling out of his hands in a fast-moving river of pics. Feeling the g-force of his spinning brain, Preston reaches for dainty morsels of leftover gourmet Martiz food from the mini-fridge and crams everything into his mouth. He then coughs, particles flying everywhere like the big bang in his head.

Preston senses that he has let himself slide too far off his medication regimen since his arrival in the Tallapoochee National Forest, popping too many pills at one time or letting himself go days without popping nearly enough. Preston wants to open the secret hatch at the top of the egg and just wander away, but instead, he curls at an angle on his narrow bed listening to the music pumped into Jasmine's room and tries to pace his breathing. Eyes clamped, he's a capsule falling through vectors of forgotten and lost selves. His insides burn. He falls and remembers. But after a while, to Preston's great relief, things begin to slow. As he starts to decompress, his mind getting clearer, Preston realizes how fragile, how narrow the wall is, how precarious everything has become. It's a matter of balance and if he does hit bottom, rock bottom, it's over. He knows how hard it is to get it back together again if he loses it. *All the king's horses, and all the king's men…*

He thinks about overpasses in San Francisco, the cold nights in the tarp with the old man, and the dumpster pizza, wandering down between where the 101 and the 280 highways meet with a mind like a damp paper sack. His mind visualizes hairline cracks representing his stress and anxiety covering the smooth dome of his consciousness. After another hour of deep meditation, Preston begins to get control of himself. With exaggerated motions, he cleans up his tiny apartment, takes a bath, clips his nails, and then uses the razor to shave both his face and head. Looking at his shiny, bald head in the mirror, Preston says to himself aloud with a confident, fatherly wag of the index finger, "No crackups, champ." He puts on the Ringo wig and uses his mouse to locate Chef Annon Martiz in his expansive kitchen. Annon is darting around the stock room with his assistant and a handful of veal shank.

"Yesterday," Annon says, shaking the shank close to Morris' face and barking like a field general, "Jasmine experienced French nouvelle cuisine at its best. Do you know what she did, Morris? She asked for 'tater tots.' Traditional French cuisine, this is what we make her and what does she say, Morris?"

Morris shrugs pooch-lipped, holding a glass of Chateau Montelena to the light.

"She has snubbed dishes cheered by Jeffery, Bill, and Hillary," Annon says. His face gleams as he looks aloft and toys with his dyed-black goatee.

"It's remarkable," Morris says. "Simply, re-maaakable."

"I mean, is she trying to destroy me or does she really not like the food? I'm at my wit's end," Chef Martiz bites at his bottom lip. "That's why I'm going with Mediterranean, Morris. Ossobuco Alla Romana."

"What? The Ossobuco?" Morris sputters. "Are you not well?"

"I'm on edge here," he says sneaking the cookbook from behind the bags of flour. "This 'Jasmine' situation calls for a new approach." He turns the pages of the cookbook. "Roman Braised Shin of Veal. This, dammit, this is objectively delicious. No pretense, nothing fancy. Since the Roman times, Morris. Salaman refers to this dish as 'meltingly sweet...with its tantalizing taste and pampering texture.' She suggests that we serve it with risotto ala Milanese, spinach, and sauteed potatoes. What do you think?"

"A flatbread as well?" Morris suggests. "The lady loves carbs."

"Why, yes," Annon smiles, waving the camerawoman forward. "We shall win her." As Morris sets to work on the risotto in the background, Annon speaks to the camera as he heats olive oil in a pan. The kitchen studio is an absolute white: white ovens, white cutting boards, white containers of herbs. The pots, pans, knives, and utensils are burnished and shiny as the chefs set to work.

"And then, here, stunning, we coat the veal in flour and brown it until it is as golden as my trophy wife's hair." The camera aimed directly above the burners records Annon as he adds fresh sage, pours in a cup of white wine, stirs, and smiles over the bubbling meat.

"Jasmine appeared to enjoy the *côtes de veau dijonnaise* last week," Annon beams at the camera, "so Morris and I are preparing a special main course for her today. In her book *Healthy Mediterranean Cooking,* Rena Salaman describes Roman Caesars sitting over just this dish, enjoying the succulence of Ossobuco Alla Romana. It smells exceptional. And then, we introduce fresh orange peel and hot chicken stock. This is a moment that makes me remember why I am a chef. The smell, a blossom of citrus zest pinned up as steamy corsage."

"Corsage." Morris says heavy lidded. "Corsaaaage."

"Morris, your breath reeks. Go stir the risotto." Annon waves him away. "Now Salaman suggests Catalan Spinach to add leafy greens to the meal. I'll chop Jasmine's organic leafy spinach…

chop chop chop...we flew this spinach in from the Netherlands... *chop chop chop*...so the greens alone are more expensive than Jasmine's car. OK, now place the spinach in the pan and cook it slowly until it wilts just a bit. Add a touch of sea salt...*shake shake shake*...stir it up and cover and let our spinach steam. Later we'll add the pine nuts, raisins, walnuts, and black pepper." Annon washes his hands and rotates his body to stand in front of the second console facing Morris and the camerawoman.

"Morris, as you see, is stirring the Risotto Alla Milanese. The arborio rice absorbs the combination of chicken stock, saffron threads, and the rare spices. Smell the onions, they are almost caramelized."

"Morris?"

"Yes, Annon."

"Don't just stand there holding the spoon motherfucker. *Stir*." Annon then walks to the end of a long prep island to peer at a monitor image of Jasmine as she lays in the bed, salty with dried sweat from her exercise with Suzie Baxter.

"And there she is," Annon raises his hands with a papal gesture. "My number-one critic. In twenty-five minutes, we will place our Roman offering, good enough for Caesars, into the dumbwaiter and see if she bites."

After Morris takes the meal to the dumbwaiter, Annon watches Jasmine on the screen as the green light goes on. Sitting up on the side of the bed, she doesn't move for thirty minutes.

"She's just toying with us," Annon says, twirling his mustache and pacing. "She knows we're watching. On 1500 calories a day, the swine has to be starving." Morris casts a wary eye at the camerawoman.

"Hold it," Morris calls down the corridor. "She's getting up."

"How's lunch?" Tick says, sauntering into the kitchen, a coy look on his face. He's wearing tan shorts and a loose earth-tone poncho. The locks of his blonde hair have lightened. He bites into a pear and leans back against a sink to stare at the monitor.

"To be so fat," Morris says pouring a glass of wine, "and the woman just *hates* food."

"She seems to have gone on a hunger strike," Tick says. He frowns, looking into the sink at the dirty pots and pans. "Dew is worried. She can't lose *all* of her weight before midseason. And we can't, you know, *starve* her."

"She's heading for the dumbwaiter," Morris says.

Jasmine opens the dumbwaiter and pulls out the Tiffany serving tray. She sniffs. Her shoulders droop.

"If she doesn't eat that veal," Annon says, jabbing his finger at the monitor. "I will fucking quit."

Jasmine stands up with the plate and goes into the bathroom.

Morris, turning pale, sits down hard on a plastic milk crate.

"What the hell is she doing?" Annon whispers grabbing the remote. "Let me see."

"Preston doesn't have a camera in the bathroom," Tick says chomping the pear. "But I do."

His cellphone rings.

"Speak of the devil," Tick says with bright eyes. "The egg man calleth." Listening to Preston on the phone, Tick taps his lips with an index finger and says, "tsk, tsk."

"Yep," Tick winks at Annon. "But you made it clear you didn't want cameras in the bathrooms... yes...yes...What makes you think...yeah you're just lucky I know the difference between what you say and what you want, pinhead." Tick toys with his iPad with his right hand, his left hand holding the cellphone to his ear. A few seconds later, the monitor reveals a close-up of Jasmine in the small bathroom.

"No," Tick says. "No way. That's my business...enough with the platitudes...yeah that's what you pay me for...just watch the monitor...yes, Preston...yes yes yes get out of my ass." He spins both devices on his fingers and stuffs them in his pockets like a gunfighter.

"She can't be doing that," Annon wheezes hoarsely and points at the monitor. Jasmine is washing the veal in the sink. After thoroughly rinsing each piece of meat, she takes her plate back to the dining area and sits down. She puts together the pieces of flatbread, the meat, and a tiny piece of spinach to fashion together a workable burger.

"Needs mayo," Jasmine says to the monitor and bites. She smells the risotto, scowls, and pushes it away. "Cheese in clear plastic and we'd be in business."

In the kitchen, Annon turns to the sink and starts washing a large, dirty pot.

"I resign too," Morris says as he turns up a glass of white wine.

"Oh no you don't, Morris," Tick says pulling a butcher knife out of a holder. "Neither one of you. You two *spoons* thought you were going to be the big TV stars here? Right? Well, now you're the comic relief. Tough titty. Such is life. Now put your chef's hats back on and get your narrow asses back in front of that goddamn camera."

"I'm ruined!" Annon screams. He punches the monitor and the plasma screen goes blobby. Annon clutches his hand and moans.

"Get him some ice," Tick says to Morris but pointing the butcher knife at Annon.

"You can't do this," Annon whimpers, looking up at the camerawoman. "If this gets out, this washing of my Ossobuco, I'm done for."

"Dinner time in four hours," Tick says as he brings the knife down hard, sticking it into a cutting board. "Cook the lady veal."

15

At dinner, Jasmine opens the dumbwaiter to see a replica of the platter she had for lunch with a double serving of veal. *They're playing dirty*, she thinks. *The gloves are off*. But this time there's also a slice of huckleberry pie.

Of all things, pie, Jasmine thinks. *They've done their homework*.

Jasmine's mind, her very soul, is a closed deep freeze full of boxed-up pies. She just hates pie, but she's so hungry she will eat this one. She stares down at the huckleberry pie, her lips trembling and face flushed. She's surprised how the abduction has stirred up things better left alone.

When Jasmine was a girl, if some of the pies fell off the forklift at work, Daddy would bring a few broken boxes home. They usually weren't messed up too bad, just some of the crust was broken or it was kind of flat on one side. Because of this, their deep freeze was usually full of white boxes with "Big Time Pies" written in big circus lettering and a grinning elephant in a big circle reared up on its hind legs in the middle of the box. Surrounding the elephant were yellow stars behind cartoon faces. Jeering clowns, giraffes, a gorilla, and a ringmaster with a black mustache, all gracing the cardboard box. The first time Jasmine had to spend the day at Big Time Pies with her daddy, she thought that she was going to the circus and would see the elephant and the clowns. But when Daddy drove through the iron gate to the yellowing warehouse, she only saw the elephant and the clowns on a rusty little sign next to a gloomy-looking factory building.

"Don't leave the break room," Daddy had said when he left her to "play." There was a wide table with a salt shaker on it and a stack of napkins. The walls were white, and the fluorescent lights above buzzed in the cigarette haze.

There's nothing to do, Jasmine thought as she sat down, *no TV or nothing.* She wished she could be over at Aunt Myrtle's watching shows with Don-Don.

A big glass window overlooked the warehouse floor where people in hairnets ran the machinery that made the pies. She could see a series of conveyor belts shuttling pies back and forth across the warehouse. She could also see her father through another glass window in the main office staring down at the floor where Jasmine's mother sometimes ran the forklift. But mama wasn't there.

Time slowed at Big Time Pies. People in hairnets and black rubber gloves would eat in shifts, opening their stained brown paper bags and black metal lunch boxes, guzzling coffee from long silver thermoses, unwrapping bologna sandwiches in wax paper, and pulling the lids off tiny cans of Vienna sausages. They tried to smile and talk to Jasmine, but it seemed as if she couldn't process what was happening when people looked at her and said words. Her mouth hung open in a bland frown, her eyes averted, her double chin resting on her chest. She sat slumped in her chair while they came and went. Invariably some lady would put one of her doughnuts or a chicken wing in front of Jasmine and she'd snatch it like a cobra handler.

When times were hard, Jasmine's family ate a lot of those broken pies. And the pies were by no stretch of the imagination "The Greatest Pie on Earth" as advertised on the box. The primary ingredient was some white vegetable grease coagulant that made Jasmine's teeth sticky. The fruit-scented filling looked like hardened cream corn juice when Mama cut into the pie and knifed a slice onto Jasmine's plate. Jasmine would fork huge clots of various pies into her smacking mouth, her face blank.

"Big time," Mama would say, exhaling slowly, as she raised a dripping fork to her pursed lips. Daddy would sit there wringing his hands, elbows on the table, knowing what was about to come next.

Mama then said, "Eating a pie somebody run over with a forklift."

"Nobody run over that pie," Daddy would say and push up his thick glasses.

"That pie's got tread marks on it," she'd say pointing.

Eyes down, Jasmine would cut herself another piece, eating fast, so as to show her father that she believed him.

"It ain't tread marks. The crust roller just got gummed up." Daddy would try to push parts of the pie together with his fork, frightened lines cutting into his weak smile.

Jasmine would pull the pie tin closer to her and stick big pieces into her stuffed mouth.

"I'm so tired," Mama said.

"Then go back to bed," Daddy replied.

"I can't sleep," Mama said.

Jasmine poked a long, curved piece of crust into her mouth and started putting dents in the tin with her fingernails while they fought.

"For God's sake slow down," Mama said to Jasmine.

"Chew it sweetie," Daddy agreed.

"I always knew this would happen to me," Mama said, staring at the olive-green appliances and stacks of dirty dishes on the counter.

"What happened to you, mama?" Jasmine said.

"Nothing," Mama said, her teeth sitting on an empty pie tin. "Nothing did."

Wiping her eyes, Jasmine looks down at the huckleberry pie. The crust is flaky, the berries newly picked, and to the side is a dollop of fresh whipped cream.

"This ain't my kind of pie," she says. "Why are you doing this to me?"

"Frankly, Jasmine," the robot voice replies without missing a beat, "you seemed dissatisfied with your life. You were morbidly obese, lonely, and unhappy. But you're here now at a state-of-the-art wellness facility with a great staff. You're losing weight and starting to open up about your feelings. Give us a chance. We care about you. I care about you. I do."

"You knew me from the bank? Kidnapping and starving me while you watch is supposed to help *me*?"

"OK, Jasmine. If you want to talk, let's talk. Let's put it all on the table. It's time for you to hear the truth. Brace yourself. OK? You, Jasmine, are the star of a reality program, a television show. It's called *Diet Extreme*, and the pilot airs on TBS this Thursday night. Like it or not, Jasmine, you are the star. Really. The first six episodes have already been green-lighted, and when we tested the pilot, the audience went nuts. They *loved* you, Jasmine. That's a fact. Especially women between the ages of twenty-five and forty. You've touched some kind of nerve, Jasmine. They were rooting for you. They want to see you, Jasmine Meadows, on her journey to fitness, beauty, and her love-self!"

"My name ain't Meadows. It's Wills."

"Sponsors didn't go for it. Try to understand how these things work."

"How long are you going to do this to me?"

"Just for a season. A few more weeks tops. In all, we'll produce twenty-four shows and a two-hour finale. The beauty of *Diet Extreme* is there will be a new cast every season. New guest chefs, guest exercise coaches, and so on. After we put the teaser up on YouTube, people started lining up to be abducted. We'll follow them, film them, then nab them. It's exciting for everybody."

"Sheeeeyet."

"Now please listen, for once. This is going to be quite lucrative for you. There's a release and a contract for you right here in my hands. If you sign, you will be able to live comfortably for decades after this is all over. You'll never have to set foot in that bank again. And we both know you needed to lose weight. I mean, come on, that sausage biscuit you've been eating might as well be a gun pointed at your heart."

"You're lying about the money."

"We're willing to offer you an advance of $750,000 that of course includes signing a waiver relieving TBS and its employees of any legal liability. Then there are royalties, Season One Jasmine Meadows' *Diet Extreme* frozen dinners, Jasmine exercise equipment, and so on. Your future is set. If you want, I'll go ahead and send the contract down the dumbwaiter."

"I'll read your contract," Jasmine smiles, "if you hand it to me yourself. You come down here and put it in my hand, and *then* we'll talk business."

"That's not advisable," the voice says. "Not yet."

"Then get ready to do some jail time sucker because I ain't signing jack. And when I get free from here my ass is heading straight for the Tallapoochee County Sheriff."

"That's your choice, but be forewarned that you'll either leave here by luxury helicopter sipping a Mello Yello with a fancy straw or on foot with a gaggle of lawyers at your heels. Believe me, it would be so easy to get lost out there. I know your room is soundproof, but you should hear the animals at night. Oooh, how the coyotes howl! I wouldn't want to be alone out there, in the dark, on the edge of this mountain. One little slip and--"

The voice whistles like a dropping missile.

"That's not funny."

"No, it's not, Jasmine. And you know I would never let that happen to you. We just need to make the deal, and then move on."

"What do you care? If I don't sign the paper, you're going to leave me out there to die?"

"I care. And I told you I would never do that. There's something about you, Jasmine. You're a strong woman, a beautiful woman."

"Shut up."

"I think you understand me."

"Buddy, you sure as shit don't understand *me*."

"Maybe when this is all over, we can be friends."

"Hmph, when pigs fly."

16

A week later, Preston is still pacing around in his cubicle holding Jasmine's contract. The pilot was a great success, the daytime talk shows are abuzz, so he just needs her to sign on the dotted line. Part of Preston yearns to go into the inner capsule and reveal himself because he has feelings for her that he hasn't been able to express. And then, just above the mirror, he sees it. For a second he can't believe it. Reaching upward, he sees himself in the mirror plucking the tiny metal object from just above the frame. It's a little eye looking back at him, recording his every move. His body visibly convulses. *Someone is watching*, Preston thinks. *But where are the feeds going?* Preston slips the tiny bug into his mouth and swallows it, his manic eyes now floating around the room as he eats a handful of nerve pills.

That bastard, Preston thinks.

Preston calls ground crew chief Jaekel Sneade to the dome. He unbolts the secret hatch at the apex where the middle-aged ex-Navy Seal crouches in dark sunglasses then slides down into the egg.

"How are things?" Preston asks as they climb down a rope ladder.

"Iffy," Sneade says with a gravelly voice.

"Iffy?"

"Morale is low, security has been compromised."

"Compromised by whom?"

"Provocateurs. Chefs."

"Who, exactly?" Preston says ducking into his quarters. "Watch your head."

"Suzie Baxter for one," Sneade says. "She is a serious threat."

"Suzie Baxter? I told you to watch Morris."

"Yes yes, Morris has been relaying information to rogue members of the camera crew. It is confirmed that he has been leaking information to E!, and frankly, Mr. Price, it's all starting quite a stir on social media. Mr. Dew is pleased with what is transpiring, so let's leave Morris alone for the time being. It's Baxter. Baxter, you need to watch."

"She's scheming with Tick," Preston says as his hands take a life of their own in his trouser pockets.

"Sure, but Godwin has no idea what she's really up to. Did you know that she now packs a semi-automatic weapon? Preston, she's planning to break Jasmine out."

"How?" Preston says, his vision now blurry.

"I'll show you. Will you pull up yesterday's feed of Suzie's exercise session?"

"OK," Preston does so and watches the women doing jumping jacks.

"See there?"

"Jumping jacks. So what?"

"Look again. You're looking right at it and don't see. Look, Preston, see how they are jumping in sequence, then down like that, the push-ups. It's a code. See? They're communicating."

"What?" Preston squints looking at the screen.

"A retired code breaker from NSA has seen this and believes that they are communicating via exercise. No doubt about it, they're planning a breakout."

"OK, keep an eye on that," Preston says. "What else you got?"

"You had better pay attention to *this*." Sneade Points at Suzie Baxter on the screen.

"Affirmative, Jaekel. Affirmative. Roger Dodger. What else?"

"It's the camera crew," Sneade says. "Constantly sneaking out of the perimeter to go to caves. At first, they were going out there to party, we thought, but now we hear them...I don't know, it sounds like chanting. We can't find the cave where they're doing what they're doing. There's talk of an uprising."

"Just keep me posted," Preston says. "Text me minute by minute."

"Will do," Sneade says looking closely at sweating Preston. "Anything else troubling you?"

"There is. I don't know how to say this. We have to get Tick off of the compound, somehow. He's losing his mind. I gotta tell you, he's compromising my ability to complete the show."

"That's not going to be easy," Sneade says. "He *is* the executive producer of *Diet Extreme*. Everybody on the compound adores him."

"You'll think of something," Preston says. "Now if you'll excuse me, I think I need to lie down." Preston clutches his stomach wondering what the camera inside him is recording. And who might be watching.

PART THREE

THE ESCAPE

17

By October, *Diet Extreme* is the most popular reality program on television. Stores can't keep the Jasmine TV dinners in stock and the ever-popular "I Don't Give A Crap" t-shirts are selling out from coast to coast. Hundreds have pre-ordered the J-ME "inaction figure" (egg dome not included). And, like most Americans on Thursday nights, Lorrie and Mandy from the bank sit mesmerized in front of their plasma screens bearing witness to a woman who remained largely unnoticed for many years right by their side. Lorrie and Mandy sit together on the couch staring at Jasmine as they rub their hands with coconut lotion, their faces idle and figures ever-widening. Without joy or relish, they stuff chili dogs into their mouths as Jasmine's media specter engulfs them in surround sound. On the other side of town, Kay-Lee Chandler sits unemployed and broken-hearted watching *Diet Extreme*, her own body now twenty pounds heavier. Portly ex-husband Parrish, laid off at the video store, moons over Jasmine's body on the screen with high cholesterol and a heart rekindled, his endless emails and texts unreturned.

Even Mrs. Salters, gated in her community, grows wide as she watches Jasmine shrink. She fills her Chesterfield sofa all alone, the fried chicken breasts on her coffee table a finger-licking testament to one woman trapped. The nation eats for Jasmine, even during commercials when attractive middle-aged women with large smiles and small hips stroll across verdant pastures waxing melodic about diet pills. A piano plays. A disembodied voice chirps about possible side effects of diet pills--kidney failure, weight gain, blindness, convulsions, stroke, instant paralysis. But after the commercial break, a made-for-TV-Jasmine shakes her thinning fist, refudiating them all. When she kicks a gourmet grilled bacon-wrapped fig high and it sticks to the glass ceiling, a generation cheers.

The show is often presented with four images on the television screen so that the viewing audience can see multiple events as they unfold across the compound. At the moment there are two feeds of Jasmine from different angles, a grainy synchronized screen of Preston's face, and footage that Jasmine herself can see on her monitor. Jasmine is sitting on the futuristic couch in white spandex suit watching the monitor as a much heavier version of herself eats a sausage biscuit on the Tallapoochee Farmers Bank commode. Face pressed down into crackling wax paper, fatter Jasmine sits wedged in the stall wearing a white polyester dress with red polka dots, smacking, her eyes squeezed shut. A purse strap hangs askew off Jasmine's round shoulder. Thinner Jasmine watches this on her monitor with a face as empty as her dinner plate.

"What do you feel when you see this?" Preston stares at his monitor in a white robe.

"I feel like saying congratulations," Jasmine utters. "You caught me at the worst point of my life, and now you are going to put it on TV for people to look at and say 'look at the loser.' But what I want to know is how can this be entertainment? I ate a biscuit on the shitter. So what? What kind of fizzle fart would sit around and watch crap like this?"

"You tell 'em, Jasmine," Mandy cheers back at home as she sniffs, her eyes glued to the set.

"Point that camera at your own know-it-all face" Jasmine says. "Let them see that if they want to see a train wreck. Your trap is worse than mine. At least I'm getting out of here."

"Wow," Preston says. "That's profound. You never cease to amaze me."

"It sure don't take much to stimulate your feeb noggin, Doofus."

"You go girl," Lorrie says, fist-pumping from her couch.

On the compound, grounds crew lieutenants with chained German Shepherds monitor the perimeter, weapons locked and loaded. Militants in aviator sunglasses and black fatigues cruise the perimeter on four-wheelers. Jaekel Sneade crouches in a camouflaged tree stand with binoculars searching nearby caves. Everyone is on alert, the constant drills and sense of anticipation making the grounds crew restless and jumpy. Last week, a CNN investigative reporter was found hogtied near the south compound entrance, and Manuelita had to medevac her to the Tallapoochee Regional Medical Center. Another reporter from *Entertainment Tonight* was found beaten on a logging road, his cameras missing. Yesterday, one of the perimeter stations burned.

Preston has struggled to keep the compound operational until he can assemble the last three episodes of *Diet Extreme* and the two-hour finale. No one can prove it, but it is believed that Tick maintains regular secret teleconferences with a small group of disgruntled camera operators and production assistants who call themselves "The Cave Wizards." Food is growing scarce in Preston's compartment, as shrinking meals come through the dumbwaiter in decreasing number. Sometimes Preston opens the dumbwaiter to find an empty plate or pieces of paper filled with strange hieroglyphs. Preston rarely communicates with compound personnel, and his increasingly hostile texts are disregarded by the frantic crew in the plantation house. Preston suspects his texts are being blocked as he tries to hack through Tick's firewall. He sits at the control center watching Suzie Baxter at the north perimeter station with uniformed members of the grounds crew. Suzie wears a 9 mm pistol in a shoulder holster, the black fatigues loose on her thinning frame. She accompanies the grounds crew on raids of the caves now, her gestures clipped and aggressive.

"Hooah!" Suzie stands at one of the rock peaks with land-scapers in riot gear. She fires a semi-automatic weapon into the darkening sky, the *crack crack crack* of the Heckler & Koch echoing off mountain walls.

On another monitor, Annon and camera girl Angelique hold one another in a walk-in pantry as Angelique tosses her silky blonde hair from shoulder to shoulder. Wearing a belly shirt and camo mini skirt, she plucks at his goatee with raven black nails. Preston can't hear their voices, but Annon is looking into Angelique's eyes whispering puckishly, their heads lowered, just touching. They titter, he turns away for a second, and then the couple slips back into an embrace. She films him as he kisses the pentagram tattoo just below her belly button ring. Morris, bald and wearing a chef's hat, chops organic strawberries for Jasmine's afternoon smoothie. Preston knows that in three minutes Annon will storm back into the kitchen to prepare Jasmine's tiny dinner. *Looks like three steamed vegetarian dumplings and one serving of seaweed salad,* Preston thinks, salivating.

Since her abduction four months ago, Jasmine has lost over 100 pounds, her body forged by shrinking cuisine and strict exercise regimen. She sits on the blue mat pulling her knees up to her chest. As Preston watches, he feels that exercise and diet have molded her body to accentuate her loveliest features, and an experimental soap shipped in directly from North Korea has resolved the problem of loose skin. Of course, Preston is reminded, millions of viewers each week now drool over her ever-changing body since TBS sold the rights for a subscription 24-hour J-ME Cam. Preston feels the envy course through his nervous system, no longer able to maintain for himself the illusion that Jasmine is his alone. After her shower, Jasmine puts on her white spandex suit and sits down on the couch. He wonders what she might look like wearing a black wig.

"Jasmine?"

"What."

"I think it's time to bring you the contract and release in person to sign, just like you demanded. But you have to promise that you won't do anything rash. It's time to get practical about this. The show is doing so well that TBS is willing to significantly up your advance. Be smart, Jasmine, please. Time is drawing short. Without your signature, you won't get a cent."

"I said I would think about it," says Jasmine as she sips mineral water from a blue glass and gingerly wipes her lips.

"Please, Jasmine. I've been watching you on these monitors for so long. You have become very important to me. I just want to touch you, you know, hold your hand, for once."

"Creepy much? Touch me and you'll draw back a nub."

"I just need--"

Glancing down at the monitors, Preston notices that the kitchen is in an uproar, again.

"I have to go, Jasmine. Chat soon."

"Put down the knife!"

Manuelita stands in the center of the kitchen pointing the stun gun at Morris. The chefs on the other side of the table shake fists and gargle in anger. Morris gets close holding two handfuls of bok choy and Manuelita jack slaps the chef's hat off his head with the stun gun. Annon chortles and flings a colander full of hot soba noodles skyward before retreating to the pantry.

"Come here you little fartknocker," Manuelita whispers and lurches forward to grab Morris by the back of his apron. "Tell me who the fuck sent those pics to *Bon Appétit!*" Manuelita holds Morris's face down to the unlit eye of the gas range.

"No no no no no!" Morris screeches as Manuelita turns on the gas.

"Watch this," Manuelita says as she looks over her shoulder to Angelique holding the camcorder. She grabs the kitchen lighter with her left hand and tries to ignite the flames, but Morris spins and gets loose of the fireball.

"Monster!" he wails and sprints out of the kitchen.

"How about you, Annon?" Manuelita growls and turns to the pantry. "You want some?"

Staring at the monitor, Preston stands up in shock as Angelique, recording with the hand-held, edges around behind Manuelita. With ferocious speed, the camera strikes Manuelita in the back of the head. She hits the ground with a flat pop. Red blood pours from the gash in Manuelita's scalp and spreads across the concrete floor.

"Oh Christ," Annon yells grasping the stun gun and staring down at the bleeding woman lying sprawled on the kitchen floor.

"She was trying to kill you," Angelique says using the dented hand-held to film Manuelita.

"She's dead. She's *dead!*" says Annon. But the bloody woman is not dead. She slowly gets to her feet and staggers out of the kitchen leaving a dripping trail.

"Get out of my way, Meghan," Manuelita whispers holding a dishtowel to the back of her head. Annon crouches behind Angelique pointing the stun gun, and Preston watches monitor after monitor as Manuelita shambles from the house to the helicopter. The chopper rises and circles the compound, then disappears to the west.

"She said Meghan," Annon says. "Who's Meghan?"

"What just happened?" Tick says to Preston from the conference room monitor. Tick is wearing a blue blazer and a crisp white shirt.

"A scuffle in the kitchen," Preston says. "Don't you think maybe you should get over there?"

"A scuffle?" Tick yells. "Manuelita just left in the helicopter *dead*, Preston. That chopper was our only way out of here. We have to contact Bill."

"Leave Bill out of this," Preston says. "After we get enough for the two-hour finale, we'll call Bill. Don't lose your cool."

"Lose *my* cool? You know everybody thinks you need to be dragged out of there and placed in a padded egg crate, don't you?"

"You sound erratic. A bit unsound."

"You know exactly what people are saying, that you've been off since your relationship with Jasmine has, how should I put it, blossomed. You're sending the wrong footage to Boulder, Preston. You've lost focus. Ratings have dipped. You seem to have forgotten that Jasmine is popular *because* she is a hick. Because she *refuses* to get with the program. You're deleting the wrong woman!"

"It's all so obvious," Preston says. "You just want to take over."

"I do." Tick says in a calm, reassuring voice. "I certainly do. But not because of whatever has been gestating in your paranoid head since you decided to lock yourself in there alone with her. Yes, yes, I admit it, I think you are too fried to produce the finale. TBS agrees."

"Traitor."

"Cut the drama and let me in the egg, Preston. Open the fuck up."

"Just like Liminoid. Letting me do all the work for two years while you bang the whole production team then grab the microphone and the checks at the last minute. Not this time. Go make out with Bobby Cleecher. Go watch Judge Roy Moore take a bath."

"You're confused again," Tick offers with as sincere a smile as he can manage. "You're seething with paranoia and self-doubt. I'm just trying to get us to the next level. Just shut up for a second and listen to my idea for the season finale."

"Not this time, rich boy."

"What can it hurt? It's just an idea," Tick says as he raises his hands staring at the camera. "Listen. Just listen. The season ends with Jasmine meeting her captor face to face inside the dome. High emotional content. Reconciliation, right, maybe even a little romance, and--"

"--I don't want to go in there until Jasmine has reconciled some things within herself."

"You?" Tick coughs back a laugh. "Who's talking about *you*?"

"You're not going in there."

"You seem to have forgotten, Preston, that we're partners. Jasmine's half mine."

"Don't go near her. She's vulnerable."

"All the more reason *I* should go inside." Tick jiggles his eyebrows. "See if we can work through her whole sexual synesthesia problem with millions of Americans watching. It's perfect."

"She could kill you," Preston says. "She beat her husband senseless. For your own sake, Tick, leave the woman alone. You don't know what she's capable of."

"No, *you* don't know," Tick says. "All those pent-up needs, just waiting to come out. That's why it's me, not you, who's going in there."

"Aging creep."

"Oh, *I'm* the creep?" Tick laughs. "Preston, are you that unaware of your own motives? I'm talking to the guy who dressed his granny up like Elvis Presley. The man who impersonated a disabled veteran trying to get laid. Do you ever stop and listen to yourself? Creating your incredible shrinking woman and seducing her on television has been *your* real desire from day one. I *know* you, Price--"

"Shut up."

"I *know* you. I know your self-esteem is so low that you can only get off with a captive audience. I know what you've got hidden under those phony Isaiah Please tapes in your closet--the prosthetic devices, the dress-up clothes, and wigs. Should I go on? You can't tell me you don't see that far into yourself you hypocritical little egghead fart-faced fucker. I mean, you're the guy who tried to set his father on *fire*. You want Jasmine more than I do, but you'll never just go for it."

"This conversation is over," Preston says. "You're fired. Don't you dare try to come in here. She'll kill you."

"No, *you're* fired," Tick says.

"I fired you first," Preston says. "You're fired."

"You're fired!" Tick's monitor goes dark.

18

In the moonless 3:00 a.m. dark, a figure in black fatigues and a ski mask crawls down the mansion's rear awning, drops to the ground, and rolls under the Jeep without a sound. Motion sensor cameras fail to register any movement, and the four German Shepherds sleeping in the grounds crew kennel fail to wake. The figure edges from a row of privets at the back of the mansion, then sprints top speed away from the compound. The ground crew perimeter station is 30 yards away, leaving only the scanty electric fence, which anybody on the premises but Preston might jump over with relative ease. After a few minutes of trekking down a steep slope, she feels safe enough to pull off the ski mask and check her GPS. Suzie Baxter is a full two miles from the rendezvous point. Three hours to get there, secure the device, and return. She removes the black fatigues and tosses them into a ditch, her jogging suit underneath. Like a mountain cat, she leaps down the slope. Ducking under branches and leaping brush piles, she gets to a clear cut and slows, the mountains of dead branches and twisted limbs making it much harder to negotiate at night. But then she finds an old logging road and is able to run again. Sunrise is two hours away.

Suzie finally reaches Grandmaw's orchard and turns to walk between rows of pear trees choked with rotting fruit. She stalks along the edge of the dead cornfield, and it's haunting and beautiful this time of the morning. She floats with low lines of fog over shadows of waning blackberry canes on barbed wire fences. Near the house, she sees a rusty old tractor and Grandmaw's Lincoln Continental. Suzie circles the house with a 9 mm pistol raised to make sure no one is out there. At the edge of the clearing, she sees the smokehouse, a windowless building black with age where old-timers used to cure hogs on hooks. She turns the piece of wood that serves as a doorknob, steps over the board at the bottom of the door, and walks inside. It's the darkest place in the world. Suzie can't see the rafters but can feel dank salt and blood.

"You in here?" Suzie says.

A flashlight in the corner clicks on.

"God you scared me," Suzie says.

"I've been here for two hours," Angelique says pointing the flashlight up at her own face with a shadowy grin. "There's a snake in the corn crib."

"What are we looking for?"

"It's here," Angelique whispers. "I can't believe it. It was here under all of these clothes and empty boxes." She drags it into the middle of the floor.

"We gotta carry *that* back to the compound?" Suzie says looking at the wooden contraption with its moldy clamps, belts, and gray straps. It looks like a dentist's chair made of aged wood. "What is it?"

"It's Preston's darkest secret."

19

Two days later, buzzards in the cloudless morning fly wide circles high above the compound. Standing in the ash of a burned-out perimeter station is the corpse of Jaekel Sneade. Flies swirl around the body and blood from the eye sockets has dried on the abandoned guard shack's gray coals. Sneade stands in an unmistakable posture wearing a baggy sweatshirt and threadbare khakis. From his hips to his feet, he stands straight, but at his torso, his body bends at a 45-degree angle like a windshield wiper blade. His midsection had been shattered, and on top of his head sits a wig brushed to mimic a Paul McCartney mop. Holding Sneade in this grotesque parody is the wooden "prosthetic entertainment system" that years ago held Preston's grandmother in the attitude of the King. It is clear that Sneade has been poisoned as well, his face contorted in a gesture of excruciating pain, his black tongue extended, his purple hands clenched as if squeezing rotten plums. But what is most shocking about this scene is the way that the tiny cameras have been inserted into Sneade's gore-caked eyes. Metal lenses bulge from the sockets like guns.

A crowd begins to collect around Sneade's corpse. Everyone is staring in horror at this work of demonic art. After a long moment of confusion and shock, two men in uniform pull at the Velcro straps attached to the murder victim's wrists, elbows, and legs. Having been killed and placed in Preston's prosthetic entertainment system before rigor mortis, Jaekel Sneade has become a grotesque mannequin with severe scoliosis. He remains frozen in the monstrous posture when he is released and falls forward into the perimeter station ash with a puff.

"Put him in the walk-in cooler," Tick says, hands on hips. "We'll have to call the authorities of course, but only after, *after*, we have a season finale. Nobody gets on this compound until shooting is finished."

"Looks like the killer wore special medical shoes," a grounds crew officer notes crouching over evidence in the ash. "Prosthetic heels."

"As I feared," Tick pronounces to onlookers and cameras. He wipes his face with a silk handkerchief.

"Price killed the chief," another grounds crew trooper says, pointing a revolver up at the dome.

"Let's smoke him out."

"Let's chop off his huevos."

"Hold it," Tick says. "Slow down. I'll get him to come out on his own, by myself. Remember, I'm his closest friend." Tick walks alone from the small crowd of people to the unused bedroom at the back of the mansion. He shuts the curtains.

It's showtime.

Like much of the unkempt plantation house, the bedroom where Jasmine spent her first night on the compound has been filled in a matter of months with random boxes, stacks of papers, and piles of soiled clothes. Clean and shaven, Tick removes his jogging suit and puts on a black tuxedo. He pushes the small button on the wall fixture behind the bedside lamp, moves the junk out of the way, rolls up the rug, and pushes the emergency code. The floor panel moves down in slow motion, twenty feet underground, down the subterranean shaft to the narrow hallway separating the mansion from the dome. Once underground, Tick tries to find a light switch as he makes his way into the adjoining cylindrical room in complete darkness. *Remembering to bring a flashlight would have been nice,* he thinks as his outstretched hands fumble from wall to wall. Twenty feet under Jasmine now, he tries the floor panel elevator. It doesn't work. This means Tick will have to climb the metal ladder up to the hatch connecting the elevator shaft to the outer egg. But at the moment Tick pushes the elevator button, floor lights flicker in the outer hallway, and a monitor next to the elevator cuts on to reveal Preston's face. He's talking slowly and methodically into the camera. As Tick climbs the steel ladder, he can hear Preston in the middle of a monologue, but not one made for Tick's benefit. He's talking to Jasmine.

"... bodies in the world create perimeters of need, and..."

Tick listens with a frown as he climbs the long ladder, metal echoes haunting the ominous shaft. The cover at the top of the ladder is unlocked and Tick quietly pushes it open a crack to peek inside the empty bunker. Tick climbs out and rubs his fingers along the bottom of the dome where he tries the hatch. It's locked.

"... what I'm saying, what I have been trying to say, Jasmine, is that I feel we..."

Tick realizes that he must unseal the outer hatch manually. He pulls the wrench out of his back pocket and jiggles it in his hand as he listens to Preston's cryptic monologue. He thinks that some of Preston's lines, if not his face, might be useful for the two-hour finale. Sweating, Tick spins the wrench around and around. He had no idea how much trouble it would be to dismantle this section of the dome.

"... and perhaps in the near future, Jasmine, we will be able to put this experience behind us..."

"Dream on," Tick says aloud as he uses pliers to rip a series of clamps from the inside of the door. He then turns the entire hatch counter-clockwise with a reassuring "clank." Dropping the hatch door onto the floor, Tick pulls himself up inside the dome's exterior wall and sees Jasmine through the two-way mirror, big as life, stretching a hamstring as Preston drones on. Excitement rushes through his body as Tick realizes that he is a mere six feet from Jasmine Meadows in the flesh, though he has no idea how to get into the shatterproof, bulletproof glass egg without Preston's key card. And to get that, he must somehow subdue Preston and take possession of the central mainframe.

"Preston?" Tick says, holding the monkey wrench over his head. The air feels hollow as he squeezes down the spiral stairwell into the pitch-black apartment. The lights are off, but multiple glowing monitors and terminals display Preston's face. He's still talking gently to Jasmine, sitting in the desk chair that Tick finds is empty.

Christ, Tick realizes, *it's pre-recorded.*

"Preston?" Tick whispers half expecting the humped rascal to leap out of the bathroom all claws and teeth. Nothing.

Feeling around Preston's quarters, Tick discerns that his old business partner is neither in the bathroom nor the tiny closet. Tick finds the light switch and sees a body-sized lump on the bed. With a cringe, he grabs the green military blanket and snatches it away. Preston is not there, but Tick is taken back by what he finds lying under Preston's sheets. On the bed is a full-sized plaster cast of an armless man with a blonde wig, its head turned as if taking a kiss from behind, and he's wearing one of Jasmine's white spandex suits. Tick runs his fingers along the edges of the spandex and stares at Preston's flickering face on the monitors. After a thorough search of the exterior bay, Tick realizes that there must be a second portal somewhere because Preston has simply vanished. But a key card is sitting prominently atop a stack of parcels on Preston's workstation and what may well be the username and password for the central mainframe has also been stuck conspicuously to the table on a yellow Post-It Note.

Where is he? How long has Jasmine been in the dome alone? Tick knows that Preston would never just up and abandon this project, even if he did flee the compound. Price lives *Diet Extreme* just like everybody else on this bizarre production. Even the camera crew lunatics in the caves exist inside their own quirky TV buzz, all enclosed in the fuzzy logic of social media and plotless television. Price's crooked orbit, let's not forget, has brought Tick to this moment. He is playing the egg man's game now. This could be dangerous.

Tick sits down at Preston's terminal and prepares to speak with Jasmine for the first time. He fixes his black bow tie. Watching her do deep-knee bends, he feels a bit uneasy. His career is on the line with Bill Dew for instigating this covert coup at the eleventh hour, but can he handle *her*? He has seen her eat Preston's lunch day after day, and now he's frankly terrified. Looking at the curves of her bending form, Tick inserts the tiny earpieces and takes a deep breath.

"Greetings, Jasmine," Tick says into the small microphone and hears himself through the earphones speaking in the computer-generated voice.

Jasmine lowers her head and peers from the corner of her eye at the camera over the exercise monitor. She already knows. Tick coughs into his palm.

"Jasmine?" Tick repeats.

"Who the hell are you? Where's Doofus?"

"Jasmine, he's on vacation."

"He was just talking to me."

"It was a recording."

"Is he alright?"

"Certainly, Jasmine. Preston's just fine. He just said he needed time off."

"Preston? You said Preston. His name is Preston?"

"That's what we call him, yes," Tick says cursing himself. He trembles, staring at the screen, suddenly realizing that he is now going to have to charm someone without being able to flash his golden hair and platinum credit cards.

"Go get him and get him quick," Jasmine says staring at the camera. "I'm not talking to anybody but Doofus. Get his ass on the phone."

"Jasmine, he's on a hiking trip, relax. He's just taking a few days off. I'll try to contact him for you, I promise, but first things first. It would be a real honor to accompany you for dinner tonight. I will bring the new contract, in person, and I am certain that you will be pleased with this final offer. You were wise to hold out, Jasmine. Now that this is all but done, dear, you will walk out of here with a net worth of over three million dollars. Three *million*, Jasmine, plus all of the aforementioned royalties. We at TBS think you're worth much more than Preston's price."

Jasmine frowns silently at the monitor as the minutes pass in silence. She takes a drink of water and wipes her lips--drinks and wipes.

"Mello Yello," Jasmine finally says. "I want three Mello Yellos, a double cheeseburger, five sausage biscuits, an order of chili cheese fries, and a Big Time Pie. Make it apple."

"Done," Tick says. "I'll have the same. Shall I bring a nice wine?"

"A bottle of Boone's Farm, Strawberry Hill."

"Indeed. See you at 7:30."

20

J asmine pulls her knees together and exhales on the workout mat. She stretches her legs and bends to touch her toes. Her body has never been so flexible, voluptuous, and toned. Her scoreboard now reads 122 pounds, and she figures that when she gets out of here and walks down the street nobody will know she's a fat person. When Jasmine looks into the mirror, she feels this sense of loss, like grieving over someone who passed. *This is not my body,* Jasmine thinks. *But this is part of the plan.* She tells herself to endure it a little while longer. With Doofus out of the picture, she feels like she might talk her way out of here tonight. And, if that doesn't work, there's always Plan B.

Jasmine shakes her head thinking about Doofus, or as the other voice just let slip, *Preston. Preston. Of course,* Jasmine thinks, *that jackass fool Preston Price from the bank.* She's disappointed with herself for not putting the pieces together before the voice gave her Preston's first name. Of course, the kidnapper was Preston Price, the crooked man she argued with over his investments. The clown who made such a spectacle, laughing insanely at the bank and making crazy shapes with his hands. The lunatic with the background in TV, of course. The crying man on the Isaiah Please tape. The man who started off trying to change her and ended up making her his goddess. It's so obvious now. He had just seemed like such a harmless dipstick at the bank, another rich crank with too much time on his hands. But all the strange things started at the bank right after Jasmine gave Price a hard time – the notes, the calls, the cameras, the stalking postmen. *Preston must have been obsessed with me*, she thought, *well before he paid Kay-Lee Chandler to wrap the rope around my neck.* The crooked man had fallen head-over-prosthetic heels in love, and for the first time in her life, Jasmine felt the discomforting sensation of being the object of genuine affection.

If I ever see Preston Price again, Jasmine thinks, *I'll kill him.*

One hour before her dinner date, Jasmine hears the dumb-waiter and slides the door open hoping for something to eat. Instead, in the dumbwaiter is a large pink gift box bound with a white bow. As she opens her present, Jasmine wonders if the new man will bring her all that junk food she asked for. In the box is a black dress, the kind of dress Jasmine associates with fancy city ladies on daytime soaps. There's also an elegant pearl necklace and a diamond bracelet, both in Tiffany boxes. Jasmine frowns at the high heel shoes, black hose, silver Victoria's Secret panties, and the chic brassiere. There's also lipstick, eyeliner, and other assorted makeup, some of the cosmetic contrivances Jasmine has never seen before. Her first impulse is to throw the stuff at the monitor and say, "I'm not wearing this crap," but she decides against it. If she does what the TV man says, he will let his guard down. And she wants his guard down if she has to go for Plan B.

Jasmine looks into the dumbwaiter again and notices that there's something else back there, a can of chilled Mello Yello.

"You talking my talk now," Jasmine says as she flops down on the couch. She pops the top, turns up the can, and guzzles.

At 7:30 p.m., Jasmine takes a last glance at the bathroom mirror. Again, she feels this wave of shock. The picture-perfect woman in the glass looks like she has been ripped from a catalog. The black dress, the pearls, the lips, even her tossed-back hair are all perfectly gorgeous. Jasmine just can't shake this sense that she is looking through someone else's eyes, or that her eyes have been transplanted into someone else's body. She looks again but doesn't let herself stare for long at the body because it gives her the creeps. When she turns back, she sees that a man has appeared in the egg studio holding a thin manila folder. In his tuxedo, let's be honest, he's one of the most perfect-looking men Jasmine has ever seen. He's tall and thin with wavy blonde hair, a copper tan, and dimpled cheeks. And he is looking at Jasmine with this bright smile, a bit sly, his lips parted. He seems relaxed, comfortable with his good looks.

"I can't believe it," Tick says clasping his hands. "The dress is lovely. Simply beautiful."

Jasmine shrugs and stares at the dumbwaiter.

"Let me introduce myself, my name is Timothy Godwin." He stretches his hand, and Jasmine makes a hawking throat-clearing sound. "I'm the executive producer of *Diet Extreme*. Believe me, Jasmine, I've waited a long time to meet the star."

"Ain't no dad-gum star."

"Let me finish," Tick grins. "You are going to be very surprised at how famous you are when shooting ends."

"Don't want to be famous," Jasmine says, her head slumped and arms crossed over her chest.

"But I guess you're excited about finishing the season," Tick says rubbing his palms together and glancing aside. Out of nowhere, he fakes a laugh. Jasmine frowns, staring at Tick's shoes, hearing the low hum of the dumbwaiter.

"Ah good," Tick says. "The wine." He slides open the dumb-waiter and pulls out the bottle of chilled strawberry-flavored wine and two champagne flutes. He unscrews the top and pours two glasses. He hands one of the glasses to Jasmine, and she snatches it, turning away from him.

"Cheers," Tick says. Jasmine leans just a bit to extend her glass for the "clink" then slugs it down. Tick pours her another glass.

"Animated," Tick smacks his lips, "with hints of corn syrup." He touches his handkerchief to his lips and puts down the glass. "I wanted candles, you know, a big candelabra, but the producers were afraid that you might burn the place down. We've learned not to underestimate you, Jasmine."

Jasmine grunts and flops down on the couch. Tick moves in beside her and opens the folder.

"Do you mind if we talk business *before* dinner? I want to get this out of the way so that we can talk, uninhibited." Tick slides a pen from his coat pocket.

"You're the abductor. Talk about whatever you want."

"I'm on your side, Jasmine. I'm here to help. The contract is pretty standard, quite simple. You will receive for your part in *Diet Extreme* an advance of $3,750,000. You will receive another $200,000 upfront for incidentals. You will also get a generous percentage of royalties accrued in association with the program and all products with the 'Jasmine Meadows' logo. We're talking in the tens of millions, Jasmine. In return, you forgo your right to sue TBS or any group or individual associated with this production, ever. Then of course there's the gag order. You don't talk to the press about your experience. You don't go to the police. If you try it, we take everything back in court. We sue *you* for libel. You spend *your* days in costly litigation. It's as simple as that. And I mean seriously, what jury would believe that someone like *you* wouldn't do anything *in the world* for all that money and fame? Feel free to take time to read it, but this is it, Jasmine. The offer is, ahem, non-negotiable."

"I don't need to read it," Jasmine says. She slides across the couch and pulls the pen from Tick's hand.

"Well played, Miss Meadows," Tick beams. "Great, well, you need to sign here, and here, and here, here, yes and here. Initial here. Great, and now I sign... and here...here, and right there. O.K., great. It's done." Tick snaps the folder closed and extends his hand. Jasmine takes it, they shake, and then Tick grasps her hand and kisses it. She snatches it away.

"Now dinner," Tick says sliding open the dumbwaiter.

As promised, there are more Mello Yellos, double cheese-burgers, sausage biscuits, orders of chili cheese fries, and even a Big Time Pie. They arrange the food together at the small booth, and Jasmine is smacking her lips before she even sits down. Tick tries to make small talk but to no avail. Jasmine is stuffing the fast-food into her mouth with such rapidity that he can only sit and watch, aghast. She picks up the double cheese-burger and licks the meat and cheese all the way around pulling back the bread and biting the meat with a sucking sound, then licking the bread and dipping it into the crusted gob of ketchup on the burger paper. She nibbles a hunk of cheese that is stuck to the burger paper, her head twisted to the side. Stuffing chili cheese fries into her chewing mouth with one hand, she dips the double cheeseburger into the chili cheese with the other, then darts with her tongue around a brown stain at the bottom of the empty cardboard container.

"Ambrosial," Tick says, sliding a can of sugary soda away, an uneaten fry limp between his thumb and index finger.

"You gonna eat that?" Jasmine says, grabbing Tick's biscuit. She takes a long minute to look at the sausage biscuit. She holds it like a chalice. She smells it, her eyes closed. And when she bites it, her face becomes slack, a long and low groan coming from deep inside.

"Save room for pie," Tick says.

"No," Jasmine says. "The pie is for you." She picks up the anemic pie and flings it hard at Tick's face. It strikes him squarely on the left side of the head but bounces away.

"Naughty," Tick says. Moving around to her side of the booth, he pulls Jasmine to him pushing the sticky side of his head into her neck, tongue and lips touching her chin and earlobe as she continues to chew the sausage biscuit, her eyes still closed and head making this very slow "no." He continues to kiss, working his way down the spots of chili grease on her throat, and she groans gently. Jasmine nibbles pie crust from Tick's forehead and pushes a fry into his mouth. Tick then takes the double cheeseburger and holds it over his lips. In ribald fashion, he licks upward at the crevices between meat and bread.

"More wine?" Jasmine says and stands up as Tick continues to molest the cheeseburger for the cameras and unbutton his shirt with his left hand.

"I'll pass."

"So I can leave tonight?" Jasmine says.

"No, not yet, I'm afraid. We haven't finished the season finale."

"Then I guess it's on to Plan B."

Standing behind him, Jasmine brings the wine bottle down hard on Tick's upturned face. He falls backward onto the floor as the burger explodes like a piñata. Jasmine stares down at Tick's flopping body and runs to the bathroom. She strikes the wine bottle on the sink and it shatters making a sharp dagger then turns to see Tick pulling himself up to the booth. Tick's broken nose is squished and bloody, the left eye already clamped in pockets of purple blood. He spits gore and capped teeth then stands upright to adjust his tie.

"What you did to me," Tick croaks, "and what I am about to do to you is not suitable for audiences under 14. Sponsors are not going to be pleased." Tick wags his head then leaps after her, just missing her shoulder. He grabs a biscuit from the table and lurches towards Jasmine with it.

"I swear to Jesus I'll stab you," Jasmine says pointing the broken wine bottle and backing toward the dumbwaiter.

"And I will stuff this biscuit so far down your throat little piggy you'll never breathe again."

With surprising force, Tick leaps forward and drags Jasmine backward onto the floor by her hair. He pulls her up onto her knees, then stuffs the biscuit between her lips. Twisting his wrist back and forth, Tick crams it into her mouth until she gags, her eyes watering.

"Again," Tick says, his eyes going flat. "Again."

Jasmine stabs Tick in the groin, then swings the bottle wildly back and forth, over and over, slashing Tick's outstretched hands and face as he emits a high-pitched shrieking laugh. Standing up, she pushes him backward over an end table, his head bashing into the floor. Sliding open the dumbwaiter, Jasmine pulls her knees to her chest then pushes her body halfway through the dumbwaiter door. Clasping her shins, she wriggles into a fetal position. *All that stretching had better work*, Jasmine thinks as she struggles to squeeze herself inside. Using the broken bottle, she pushes the button and slides the door closed.

Click, Jasmine thinks. *Click, damn you.*

The dumbwaiter clicks. She feels herself descending down the long metal shaft and clutches the bottle, ready to stab. When the dumbwaiter opens, Jasmine can't see or hear anybody in the hum of fluorescent lights. The lights are off halfway down the long hall. Jasmine pries her lithe body out of the tiny elevator and stalks down the empty corridor. Opening a set of double doors, she finds a small laundry room and her own bedsheets, white spandex suits, and slippers stacked neatly on shelves. There's a row of lockers across from the washer-dryer units, the kind they used to stuff her into at Camp Calvary.

Somewhere a door closes.

Jasmine leaps into one of the lockers and peeps through the holes. A tired-looking woman in a gray jumpsuit trudges into Jasmine's view pushing a bucket on wheels with a mop to

202 | Ballad of Jasmine Wills

an adjacent broom closet. The woman exhales loudly. Jasmine hears the sound of running water.

Cut her, something inside Jasmine's head says, and she slips out of the closet holding the bottle like a butcher's knife as she moves in behind the janitor. Jasmine snaps forward like a movie slasher and pushes the shard of glass against the woman's throat, her sweaty fingers covering the scream.

"Hush up," Jasmine whispers into her ear. "Or I'll slit your fat throat."

Eyes agape, the woman nods.

"And I'll do it," Jasmine says.

The woman nods again.

"Now I'm going to let go of your mouth. Just tell me how to get out and I won't kill you." The woman peeps at Jasmine out of the corner of her eye and her face becomes animated.

"Omigod!" the woman says. "You're Jasmine Meadows on *Diet Extreme*! I watch you every Thursday night! You don't know how much your show means to me. Your strength, Jasmine--"

"Shut up lady and tell me how to get out of here."

"Jasmine, what are you doing *here*?"

"Like you don't know, liar. I've been trapped in this shit-house for months." Jasmine points at the dumbwaiter.

"I have been here for six weeks not knowing right above me is *the* Jasmine Meadows. God! I'm just a custodial engineer."

"My name ain't Meadows. It never was. It's Wills. Now show me how to get my ass out of here."

"There's a stairwell on the other side of that door." The woman points down a dark hallway. Jasmine turns and like a bolt of lightning, the woman clamps the mop around her throat.

Jasmine spins and pokes the woman in the stomach with the broken bottle. The woman staggers back and emits a low hissing groan.

"Shut up, I didn't stick you but a little bit," Jasmine says with her hands on her hips. "Now give me your clothes."

The whimpering, punctured woman points at the middle locker, a small patch of blood forming on the front of her jumpsuit.

"Just stay put," Jasmine says putting on the woman's oversized jeans and flannel shirt. "I just nicked you. Better yet, get your ass in that locker."

"I can't fit in there," the woman whines.

"Take my word," Jasmine says. "You'll fit." With some effort, the janitor stuffs herself into the locker, and Jasmine slams it shut, but then she opens it again.

"Give me one of them coat hangers," Jasmine says. She flattens the wire hanger, squeezes it into the little hole where the lock should be, and wraps it around and around so the janitor can't get out.

"How do *you* like it?" Jasmine says. "You fattening hog." Jasmine kicks the locker. "You…you…*extra.*" She slams into the front of the locker with her chest.

"It's cold out there at night, Miss Meadows," the woman says. "You are going to need a coat. Bobby's stuff is in locker two. He keeps gloves in there."

"What I need is a belt," Jasmine says pulling at the loose jeans.

"Bobby's combination is 22-4-16. He might have one."

"Shut up!" Jasmine yells and slams the locker with an open palm. She easily pops Bobby's locker open and finds not only a belt but an olive-drab military-style jacket, leather gloves, and a pork pie hat. There's a white plaster bear's head in there as well. Jasmine stares for a minute and shakes her head. She thinks she hears a scratching sound down the hallway.

"Is anybody else in this building?" Jasmine asks.

"Not down here. There are always people at the mansion." A door creaks down the dark hall.

"*Who's that!*" Jasmine shrieks. Out of the door comes a human shadow holding what looks at first like a flashlight. Then, as the figure gets closer, Jasmine realizes that the person has a hand-held camcorder on her shoulder. Pointing it at her and grinning in the darkness is Angelique.

"Well, well," Jasmine says, grabbing her glass dagger from Bobby's locker. "If it isn't Meghan Oswell. Girl, I owe you big time."

"I release you from your debt, crone."

"Quit pointing that camera at me."

"See it or no," Angelique says, "the camera is always on you."

"You may think somebody's always got to be looking at you, you stupid little camera whore, but that's your problem, not mine. All your life, you've tried to make yourself look like Little Miss Fancy, and what has it got you selfie slut?"

"Stop calling me Little Miss Fancy. My name is Angelique."

"Give me that camera."

"Step off!" Angelique yells as Jasmine grabs at the camera.

"Gimme that damn thing!" she says, sticking the dagger in her belt. Jasmine wrests the camera from Angelique and knocks her to the floor with an elbow. "Is this what you want?" Jasmine pushes the camera lens hard against Angelique's right eye. "Is this thing even on?"

"Stop it!" Angelique squeals as she twists and covers her face.

"You think this camera is going to change things," Jasmine says. "That it's going to fill that empty place in you? Make you reborn? Let me tell you from experience sister it ain't."

"Gimme my camera!" Angelique begs from the floor.

"I know your secret, tramp. Yeah. The men say you're a hot tail, so good looking, everything a horny piece of crap with a goober can say, but every day you look in the mirror and you know down deep in your soul that you're ugly. Don't you? I know that just like I know that it don't matter how much weight I lose I'm still going to be as fat as a goddamned hog. How come I know that? This camera right here told me." Jasmine smashes the camcorder to the floor and it shatters into a million pieces. "You got over this time because I feel sorry for you, but if you ever point a camera at me again I'll knock out your teeth. Bitch I'll roll you. *Now get your gimlet ass in that locker!*"

After using another coat hanger to trap Angelique in the locker next to the custodian, Jasmine runs down the dark hallway, up the long spiral of white stairs, and through the double doors into a starry night sky.

German shepherds howl in the distance and wake distant wolves who join the chorus, all singing the howlin' blues. Owls stare down with caution light eyes, satellites in space orbit and wink, and Jasmine sees a world remastered. Looking back for an instant at the dome, the white egg glowing like a misshapen moon, Jasmine turns and runs. She runs faster than she ever has. And for a brief moment, as she climbs the mountain with pumping legs and beating heart, for just a second, under vectors of starlight and spotlight, Jasmine flies the sky bionic.

PART FOUR

THE LONG AND WINDING ROAD

21

J asmine Wills spent most of the summer of 1985 watching *The Price is Right* and *The $25,000 Pyramid* with her cousin Don-Don. Her mother would drop her off at Aunt Myrtle's on the way to work, and on the rare occasion that Jasmine saw Uncle Patrick's white eighteen-wheeler parked sideways in the middle of the front yard--parked precariously close to Aunt Myrtle's antique rose bushes--Don-Don would be waiting at the mailbox. When Uncle Patrick was home, the third-grade cousins would spend long hours playing out back behind the house in abandoned buildings half-destroyed by a twister. When they were nothing more than dots at the edge of a vast residential hayfield, stumbling around in Black-Eyed Susans and knee-high thistle, Jasmine would sometimes break out in the sweet sound of a child's open laughter. It was strange and precious as it floated over the dense neighborhood like a lost balloon.

When at home, Uncle Patrick knocked over glasses of juice at the kitchen table, tracked in mud, complained of mysterious ailments, and left open the back door allowing Aunt Myrtle's prized Shih Tzus Wiggles and Tuggy to escape from the house. Wiggles and Tuggy often wallowed in roadkill and cow manure upon escape then returned home to the sound of Aunt Myrtle's hyponasal ravings and furniture flung end-over-end from one room to the other. Everybody agreed that the huge man was just in the way, and family members even became irritated by the shadow of his colossal head through the window of his Airstream trailer out back. Aunt Myrtle would yell at Uncle Patrick through the kitchen window day and night until, finally, the call came for him to get up to Tallapoochee to pick up a load. To everyone's great relief, Uncle Patrick would drive truckloads of frozen Big Time Pies to places like Louisville and Pittsburgh for weeks at a time. Uncle Patrick had pictures of Aunt Myrtle, Don-Don, Wiggles, and Tuggy taped across the dash of his refrigerated truck and a dated Ten Commandments air freshener dangling from the rearview mirror. Uncle Patrick liked it on the road.

People said mean things about Uncle Patrick's body. Kids at school said Uncle Patrick had "a big ol' set of titties." To Jasmine, the idea of having a "set" meant there were at least four, but she never thought to investigate. It was also rumored that Uncle Patrick had a hemorrhoid as large as a water balloon extending from his rear end because he had to sit behind the wheel of the refrigerated truck every week. Jasmine heard many people in the community say of the famed hemorrhoid, "if it ever pops it'll kill 'eem." But it didn't kill him. He died in his Airstream of coronary heart disease in 1997, clutching his chest as Aunt Myrtle recounted his various misdeeds through the kitchen window.

A tornado damaged two homes on the dirt road behind Aunt Myrtle's house between Tallapoochee and Peachtree back in '81, and a giant water oak fell on the old Peachtree Tabernacle of Baptismal Flame, making a hole in its side. The east wall of the tabernacle was reduced to rubble, but on the west wall were large stained-glass windows, each a high-columned patchworks of colored squares. There were only a couple of broken pews left in the high-ceilinged church, and a stack of damaged hymnals grew moldy in a back corner. Other than that, nothing remained on the dirty wooden floor but a few soda bottles and cigarette butts left by neglected neighborhood children. Jasmine and Don-Don would wait out Uncle Patrick in the church with Kool-Aid mustaches, listening in anticipation for the sound of his diesel engine coming to life. Don-Don was a skinny boy who always needed a haircut and was the only kid in school who had both an *Iron Maiden* t-shirt and a *Twisted Sister* tape. His energetic hands darted wildly around his thin body as he jumped about next to the lethargic Jasmine, who was his best friend at the time, describing slasher film murders faster than Jasmine could recount. In another age, he might have been given the medication Ritalin, but in 1985 he was prescribed the belt. People in Tallapoochee described Don-Don with the Alabama catch-all reserved for the fool, the criminal, and the poet.

"He ain't right," people said.

Nobody had any idea what Jasmine and Don-Don could be talking about all day long, but Jasmine's mother was certain that it involved Satanism, guitars, and biting the heads off bats. Don-Don was going to Graves Military Academy the next year after being expelled from Tallapoochee Elementary. He'd always been a class clown and, sure, he had the occasional fight or F- on his report card, but he was doing just fine at school until he got into Miss Cleecher's class. Jasmine lucked out that year and got in Mrs. Chandler's instead. Everybody loved Mrs. Chandler's class because she was a good teacher. She let her students watch educational videos like *The Return of the Pink Panther* and *Revenge of the Pink Panther* while Miss Cleecher across the hall ran her class like a work camp. The kids called Miss Cleecher's class "Alcatraz." Miss Cleecher looked like a pro wrestler with bulging muscles and a unibrow, but she had this mincing hairstyle that curled daintily at her shoulders and forehead. An outsider in the small Alabama town of Tallapoochee, Miss Cleecher was a stern and rigorous teacher who was the butt of many cruel jokes. One day after being admonished by Miss Cleecher for missing seven words out of ten on his spelling quiz, Don-Don went to the boy's bathroom and came back with his wet hair curled just so on his shoulders and forehead. When Don-Don sat back down at his desk with Miss Cleecher's curls, the kids roared with laughter. When Miss Cleecher looked up from her grade book at Don-Don as he imitated her scowl, her face purpled with eyes like hollow-point bullets. Don-Don was sent out to the hall and given the choice of three hundred sentences or three licks with a paddle. Bouncing on the balls of his feet and fidgeting with his hands, Don-Don chose the paddle but included the codicil that Principal Comer should administer the paddling, not Miss Cleecher. And not with Big Freddy, the legendary paddle in Miss Cleecher's desk that was rumored to have caused children to age prematurely and lose teeth. But Miss Cleecher already had Big

Freddy in her iron fist. She had been hiding Big Freddy behind her back the whole time. Students with scared opossum eyes could hear the *thwack, thwack, thwack* of the wood on little Don-Don's denim in the hallway followed by high-pitched gargling screeches.

Things were never good for Don-Don and Miss Cleecher after that. Walking in line to the lunchroom, Jasmine would often see Don-Don standing outside Miss Cleecher's door waiting for the principal to give him additional licks with the paddle. In the hall he would waste time, his hands and feet always filled with energy, making a ball of paper into an airplane or drawing muscular Sasquatches with dainty curls on the wall with his pencil. Uncle Patrick and Aunt Myrtle were brought in to have conferences about Don-Don's behavior, and at night Aunt Myrtle would lay into Don-Don with a Pabst Blue Ribbon in one hand and a leather belt in the other. A king-sized cigarette would dangle from the crook of Aunt Myrtle's mouth as she'd strike multiple targets with a wild back-and-forth motion while howling admonitions with a squeaky voice. And then, after two fistfights with first graders, drawing large naked animals on the walls in the hallways, and finally pooping in the bathroom trash can, Don-Don was expelled from Tallapoochee Elementary. His mother had to drive all the way to Birmingham to find used military suits in his size.

In the meantime, Don-Don sat in the summer shade with Jasmine in the abandoned tabernacle spinning wild tales about Miss Cleecher and Bobby Cleecher. He said that when Miss Cleecher was a little girl, she had strangled a petting zoo cow with her bare hands. He said that her brother, Bobby Cleecher, was once at his two-acre marijuana patch up in the Tallapoochee when he saw a Sasquatch and Miss Cleecher making a lover's burrow out of pine straw and logs.

Wearing a black cloak that he'd found in the fellowship hall, Don-Don would dance at the front of the tabernacle and preach the gospel. He would close his eyes, lean back, open his palms and say "Jeeeezuss." When the sun started going down, the sunlight struck the panes of colored glass and the children's skin glowed like Christmas trees. The entire room would become a kaleidoscope of greens, oranges, reds, and blues moving up the wall. When this happened, Don-Don and Jasmine would just sit there looking up at the slowly passing colors without saying a word. These were the best moments in Jasmine's life.

Before Don-Don was to report to Graves Military Academy, he and Jasmine spent one last day hanging out in the tabernacle. They played Old Maid and watched the colors float across the room until the waning stained-glass sunlight grew purple. When the last bands of color were gone, Don-Don jumped up and ran outside the tabernacle, his face jumbled and angry. He picked up a rock and threw it hard through one of the colored glass panes. One little square shattered. But when he picked up the second rock, Jasmine grabbed at his hands.

"You ain't supposed to do that Don-Don," she said, squeezing his hands in hers for a second. "This is a place of worship."

The next morning, Don-Don was on the bus for Graves.

Jasmine didn't hear much news about cousin Don-Don, but at the end of the school year Jasmine's mama and daddy drove her up near Bankhead to see his elementary graduation. He wasn't called Don-Don anymore. Jasmine sat slumped watching the lines of military academy students in dress blues, their white captain's hats immense on diminutive shaven heads. Pink-faced, they marched in time holding polished wooden rifles, their little legs kicking out as they stomped left-right-left in patent leather shoes. A student military band played a troubled version of "Pershing's Own," and Jasmine was shocked to see "Don" in the front of his class holding a flapping flag on a spear. He strutted with the rest of them, no clownishness. And afterward, when the family went to a steakhouse, Don sat at the head of the long table, posture straight, in his dress uniform, still wearing the white captain's hat with chinstrap. He didn't laugh or say much but responded to questions from family members with quick responses that ended with a "sir" or a "ma'am." The family was delighted with Don's transformation, but Jasmine just sat at the far end of the table with an empty face, her eyes down as she gobbled country-fried steak with gravy. Jasmine and Don didn't say one word to each other, but she did see for a second before he got into the family sedan a goofy little jiggle in the knees and shoulders. He did a barely noticeable robot move, and that was it. He was gone. Don-Don was gone. And when Jasmine got back home in the late afternoon sun, she collected a big pile of rocks and finished the job on the stained-glass windows.

Only after her escape from the egg is Jasmine able to feel a feeble twinge of Don-Don somewhere inside her. Despite everything, those tender and all-but-forgotten emotions are still there. She kneels between two boulders on a cliff face, her eyes following a small hawk soaring over the long valley. Orange and yellow lines of sunlight burn her eyes because she hasn't seen the sun in over one hundred days. She exhales steam, her clothes moist from the dew, then standing up rubs her shoulders and stretches hands to the sky, her back popping from lying on uneven ground knotted with pine root and stone. *The compound,* Jasmine thinks, *must be only two miles away. Time to start walking,* she thinks, *but in which direction?* Jasmine knows that if she walks west, down the mountain, she will be heading toward her home in Tallapoochee. But if she went that way, she could remain in the national forest for a week. Seven days without food, that's not a plan. The compound is to the south and there's no going back there. North, Jasmine thinks, is nothing but forest all the way to Tennessee. That leaves east, towards the morning sun, and over the mountain. Walking east, she figures that she can probably be out of the forest in two days, but she will have to climb some dangerous cliffs and high-rock faces to do that.

Hungry, she thinks back to all that wasted food from her dinner party with Timothy Godwin. Things happened too fast for her to grab even a few greasy fries. What she wouldn't do right now for a burger, a biscuit, even a scrap of Big Time Pie –just a tiny piece. Or even one of those strange vegetables or tortured meats the TV chefs had kept sending down the dumbwaiter. Anything. Jasmine licks dew off leaves and cracks acorns for breakfast, disappointed that huckleberry season is over. Maybe if she hits a clear cut there might still be a few dried-up blackberries in the shady brambles. She drinks from a rock indentation filled with rainwater.

Crunch crunch crunch crunch crunch crunch, Jasmine trudges up the mountain. Sweating, she flops down on a rock, her lungs pained in the cool air. *The problem with fall,* Jasmine realizes, *is that they can hear you coming.*

Crunch crunch crunch crunch, another switchback mile. Chest heaving, she takes off the leather gloves, adjusts the oversized jeans, and pulls the belt with rebel flag buckle one notch tighter. Despite everything, as she sits on the side of this steep incline, Jasmine has this odd sensation that she can scarcely recall. It's happiness. But before she can grasp the feeling, it brushes by with the northern breeze that lifts and drops her ponytail. She faces north and inhales deeply. The wind now has a smell, a scent that Jasmine knows all too well. It is perhaps the most welcome aroma she could have hoped for out here in the wild.

Hello sausage my old friend. I've come to eat the pig again.

Squinting due north, Jasmine sees a leaning line of white smoke on a low-lying ledge a half-mile away and decides to change direction and hike as quietly as possible toward what she hopes is the campsite of well-larded deer hunters. She proceeds to flank the site to the east so that she might peek from a safe, elevated distance. To reduce the noise from crunching leaves, she leaps from rock to rock, glass dagger in hand. It takes her almost a half hour to wind her way up through the rock cliffs, sweat evaporating from her thinning body at this elevation. On top of a jutting boulder, she peers down at a long ledge and sees the campsite. There's a green pup tent and a circle of rocks next to a thicket of short-leaf pine trees where a small fire smolders. Jasmine smells coffee, the aroma of the cooking link sausages making her drool, but taking a quick peek she can't see anyone down there. *Maybe they're in the tent,* Jasmine thinks. She sits for a while longer on the boulder clutching her crude weapon, then pokes her head up to take another look at the camp. There's no movement inside the tent, but two backpacks lean against a majestic pine. Jasmine sneaks around the boulder and moves in closer. She hides behind a hickory tree for a minute, then eases toward the tent. Jasmine's heart begins to thud and she hears the sound of water slapping on rock from a small waterfall on the far side of the ledge. Crouching to look into the tent, Jasmine sees only camping equipment and bedding. Three links of what has to be Conecuh County sausage cool in the frying pan. Jasmine snaps one up, blows it for a minute, and pops it into her mouth feeling a momentary burst of greasy bliss. Edging around the tent as she chews, she looks up to see a thin stream of water running down a flat rock face. Beside this trickle, Jasmine is mortified to see a bald and crooked man, soaped from head to foot, trying to splash himself clean. She freezes for a minute looking for his weapons but sees none. *It's that little asshole kidnapper Preston Price, naked as a jaybird with soap in his eyes.* A craven smile comes to her face as she picks up a handful of stones.

"Hey Doofus!" she yells as she hurls the first rock. It strikes him in the back and he emits a startled yawp. The second rock tags the side of his head and bounces upward. Dazed, Preston whirls around rubbing his face and uttering incomprehensible threats. Putting on his glasses with both hands, he slips in the soapy water and flops backward against the rock. Jasmine is filled with uncontrollable laughter as she pelts Preston with four more choice stones and then rushes in fists high. First, she strikes him with a hook punch to the head, then an uppercut in the guts followed by a right jab to the spine. After kicking him repeatedly in the nether regions, she snatches the belt from her jeans and whips it around Preston's throat pulling the man back from the small waterfall to the pine thicket.

"Jasmine," Preston gargles, frothing with a look of glee on his battered face. "You've arrived."

Using the belt buckle, Jasmine ties Preston by his neck to a hickory tree. She sits down on a rock next to the fire, pours hot coffee into Preston's field cup, and sips. Jasmine smiles and holds the tin cup to her lips as Preston gags, spits, and struggles. She likes the dark roast gourmet stuff now. Preston's face purples as he grabs at his throat, his eyes still giddy. She picks up the second piece of sausage and bites it noticing that Preston has leaned backward in the tree just so and can now breathe a little.

"Jasmine," he croaks. "I find it interesting that after all this time you put me here just so, in just the right place for me to watch you eat."

Stuffing the third sausage into her mouth, Jasmine stands up and pulls off Preston's round glasses. With a dead-pan face, she puts the glasses down on a rock.

"No, Jasmine, I--"

The glass makes snapping sounds under her boot.

"Say something else smart." Jasmine walks over to Preston's pile of folded clothes and picks up his Ringo wig. It sizzles and crackles when she tosses it onto the campfire's red coals then bursts into a short-lived flame. Jasmine digs into Preston's pocket and finds his billfold, searches through his identification and credit cards. In his personal effects, there is only one picture. It is a photograph of little Preston in a striped shirt holding up a turtle. She puts it into her pocket.

"Your friend Godwin," Jasmine says leaning over the fire. "I think I killed him."

"No, you gave him quite a wallop, but he's alive."

"How do you know?"

"I can show you the link if you let me loose and promise not to beat me up again."

"I won't hurt you if you act right," Jasmine says. "Mama taught me never to pick on cripples."

"Making fun of a person's disabilities. That hurts worse."

"Shut up," Jasmine says untying the belt around his neck. "Put some damn clothes on."

After putting on olive drab trousers and a black turtleneck sweater, Preston pushes buttons on his device for a while then hands it to Jasmine. She watches herself from a high angle strike Tick with the wine bottle, watches Tick stuff the biscuit into her mouth, his head-splitting fall, and finally Jasmine's daring escape through the dumbwaiter.

"Lord have mercy," Jasmine says.

"Oh yeah," Preston says nodding. "It's very graphic, Jasmine. Bloody too. You made mincemeat out of him. But look." He fast-forwards the feed to show Tick standing up and using the key card to make a shaky exit through the glass door.

"So he's OK?" Jasmine asks.

"I wouldn't go that far," Preston says. "His face and hands are mummified in gauze and his nose looks like a half-eaten rutabaga.

You've stolen Tim's most prized possession, Jasmine. His face. I can probably find him in real-time if you'd like," Preston says as he pushes more buttons.

"I believe you," Jasmine says.

"This thing is great," Preston says. "I got our GPS, we can watch *Diet Extreme* Thursday night if you want. Hey, look at this!" Preston pushes another button to reveal a point of view shot of Jasmine sitting by the campfire, live.

"So you are filming us now?"

"Yep," Preston grins pointing at a tiny camera on his sweater. "This very moment might well end up on the show."

"Woo, let me see that again," Jasmine says. Preston hands the phone to her, and she stands up and walks to the ledge.

"Check this out, Doofus," Jasmine says and hurls the phone off the cliff. Preston shrugs when he hears it smack against the rocks below.

"Please, call me Preston." He takes a phone from his pocket. "I'm glad to see that you signed the contract. How does it feel to be famous *and* rich?"

"Shoot. I'll be asking for a pay cut at the bank when I get back, if they'll take me."

"Jasmine, I still don't think you get it. The very day your show aired, Oprah *Winfrey* called our office for an exclusive. They're all calling. Jasmine, you've been invited to give the commencement speech at Smith! You should see what *People* magazine has to say about what they're calling 'Meadows swank.' Like it or not, Jasmine, you're a celebrity. You made it babe. You're a real live star."

"No. I work at the bank."

"OK, fine, you work at the bank, Jasmine. You work at the bank."

Jasmine pokes coals with a stick. Preston stands hunched at the edge of a cliff.

"In that pack," Preston says, "you'll find two sets of clothes, your size, a pair of proper shoes, field binoculars, canteen, a sleeping bag, flashlight, a compass, Swiss Army Knife, mess kit, matches, and food for one week. No more sausages though, I'm afraid. Nothing too heavy to carry from here on out."

"What the hell are *you* doing out here?" Jasmine glowers.

"I had to leave the compound because rumor has it I murdered a man in my employ. A man named Jaekel Sneade." Preston puts a few leaves and sticks on the smoldering coals.

"Did you?"

"Of course not. It's a setup. He was poisoned by your exercise trainer, Suzie Baxter. She also desecrated his body. I also have reason to believe that that Angelique may be involved."

"That exercise trainer," Jasmine utters. "She's a psycho."

"I have proof of my innocence. There were cameras in an automobile near the crime scene. Some cameras were turned off before the murder, but Suzie failed to find them all."

"There are cameras everywhere."

"You said a mouthful, Jasmine. You have to realize that *Diet Extreme* involves the chefs, exercise, the interactions among all the people at the compound. Even in the woods. So we used a variety of hidden spy cams."

"And you're still recording me?"

"I'm not going to lie to you. There are a half dozen cameras pointed at you right now. All the live feeds I record today will be forwarded to the editing team in Colorado. The team there is trying to take all of the feeds and finish the season. We have a two-hour finale that has to be produced."

"Is Godwin recording me too?"

"Maybe," Preston says as he glances up at the sky. "I don't know. They are using drones and satellite images. My guess is they've filmed your every move since your escape. In any event, they'll be coming after you."

"With cameras?" Jasmine asks, her face red.

"With cameras." Preston rubs his hands together over the fire.

"I'm getting out of here," Jasmine says as she spits into the fire. She turns, hearing a sound, panicking, but it's only squirrels scrambling in the boughs of hickory trees.

"East I take it?" Preston says.

"Leave me alone," she says staring at the orange embers. "Where I go is none-ya damn beeswax."

"Check this out." Preston unfolds a government map and lays it out on the ground. He places a small rock on each of the corners. The map's terrain features are marked in brown wavy lines on olive green, and Preston has made numerous circles with a blue magic marker. Standing sideways, he uses a crooked stick to point.

"Here we are, right about here. Tallapoochee Gap over here. Down here is the compound, mansion, egg dome. Grandmaw's house is due west. This is the mountain range running north to south. But look here, this little dotted line. That's the Tsoyaha Trail."

"So?" Crossing her arms, Jasmine kicks at the map.

"The Tsoyaha, Jasmine, intersects with the Appalachian Trail, which goes all the way to Maine."

"So hit the road, toots. Take off."

"Maybe you and I, we both take off--"

"--forget you," she shoos at him with her hand. "Just get out of my face you goofy-ass rascal. You're just lucky I don't tie you back up and leave you for the buzzards."

Exhaling, Preston folds his map and starts to break down the pup tent.

"Your backpack is over there," he points at a gray pack leaning against a tree. "There's a water purification kit in there as well. I can show you how to use it."

"Go away," Jasmine says, standing up. She walks over to her backpack and slides her right arm into the shoulder harness, but her left arm can't quite slide in. Her elbow pokes out at an angle as she spins and bounces around.

"Here, let me show you," Preston says and presses the clasp loosening the strap. "This strap goes around your waist. It helps." He moves in closer, reaching with his hands to slide the straps around her hips to her stomach, then slides the clasps together with a click, letting his fingers rest for a second between the tight strap and Jasmine's belly.

"Get off me!" With both hands, Jasmine pushes Preston away. "Don't touch me!"

"I'm sorry, I apologize."

"Uggh, just get away from me," Jasmine says. "I don't like you or your kind. You're all going to the jailhouse when I'm done with you."

With a grunt, Jasmine starts hiking east, straight up the side of a gorge. Preston sits at the edge of the cliff listening to her feet crunch in the fallen leaves then starts to gather small twigs for a new fire. Once it has burned down a bit, he slides two rocks close together at the flame's edge and rests his gray cup on the rocks to warm water for tea. He opens his phone and calls Manuelita, who is convalescing in Birmingham after her injuries.

"Good morning, Mr. Price," Manuelita says, alert.

"Morning. I need you to fly a pair of my glasses and a new hairpiece to Grandmaw's house. Just put them on the mantelpiece."

"What happened?"

"Great news," Preston beams. "Jasmine escaped. She's heading east."

"Don't tell me she got out through the dumbwaiter."

"Yep. Heh heh heh."

"You were right again, Mr. Price."

"At the moment I'm blind as a bat." Preston sips his tea. "I'll have to get to Grandmaw's without my glasses, but that shouldn't be a problem. Like I said, she's heading due east from my current coordinates, so no matter what happens, keep the cameras rolling."

A warm wind blows at the fire and Preston tries to meditate on everything that's happening. He sits quietly on the pine needles and tries to focus on his breathing, but for some strange reason images of his father's tea table flash into consciousness. *That stupid white table with all the plates covered in dried-up tea bags he kept for re-use. Why now? Why that stupid tea table of all things? Why do such rare slivers of memory, things all but forgotten, come into brief focus then disappear?* Staring into the fire, Preston plucks at the memory embedded deep like a wood tick.

22

Preston and his father Ackerman never quite connected after his mother died in the crash. Passing in the hallway, they spoke at each other in strange tones with smirks and knowing looks. Ackerman would breathe heavily out of his nose, his nostril hairs producing a pretentious hiss. He would lean his thin head, pull off his tortoiseshell glasses, and look through the lenses like he did with his patients, hissing heavily from his nose. There were always plans for road trips to Seattle and canoe rides in Colorado, "doing things together" as "father and son" in some abstract future, but they never did those things. Usually, Preston's father went on the trips and boat rides alone, or in a van with a group of recovering addicts from Megargel State Hospital. But most of the time Ackerman just stayed in his home office with the door locked listening to the Beatles.

Preston cringes, remembering all those uncomfortable moments at the threshold of his father's home office, eight-year-old Preston standing in the long hallway staring at dried tea bags like cat turds littering the white tea table. Ackerman would wait there in perturbed silence for his son to turn and leave. Preston, always with his camera on the leather strap around his neck, usually wanted a ride into King City to get pictures developed. His father's office contained stacks of books, Monterey Pop Festival posters and framed album covers on the walls, the prominent tea table in the middle of the room. Preston remembers standing at the door hearing his father's radio playing "Morning Edition" on NPR, his father wearing a gray V-necked sweater with a black t-shirt underneath, his lips pooched in consternation. After listening to the radio, his dad would take a long run, and then sometimes they would ride together to Monterey in Ackerman's green MG for lunch and a stroll along the pier to watch sea lions on the rocks. On that fateful day, Preston hesitated at the office door, hoping that his father would invite him to go for a ride later, but Ackerman just offered a noncommittal stare.

"Preston," his father finally said. "I have a present for you. It was meant to be for your birthday." Ackerman cleared the cups and dried teabags off a mustard-colored box and handed it to Preston. The teabags had made brown stains on his present. Grabbing the gift, Preston plopped on the floor in the doorway and opened it. What he found was a brand-new movie camera, a Super 8. Preston knew that there was a projector in the attic that played movies, but the Price family never had a camera until now.

"Your mother bought it," Ackerman said, "because of your talent."

Preston grasped the handle of the camera and looked through, seeing the tea table. He toyed with the focus.

"Now please go play," Ackerman said. "Buddy I have work to do."

"Ackerman, I need film," Preston said. "Can we go into King City? Please?"

"Preston, you little reaction formation, no," Ackerman turned to face the radio. "Go play."

Preston did finally get film and batteries for his new camera, but on this hilly stretch of California farmland turned residential community, there wasn't anything much to shoot. Preston wasted twenty minutes of film pointing his camera at his brown two-story farmhouse, the rusty swing set in his backyard, and two trees on a hill. He filmed his room, his toys, and his father's British sports car. Preston learned after watching his first efforts in the attic that a movie without action is just a picture, so he turned his camera to the only living creature he could find, his father. Preston would film Ackerman through the keyhole, watching his father talk to himself while breathing through his nose and looking into his glasses as if he were talking to a patient. Occasionally, Ackerman would masturbate with his feet on the tea table while looking at a *Playboy* magazine. Preston hid behind the shower curtain filming while his father sat on the commode reading the funny pages of the *San Francisco Chronicle*. But what was weirdest was when father would stay in the office for long periods listening to the Beatles. For Ackerman Price Jr., listening to the Fab Four was a sacred thing. Preston realized after Ackerman's death that the Beatles rituals were his father's only chance to experience open-hearted reverence, even atonement, in an otherwise peevish and snarky existence. Ackerman would start to sing with the Beatles, and if so moved would put on his secret mop-top wig and, using an old acoustic guitar, would pantomime entire albums three or four times. These sessions could last until two in the morning. You could tell by his facial expressions whether Ackerman was being Paul or John. Mostly he wobbled and grinned like early Paul. Preston preferred the late John.

A few weeks after Preston had begun filming his father, he taped up hand-drawn movie posters all over the house with "Come to the Big Show" and "Movie Premier" on them. Ackerman brought the film projector down from the attic to the living room and made popcorn for Preston's directorial debut. Preston and Ackerman sat on opposite ends of the couch eating popcorn in quaint plastic containers fashioned to look like the cardboard cartons people got at the movies in the 1950s. A blank white rectangle flashed on the slide projector screen and the credits rolled. Preston had written words on pieces of notebook paper in crayon and taped them on the wall so that he could pan to each one: "Father"--"By"--"Preston Price."

"Inventive way to handle the credits," Ackerman said smiling over at his son. The movie starts with a picture of Ackerman's office door and then advances slowly to the keyhole.

"Oh, you little *voyeur*," Ackerman said watching himself through the keyhole gesturing to himself while masturbating in fading black and white. The next scene is a close-up of Ackerman's sweating face straining to defecate on the commode as he reads the funny pages. His mouth appears to be opening and closing, opening and closing. Scene three is a long shot of Ackerman pushing a cart through the grocery store with a little piece of notebook paper taped to his back, scrawled in Preston's hand with the words, "Goober Pyle." In the film, Ackerman shakes his head at an old woman reaching for a can of soup, wheels impatiently past a mother with children, and bites down on his bottom lip with impatience at the checkout line. People point at the "Goober Pyle" sign when a perturbed Ackerman passes.

"Goober Pyle," Ackerman chuckles with eyes aflicker.

The film ends with a very elaborate performance of "When I Saw Her Standing There," Ackerman wearing the Beatles wig, his face shaking wildly. There was no soundtrack, but it was clear what Ackerman was singing.

"I held her hand in miyeeeeeeeeeene," Ackerman sang along with the silent film watching himself in costume. As the film ended with flapping reels, Preston sat on his end of the couch staring at the white screen with a startled look on his face.

"Bravo!" Ackerman clapped, seemingly unperturbed by the exposé. "Brilliant camera angles. Very *avant-garde!*" Ackerman patted his son on the back and with a beaming face walked back into his office. Preston went to bed exhilarated and did not dream. But the next day when Preston woke up, he found that his movie camera and film had disappeared in the night. Even his 35 mm had been removed from his bedside. Preston stomped down the stairs to find that his father had prepared Eggs Benedict with fresh-squeezed orange juice, the plate and juice placed on the table just so. Preston knew something was amiss.

"Have a seat, me boy!" Ackerman said, sipping his tea by the oven. "I made your favorite breakfast."

"Where's my camera?" Preston said.

"I've put it away for a while," Ackerman said. "After considering your film a bit more, I am not quite sure you are ready. This is not to say that you aren't very talented. Some of the shots were just stunning. Believe me, son, I am overall proud of your visual *sense."* Despite himself, Preston's face gleamed as the smile broke through the sardonic posture that father and son commonly used to communicate.

"Nevertheless," Ackerman continued, "there are editorial concerns. You see, my office is my own private space. What I do in there is for me and me alone. Understand? We on the other end of the camera are more than images, my son. Think about that. How would you like it if I made a film of your naked body and played it for your class at school? What if I did a close-up of your bald pubis and showed it to the other children? You wouldn't like it, would you buddy? No. And that is exactly what I am going to have to do, to help teach you this lesson."

"No!" Preston cried, face red and suddenly bellowing. "No daddy no!"

"Son, I have no choice. I am just going to have to film you nude and show it to your class at school." Ackerman pulled a slip of paper from his slacks as tears burst from his son's red face.

"No, heh heh," Ackerman said after a few minutes of sobbing. "I wouldn't do that. I just wanted you to understand what it would feel like. But I do have news. You see this piece of paper," he waved a slip. "It's a bus ticket. I called your Grandmaw this morning on the phone and we both decided that it would be good for you to spend the rest of the summer in the country. You need to spend some time with your mother's side of the family, maybe put filmmaking aside for a while. Maybe you two can play dress-up together or shuck corn. You need to put things in their proper context."

"No daddy!" Preston cried. "Please don't send me to Alabama!"

"Summering in Dixie doesn't suit you?"

"Daddy pleeeeease let me stay home. Don't let them lynch me! I promise I won't do it again. Please don't send me to Grandmaw's house! Please don't send me to Grandmaw's house!"

"To Grandmaw's house you go," Ackerman put his hand on Preston's shoulder. "Next week you leave on a Greyhound bus. But if you behave yourself, Preston, I promise that I will forget about the little film I planned for you. OK, chief? Now eat your Eggs Benedict." His breath hitching, Preston ate his cold breakfast, realizing that he was again being abandoned by his father.

Preston never felt so alone until this moment, out on the side of Tallapoochee Gap Mountain. He can still smell Jasmine as he stares down at the Yoko Ono wig in his hands, his mind awash in magical mystery.

23

Jasmine sniffs her armpits and scowls as she trudges along the mountainside with her new backpack. A small cavern appears overhead as she rounds a bend shaded by beech trees and thin lines of water dripping from the cavern's mouth into a stream where flat rocks shine. Climbing up a narrow ledge using rock outcroppings and tree limbs for balance, Jasmine finds a flashlight in the backpack's side pocket and edges into the cave. She pans around the small enclosure, the dim circles of light on the damp rock face giving her the shivers. Jasmine's light freezes on odd silver graffiti scrawled across the far cavern wall, a strange hieroglyph in silver spray paint depicting two figures emerging from the top of a large oval structure. The man's back is bent at an angle, his arms extended in a position of veneration toward a pear-shaped woman at the apex of the dome. Lines like a child's crayon sun extend outward from the transcendent female form. Jasmine drops the backpack to the floor and the clank of steel on rock echoes in the small chamber. Clicking off the flashlight, she stands facing the picture on the cave wall. The image shines luminous in the dark, an occasional strand of sunlight reflecting off the collected water on the cave floor to illuminate the space in wavy bands. Jasmine allows herself to touch the clammy black wall with her fingertips and stands still in the blackness, her hands caressing the wet wall as she listens to the trickling water. She hasn't felt unwatched and all alone in months. She savors it as a full hour passes. As the sun sets, Jasmine's eyes adjust to the expanding dark, and she perceives the gray contours of the smooth room worn flat by centuries of flowing water. There is a small puddle at the far end of the cave and Jasmine crouches down toward it seeing her eyes glitter in the dark reflection. She touches her tongue to the clean water and an image of her own brick house in Tallapoochee comes to mind. She thinks of gallon cans of cheese dip, unused plastic patio chairs, plus-sized rayon shirts on wire hangers, and her mama's crockpot on the bottom shelf. At that moment, Jasmine knows she will never set foot in that little brick and stucco house again.

The cave's walls contain mica, and after some time in the dark, she sees it shimmering in the rock like her baby's polished tombstone. She knows there aren't any flowers on her baby's grave. There never have been flowers there. The air near the floor of the cave feels cool and she curls up there feeling colors in her mind hanging motionless like bubbles in old glass. Memories coil around her heart and squeeze like great, wet hands. Wiping away unforeseen tears, Jasmine opens her backpack and finds the poncho. She lays it down on the floor of the cave, then shakes the backpack letting everything fall.

Cut the crybaby crap, Jasmine thinks, wiping her face with the back of her hand. *Get yourself over this mountain.*

Someone has taken a long time to choose these clothes, Jasmine finds, as she points her flashlight down at the pile. And it's more than a little weird. The clothes are *too* right. There's a loose gray shirt with ruffles identical to the one she wore to work, only in a much smaller size. There are the gray tennis shoes that she likes, her favorite brand of pants, and three pairs of pink panties. Secretly, Jasmine likes pink panties, but nobody in the world would know that. After finding a washrag and travel-sized body wash, Jasmine peels off the dirty cleaning lady's clothes she swiped from the compound. The trickling water makes goosebumps at first, but it's not too cold for a good shower. Jasmine exhales as she lathers the washrag and rubs soapy water onto her body, then looks up to the mouth of the cave as the thin stream rinses her. Looking at the vast valley below from the cave, Jasmine towels herself dry. She looks down at her own body in the reflection and acknowledges that she now looks like the kind of girl that you might see on a mechanic's calendar. With full breasts, athletic thighs, rounded hips, and a trim waist Jasmine knows that if men saw this body, they would want it. They would treat her like Meghan Oswell, all smiles with funny looks in their eyes, with all the sucking up. The thought fills Jasmine with intense revulsion. She tells herself that she can't wait to get fat again.

Dogs howl down the mountain. They sound to Jasmine like blueticks and bloodhounds, hunting dogs heading her way. Jasmine hears leaves crunching as loud male voices shock the air. Naked, Jasmine crouches in the cave looking down the cliff with her field binoculars. There are three men with shotguns and dogs moving north from the direction of the compound. The red-faced man in the front has a buzz cut and wears a sleeveless plaid shirt. His bloodhound on leather leash sniffs the ground, snuffling and moaning up the path. The hunched-over man in the yellow CAT hat behind him spits black tobacco juice and wipes his dirty face, a bluetick on his leash. Taking up the rear is a young guy of maybe nineteen, wearing an Aryan nation t-shirt with long red mutton chops and a bald head. He has a Boston terrier on a doggie walker. All three of the men are holding brand new twelve-gauge double-barrel shotguns. Two of the dogs get wrapped around a small oak tree and the men stop to untangle them. Jasmine cups her ears and tries to hear what they're saying.

"He's moving in the other direction," CAT Hat says pointing north staring down at his GPS.

"He's going that way, yeah?" says Buzz Cut. "North by north-east, innit." As the hillbillies trudge up the side of the mountain, Jasmine wonders why they have British accents.

24

Early in the evening, as black-bottomed clouds go pink, Preston finds a dry tulip tree grove in a creek bed to make a campsite. As the blackbird flies, he is one mile away from Jasmine. He knows this because the GPS sewn into her backpack pulses a little red dot on Preston's phone app. He hasn't made good time today because he had to pick up supplies at Grandmaw's house, but he has found a fantastic spot to camp. He tells himself that he loves his campsite, that being alone in the outdoors like this is great. *Just great. This is fun.* He's close to a stream that meanders down the mountain. Wide ferns grow from gray rock faces. Magnolia and Catalpa branches make parasols over moss carpets. *It's just great.* He finds a wood tick behind his right ear. *Here a pool, there a tiny waterfall, everywhere the sound of moving water over rock.* Preston snatches limbs from a small space under some tulip trees and strikes stakes with the hammer end of his small hatchet. He misses one of the stakes and then pummels it into the ground in a fit of rage. After getting the tent up, Preston unrolls his blue sleeping bag and attaches a small field lamp to the mesh ceiling so that it will glow at night. He finds his book, *Facing the Hate-Self,* and flings it at his unrolled sleeping bag. The book is getting heavy and something deep within him wants to toss it page-by-page into the fire. Preston uses his water purification kit to fill his shiny US Army canteen, then gathers a nice stack of firewood for the long night ahead. He decides that he will keep a fire burning all night. If Jasmine's still heading due east, she will be able to look north from any fixed position and see his flame. Preston's pile of twigs is easy to light, and an excellent piece of heart pine blazes and crackles to life. Preston wishes that he had a long piece of sausage to fry, but he has only dehydrated strawberries and nuts. Instead of eating his meager rations, he flings handfuls of food over his shoulder and chews pills out of random brown bottles.

An hour later, after the meds kick in, Preston slides another piece of kindling onto the fire and watches splinters of flame burst upward into the atmosphere and become diamonds. Clouds decorate the sparkling sky in sunset pinks, while Preston stands over the fire holding the Yoko Ono wig. He holds it just over the fire, flames licking up to melt one long black strand, but pulls it back to his heart, the black hair hanging through his fingers long and silky. Preston slides the wig into his backpack and puts on water for tea, but before the water boils Preston hears the distant sound of howling dogs. Preston sits in a half-lotus position as dogs and men tramp closer and closer to the campfire. They're loud, seeming at one moment high up on the mountain and the next heading away from the fire, then moving back west. From the ruckus, they also seem to be falling down a lot, the dogs snapping at one another when their leashes become intertwined. The sky now dark, Preston sees three flashlights swinging in the night and hears the bombastic voices thirty feet away.

"Tie up your dogs," Preston yells as he stands at an angle, but the men pay him no mind. The barking dogs and countrified men are suddenly crowding Preston's campfire, shotgun barrels swinging in all directions. Flat Top frowns down at Preston while CAT Hat and Skinhead jeer.

"You not from around here are ya *boy*?" CAT Hat says and spits tobacco into the fire. He curls his face back into an ugly capped-toothed grin.

"I could say the same of you," Preston says. "What are you doing out here?"

"Nuthin' much," Flat Top says and they all let out this mean chuckle, "we just on a little *pig* hunt."

"Then why aren't you closer to a creek," Preston offers, "or maybe a swamp? You are on a protected wildlife preserve, you know."

"Fiddle dee frickin' dee," CAT Hat says and the hunters laugh.

"Mind if we warm ourselves by your nice fire?" Flat Top says and the men sit down on the ground holding shotguns on their laps. Flat Top and CAT Hat squeeze in close to Preston.

"Spot of tea?" Skinhead dips Preston's Darjeeling into the hot water.

"Please do." Preston exhales from his nose and shakes his head while they wait for the tea. Skinhead plays a flawless rendition of "Old Folks at Home" with his harmonica.

"Hey Preston," Skinhead says in the firelight. "Dance for us a little bit. Do a Cotton-Eyed Joe for me and the boys here."

"How do you know my name?"

The boys laugh as they pass the metal tea-cup around and slurp, pinkies up.

"Shake that crooked moneymaker for us," Flat Top chuckles. "Randy here thanks you got a real purty ass."

"I'm not into that scene," Preston says staring into the fire.

"Scene?" CAT Hat stands and points the shotgun at Preston. "Oh, you in the *scene*, bubba. Now get your asymmetrical bum up here and give us a dance."

"So this is how Tick settles the score? He can't get to Jasmine so he does *this*?"

"Stand up!" Flat Top barks.

"If he don't get up, I'm gone have to make him *my* wet nurse," CAT Hat says. "Come here, nanny nanny nanny nanny."

The boys chuckle.

"OK, OK, n-no wet nurse stuff." Preston stands. With arms raised, all eyes and gun barrels on him, he begins a routine for a country exercise video he once did to the Oak Ridge Boys song "Elvira," his elbows moving up and down and knees extended in fast-paced clod hopping.

"Now git that shirt off," Skinhead says as the men surround Preston. "Slow it down a little and rotate them special hips."

Eyes glazed from the prescription meds, Preston pulls half-heartedly at his sweater, his crooked hips snapping to his singing.

"I like that," says Skinhead, beads of sweat on his upper lip. "I like that a bunch. Now cockle doodle doo like a rooster."

"*What*?"

"You heard 'eem!" Flat Top says, giving Preston a love tap in the stomach with the butt of his shotgun. "Cockle doodle doo like a buttfuckin' rooster."

"Cockle doodle doo!" squeals CAT Hat into Preston's ear.

"OK," Preston wheezes hoarsely. "Cockle doodle doo. Cockle doodle doo."

Seeing this, the dogs back away from the fire, whimpering.

"I *know* you can do better than that," Skinhead whispers.

"I think he's more a layin' hen than a rooster," CAT Hat says and they all snigger.

"You lay eggs, boy?" Flat Top says.

"Why don't you get down on your knees right there and lay us an egg," CAT Hat says.

"Get away from me," Preston wheezes. "Joke's over, chumps. I've seen *Deliverance*."

"Henny Penny, it's time for you to meet Rhode Island Red," Flat Top says jabbing Preston in the stomach again with the shotgun.

Gasping, Preston drops to his knees as the men move in closer.

"Here chicky chicky chicky," Skinhead says, his hands deep in his pockets. Leaning toward Skinhead, Preston grabs a burning log from the fire and swings it at the men as he backs into the wooded darkness.

"Put that torch down," Flat Top says, aiming the shotgun at Preston.

Preston tosses the torch at CAT Hat, backs further into the dark, and turns to flee.

"Get 'eem!" Flat Top yells running after him.

Dashing by a rock formation with Flat Top right behind him, Preston sees a glint out of the corner of his eye and spins to see kneeling Jasmine stick a knife deep into Flat Top's stomach. Flat Top groans and falls, sliding down the mountain of dead leaves. Preston grabs the shotgun and they both crouch now, waiting.

"Your man's been stabbed," Preston yells after a few minutes pass. "He's in shock." Preston peers around the tree and sees that Skinhead and CAT Hat are standing by the fire whispering to one another looking scared to death. Their shotguns droop. "We're coming up," Preston yells again. "We're armed and we can see you. Put your guns in the tent, and walk slowly back toward the fire."

Preston and Jasmine slowly walk back up to the hill, Preston pointing Flat Top's shotgun at the men and Jasmine wielding her bloody Swiss Army Knife. CAT Hat and Skinhead stand slack-jawed with their hands in the air.

"I see ya!" Jasmine screams at someone holding a camera some thirty feet up the mountain. "I see ya!" The figure disappears into the undergrowth.

"You're not Alabama boys at all, are you?" Preston says.

Both men shake their heads, sulking.

"What's your name?" Preston points at Skinhead.

"Nigel."

"Nigel, where do you hail from?"

"Manchester."

"You're a bad actor, Nigel. I don't know many rednecks out here with perfect manicures. How did you get this gig?"

"Piss off."

"Talk, or I stomp your GPS and leave you to your own devices. Where did that prick Godwin hire you?"

"We were doing this musical dance show--"

"Speak up!" Preston taps CAT Hat on the head with the barrel of the shotgun. "A *dance show*, you say?"

"--called 'Songs of the South,' at Disneyland Paris."

"*Euro Disney?*" Preston points the gun at Skinhead. "Godwin sent Euro Disney hillbillies after *me*? Now listen to me, mates. This ain't no puppet show. Your man down the hill is dying. He's been stabbed in self-defense. I want you two to drag him and these pooches back to the compound and tell that dickweed Godwin he's going to have to do better than this. You're all fired."

Preston fires a shotgun into the air and one of the hounds falls over dead from the shock.

"That dog comes out of your pay," Preston says. "Now get out of here."

Tick's posse trudges back down the mountain as Jasmine and Preston sit silently by the fire. The flame burns down, and things grow quiet, the flowing stream lulling Jasmine's tired body until her head begins to bob. She rubs her eyes and looks hard at Preston who returns her stare. They say nothing.

"Sleep in the tent," Preston finally says rubbing his sore back. "I'll crash out here in the sleeping bag." Without a word Jasmine stands up and goes to the tent, unzipping the oval door and crawling inside. A few seconds later she pokes her head out and looks at Preston who is still sitting at the fire.

"I'm leavin'," she says.

"Don't," he says. But she has already disappeared into the darkness.

Frazzled, he stands and looks down at the dead hound curled up on its side. *The poor bastard must have died of a coronary*, Preston thinks. Deciding to get out his e-tool to dig the dog a grave, he sees the bouncing arc from his flashlight more than fifty yards away. She's climbing straight up the mountain again. He wants to yell out Jasmine's name, beg her to come back to the fire, but he doesn't. He digs a shallow hole in the ground and buries the dog, then staggers back to the tent. He notices that most of his dehydrated fruit is gone. Face in dirty hands, Preston breathes the smoke that now floats in a perfect line from the fire to his tent. Coughing, Preston lies down flat hoping that the wind will change. It doesn't, but he's too tired to budge.

Preston suffered from mild smoke inhalation once before, when as a youngster he started a fire inside his own home. It was, as he recalls, right before his father put him on the bus to Grandmaw's. Preston doesn't want to think about this right now, but the smoke and stress make bad memories unavoidable. *When you're weak*, Preston thinks, *bad things come home to roost.* Preston is now haunted by Ackerman, and it's as if his stuffy father is curled up in the tent with him, finally around for some father-son fun. Preston thinks about the day he swiped back the Super 8 camera and plotted revenge on his father. He'd found the camera behind a bookshelf when Ackerman had puttered away in his MG to lunch leaving Preston alone to eat leftovers. Looking through the eyepiece of his movie camera, Preston decided that he would make one more movie before leaving for Alabama. The title of his new film would be "Fire."

For pre-production, Preston first went down to the deep freeze in the cellar and got out five frozen pies, the Big Time Pies his mother had loved so much because they reminded her of home. Preston and Ackerman, of course, would not touch the repugnant frozen pastries, and it was only a matter of time before they would be tossed into the garbage with his mother's frozen black-eyed peas and collards. Preston preheated the oven to 375 degrees, crammed all five pies in the oven, then ran down to the pasture behind his house. Preston used one of his father's brown wingtips to shovel the horse manure into a brown paper grocery bag, then ran home to secure his father's papers. Parts of Ackerman's book project were stacked in yellowing piles all over the office, but the heart of "Jung and Addiction" could be found in folders under Ackerman's tea table in a cardboard box. Preston took the files to his room and hid them under his bed alongside the pies and the brown paper bag. Ackerman might smell the pie or find the camera gone when he returned, but he would never notice the missing manuscript. Preston knew that his father took great pains never to look under the tea table at his unfinished *magnum opus* underneath.

Around four in the afternoon, Ackerman's sports car sputtered back into the wooden stable, then he traipsed back to his office. He had lunched at Monterey then loafed along the pier before drinking two glasses of Bordeaux at the Wine Loft. Ackerman closed the office door behind him and Preston listened hoping to hear the Beatles, but it was only NPR. Preston set up his tripod and camera at the end of the hallway then ran to the stable for the lighter fluid. He crouched under the office window waiting to hear the Fab Four. Public radio droned on for an hour as Ackerman sat with his feet propped on the tea table, the occasional hiss emanating from his nostrils. At dusk, Preston heard the first licks of "I Want to Hold Your Hand."

Things had to be just so. During "She Loves You," Preston put the bag of horse droppings in the hallway just outside Ackerman's office then piled the manuscript folders on top in a big mound. Then he brought out the Big Time Pies one by one and placed them on the mahogany buffet at the end of the hall next to the tripod. Preston peeped into the keyhole to see his father swaying and singing along to "All You Need is Love" but not yet wearing the mop-top wig or clutching the guitar. Preston knew that Ackerman would have to go full McCartney before the night was over. Preston peeped in again, and his father was wearing the wig, standing up, his trousers unbuttoned. Preston locked his father's door with a skeleton key, doused the manuscript in lighter fluid, and lit the fire. Turning the small fan on "lo," Preston giggled into his hands as the smoke began to boil under the door. Preston turned on the camera when he heard his father's Italian leather boots kicking the locked office door. Hearing his dad kicking and grousing, Preston readied himself with one of the Big Time Pies. Preston saw his father's boot protruding from a crack in the door and Preston threw a pie at the foot but missed. A few seconds later the door burst open and father, wearing the wig, darted into the smoke-filled hallway swinging his arms stomping wildly at the manuscript while Preston flung pies in playful arcs. One of the pies hit Ackerman in the back and stuck there then another splattered against the top of his head. Ackerman fell to the floor and began to roll back and forth over his flaming book. Preston took the camera from the tripod and edged toward the front door, still filming his father, the wig now scarcely clinging to the right side of Ackerman's head. That's when Preston started choking, the overwhelming feeling of being suffocated by the smoke making him cough and gag.

"Quite inventive," his father had said looking around at the chaos, still sitting on his charred book project. "Profound." Wheezing, Preston bolted out of the door and ran through the high grass of a neighbor's field. He slept that night in an abandoned rabbit hutch knowing that he would soon have to face the music. Preston was never formally punished, but within 24 hours he was on a bus for Tallapoochee.

Ackerman would die seven years later of colon cancer, the relationship between father and son after "Fire" not much more than a muddled series of terse transactions. The eight-year-old boy had made his father enact his neuroses on a three-minute reel and the moment was terrifying for them both. It was the closest thing the pair had ever gotten to an emotional father-son moment. The event had helped Ackerman's career, however, as he later devised a transactional role play technique that prompted family members to act out their addiction problems in staged performances choreographed to songs by 1960s bands such as The Monkees and Herman's Hermits. Ackerman's technique went over well on the West Coast, and he was interviewed on NPR after his findings were published in *Psychology Today*. And even now, after all these years, Preston cringes when he re-watches "Fire." Even when digitally remastered, the low quality of the film gives Preston this feeling that he can't breathe when his father kicks through the door and emerges on the grainy film, his arms flapping, the wig bouncing, dodging pies, and slipping about in his Italian boots. Seeing Ackerman stop-drop-and roll over his failed book, shit-stained in the flames, still brings a twinge of joy. But the feeling never lasts.

25

When Preston wakes up just before dawn, he has a bad headache. His temples throb from the smoke inhalation in the damp tent. After struggling to get on his muck-caked shoes, he unzips the mosquito net and staggers out to cough in the cold, wet air. The fire's dead. Preston shivers, hacks, and spits before going to pee off the nearest cliff. The first touches of sunlight turn the sky a milky gray as Preston piles up leaves and limbs for the fire. His body trembles in the cold. Once the fire starts to blaze, Preston walks down to the edge of the stream and dips his face deep in the water, getting the tips of his wig wet. Preston raises his head, gargles, and spits again before filling his pot for coffee. When he returns, Jasmine is sitting on a rock next to the fire. He says nothing as he puts the water on his rock stove and sits down beside her.

"I heard somebody on the ridge," she says. "Somebody a whole lot sneakier than the Apple Dumpling Gang."

"It's probably that lunatic Suzie Baxter."

"Don't scare me like that," Jasmine utters.

"I've been thinking about how to get us out of here."

"I'm not going anywhere with you. I came back for food."

"We're running low," Preston says. "You stole most of it. I think we have a better chance of getting out of here safely if we hike out together."

"Not while you're filming me," Jasmine says. "Show's over."

Without a word, Preston goes to his tent and pulls a small silver case from his backpack. He produces an object that looks like a black hospital straw and a pair of needle-nosed pliers.

"This," he says, "finds the cameras. Just push this little button and wave it like so, and you hear it, hear the beeps? See the light turn red? That tells you where the camera is. Then, when you locate it, you can crunch it with the pliers. Go ahead, Jasmine. Have at it."

Jasmine points the detector at Preston and instantly finds a tiny one attached to Preston's John Lennon glasses. She crunches it and finds one more on Preston's clothes. Then she checks Preston's tent, his equipment, her equipment, and the surrounding woods.

"Why do you have this?" Jasmine asks.

"People bug me, heh heh."

"Sickenin'," Jasmine grunts. It takes her a half hour to find all the cameras. "I found eight," Jasmine says after surveying the campsite. "Are there more?"

"Just this one," Preston says pulling his cellphone out of his pants pocket. "But it's the last phone I have and we are going to need it when we get up to Sukhuce State Park. Want to look at a map?" Preston excitedly opens the large US Forest Service map and lays it flat on the ground. "We're here, north of where we talked last time. I still think we should head up the Tsoyaha Trail. We can do the press conference at the Sukhuce Lodge."

"*Press* conference! You're crazy."

"I'm going to have to get my side of the story out, and your fans will need to know that you are safe. You are going to need a good press agent."

"A *what*? I'm not talking to nobody."

"At Sukhuce we can get our clothes washed, sleep in a real bed, get some warm food, and think about our next step."

"There is no *our* next step," Jasmine says. "I'm going back to Tallapoochee and you're going to the pen."

"Jasmine," Preston says. "Let's check your bank account balances online. Please, just take a look." Preston clicks on his phone pad for a second and hands it to Jasmine. She types in her login number and password with a scowl. The checking account balance is the same as when she left, $811.03. But her savings balance, which was just over three thousand dollars, is now $2,003,231.44.

"Two million smackers?" Jasmine says. "Bull."

"And that's just part of your advance, Jasmine. Two *million*. Your boss Joanne Salters put it there because you didn't have accounts that earn interest. Time to diversify your portfolio, Jasmine. I suggest you start with index funds."

"I don't want any of the damned money, if you can understand that," Jasmine says. "I just want to be left alone."

"One more favor," Preston says. "Google the name 'Jasmine Meadows.'" With a grunt, Jasmine does so, and her eyes widen.

"Oh My God," she gasps, hand to mouth.

Days pass and the Tsoyaha Trail is just plain mean. It's an ankle-twisting, rock sliding, slippery, switchbacking, dehydrating, sunburning, chafing, narrow zig-zag in the woods that goes from the middle of Alabama to Tennessee, across the length of Kentucky, then east to the Appalachian Trail. Jasmine and Preston plod along on the Tsoyaha for three long days feeling hunger pangs as their supplies diminish and the trail burns calories faster than they can be stored. They leap over dried-out ravines, pull themselves over rock faces, and negotiate gravel patches prone to slide as their bodies continually adjust to the crooked logic of the trail. Photogenic mountain peaks and waterfalls are trudged by without comment, their hikers' sunburned faces down and serious. It's a strange part of the fall season on this mountain because the nights are bitter cold, but by midday it can get over 90 degrees. The Tsoyaha is especially hard on Preston, who has to lean left on the west side of the mountain. That means that his body has to hang over every cliff and spur, his left leg struggling to compensate for the crook. When they found the trail three days ago, Jasmine took the lead but found that Preston just couldn't keep up. He looked like a broken troll back there, his face contorted in constant pain as he pulled himself along from rock to tree, his head and backpack jouncing side-to-side. He never complained, but she could tell that Preston wouldn't be able to keep the pace for much longer. She considered stealing the remaining food and abandoning him, but after stopping to eat a lunch of five dehydrated strawberries two days ago, Jasmine let him take the lead. Now she's reconciled with pulling him up the side of rocks and holding his hands while maneuvering narrow draws and spurs. They cling to muscadine vines together and step from rock to rock over wide streams. She takes his hand when he seems confused.

Walking at his own pace, Preston sometimes spaces out, his face loosening. Sometimes he stumbles on high ledges. When they walk for more than an hour without talking, Preston will often wipe tears from his wind-burned face and mumble with an odd smile.

"Wash our socks," Jasmine says standing next to a small creek. It's noon without a cloud in the sky and the groaning hikers take off their packs. The wind blows their sweaty backs and makes them shiver while their red faces and arms sting from overexposure to the sun. They kneel and dip their faces in a clear pool, the water purification system tossed days ago with the heavier gear. Preston's shoes are muddy and wet as he washes socks in the stream water, squeezes them as dry as possible, and clamps them to his backpack like pelts to hang and flap in the sun.

"Preston, there's blood coming out of your shoe."

"There isn't."

"Yes, there is, Doofus. Take your shoe off and let me see."

"That's dewberry juice."

"No the hell it ain't. Dewberries were over months ago. Now cut the crap and take your shoe off. I'm not gone carry you up this mountain 'cause you let yourself get trench foot."

"Jasmine, what do *you* know about trench foot?"

"Plenty. Uncle Patrick had it in the Army."

"The one with man boobs? C'mon."

"You can have trench foot and man boobs at the same time dummy now take off them shoes." The heel and inside of his left foot have been worn raw. Blisters had formed days ago, but they were rubbed to pulp due to negligence. Jasmine rolls up Preston's pants to his knees and makes him sit on a rock so his feet can cool in the stream. She gives him two Ibuprofen tablets from her first-aid kit and washes off his soiled medical shoes. She pulls open the shoes and puts them out on a sunbaked rock to dry then sits down to wash his feet with brown antibacterial field soap. After a thorough washing, she makes him put his feet in her lap. She takes the time to massage each damaged toe and rubs his arches as he leans back, closing his eyes. Jasmine dries his feet with a washcloth then uses band-aids and gauze to cover his wounds. Finally, she fishes her one last pair of dry socks from her backpack and tosses them into Preston's hands.

"I'm not taking your last pair," Preston says.

"Take them or I leave you here," Jasmine says. "I'm not walking behind your hunchback ass for another week. Keep your feet dry, Doofus. I seen you just walking right through mud holes. Look at my shoes, fool. Clean! Dry! Why, because I walk *around* the mud hole."

"Walk around the mud hole," Preston mutters. "Walk around the mud hole."

"Quit acting stupid and get your shoes on. Let's go."

"Go on ahead," Preston says. "I'll catch up." He waits until Jasmine has walked up the trail a few hundred feet then pulls off his backpack and digs around inside. He finds the Yoko Ono wig. He caresses the dark artificial hair for a moment, presses it to his lips, then drops it on the trail.

Around three in the afternoon, dark clouds from the west swirl over Slash Pine Ridge. Distant lightning flashes as cliffside trees bend back and forth along the path. Jasmine gets dirt in her eye as air spins around them, Preston's drying socks flying outward in all directions. The wind dies down, then kicks up again, and the sudden rain stings their sunburned skin. Preston pulls off his backpack and grabs his poncho and twine. He tightens a line between two trees, throws the poncho on top, and stakes down a makeshift pup tent. Under the tent, Preston ties up his hammock. Preston and Jasmine tie their backpacks to the trees under the poncho tent and sit down together in the hammock as heavy drops of rain fall. The sound of rain pelting plastic is almost deafening as rivulets of water flow beneath them. The hammock rocks slowly back and forth. After removing the dirt from Jasmine's eye with a torn page from his book, Preston pulls four almonds out of his shirt pocket. They chew slowly, Jasmine's head resting on Preston's shoulder. Her head bobs, slides down his crooked torso, then pops back up. Wordlessly, they maneuver around in the hammock until they are both stretched out, almost comfortable. Within minutes they are asleep, the heaviness of their bodies borne by the rain's lull and thrust, snoring in a rainstorm, hands and fingers touching without knowing it, faces cheek to cheek. When Jasmine wakes, the sun raging again, Preston is studying his map, scratching the growing hair under his new Beatles wig, and charting their path home.

Late in the afternoon, they come to County Highway 3, the first paved road Jasmine and Preston have seen in quite some time. They trot across in the rising asphalt steam as a rusty Hummer clatters by full of nanny goats. Preston has this eerie sensation, like a spell broken, when he sets foot on the slippery road. *Jasmine could wave down any passing car and this would all be over,* Preston thinks, as they slip back into the woods looking like laid-off carnies. Two SUVs with bumper stickers and canoe racks are parked at the gravel trailhead lot on the side of the road and the first half-mile of the trail is littered with plastic water bottles, soda cans, potato chip bags, and Starbucks cups. But it doesn't take long before the trail is clean again. *People who take Frappuccinos into the woods,* Preston guesses, *don't get out that far.* Two miles in, college-aged hikers fast-walking south in a line nod and smile as they brush by. Cringing, Preston wonders if they noticed that the hiker with him is *the* Jasmine Meadows.

A decent campsite is hard to find after the rainstorm and Preston finds it even harder to make a fire. He finally has to rip out entire chapters of *Facing the Hate-Self* to get the damp kindling to burn. Late afternoon comes with owls and whippoorwills, the evening sun sneaking a glance between two long slats of black cloud. Preston takes in the crisp air and inhales rain, pine, and mountain soil. He finds a tick on his leg and pulls it off with his needle-nosed pliers. Nothing is quite dry, but the sleeping bags were largely spared from the rain. Jasmine and Preston set up their tents and make a long clothesline to hang wet gear and clothes. Preston makes the last of the hot tea as Jasmine collects firewood. They sit for nearly an hour in silence as the sky grows dark. They avoid the topic of food.

"Wait!" Preston's eyes brighten. "I can't believe I forgot, I--," Preston opens his backpack's outside pockets. "Yep, here it is!" He holds a silver flask aloft. "Whiskey!" He tosses it to Jasmine.

"Dang that burns," she scowls after taking a quick nip.

"Gentleman Jack." Preston turns up the bottle as the fire crackles.

"Why did you do all this to me?" Jasmine asks. "I mean, how did you get into this, this--"

"This *business*."

"If that's what you want to call it."

"Fair question," Preston replies and takes a long pull. "After I graduated from high school in 1991, I went to a rinky-dink school called the Los Angeles College of Media Arts. I was going to get a degree in film, be the next Kubrick, all that," Preston tries to fix his wig, his face twitching. "So, I was taking this directing class, and my final project was a black and white documentary about a local man, this guy I heard of in LA that they called Greco -- Greco, the Homeless Magician and Mystic." Preston turns his head skyward and smiles. "Greco had this plan to make all of the animals in the LA Zoo disappear."

"*What?*" Jasmine says, grabbing the flask.

"He was going to make the animals," Preston giggled, the liquor already going to his medicated head, "levitate to a faraway planet. Greco was a no-neck guy who passed out leaflets on street corners with titles such as 'Animal Auschwitz' and 'Meat is Manslaughter.' He raved about the use of primates in space exploration, cosmic vegetarianism, and the psychology of the planned zoo performance."

"You lost me."

"I was lost too, Jasmine. Utterly lost. But I was trying so hard to make a good film. So, Greco and his sidekick Francis the Freak break into the zoo at midnight, you know, and eat some peyote near the entrance, then they start a small ceremonial fire at the

Australian Outback exhibit and the fire instantly burns down a grove of Eucalyptus trees. A few koalas suffer from smoke inhalation, blah blah blah. And I am following them around with my camera filming everything and the authorities arrive almost immediately. In the movie, you can see me chasing the cops as they chase Greco and Francis the Freak all around the zoo. An emu is allegedly trampled. Whatever. That's what got Greco and Francis the jail time -- the dead emu."

"Preston, I gotta tell you buddy that sounds, uh, stupid."

"I can't dispute that," Preston says, his smile long and immeasurably sad. "But to me, at the time, it was an important social statement. When the film students in my class watched the footage, they all just laughed and laughed, like it was a slapstick comedy. They even stood up and cheered at the end when 'Directed by Preston Price' flashed on the screen. They called it a work of 'comedic genius.' But I wasn't laughing. I wanted to jump in front of a train."

"So what did you do?" Jasmine says.

"I quit," Preston says. "I withdrew from the university. I never went on campus again. But that film was to establish one crucial connection for me. I met a young student there named Bill Dew, a guy who remembered my documentary years later. He gave me my break with my first exercise video, *Pumpin' In Da Hood*. He worked with me on other projects and then later helped produce *Diet Extreme*."

"So *he's* the one that messed up your life."

"No," Preston whispers after a long glug of whiskey. "If it weren't for that one movie, I would never have gotten to know *you*, Jasmine."

"Huh, then he messed up *my* life."

"Look, there's Orion," Preston slurs taking a drink while pointing up wide-eyed at the night sky. "And right there you can see a satellite flashing its lights, orbiting the earth. Sometimes I think about those robots they shoot out to Mars, Jasmine, the Hubble Telescope, Perseverance, deep space – still out there. One day their batteries are going to run out and they will send their last transmission, then they will go silent. And they'll be alone in the darkness and quiet of space. Like a space monkey starving in his capsule still pushing buttons and pulling levers. The loneliness of that. It's so sad to me."

"That don't make a lick of sense," Jasmine says, glancing for a second at the stars. Preston stands aslant with the flask in his hand and breaks into song:

> She walks these hills
> In long black veiiiiiil--
> She visits my grave
> When the night winds waiiiiil–
> Nobody knows, nobody sees
> Nobody--

"—*Damn*, shut up," Jasmine says. "I hear something."

"What?" Preston says as he sits down and cranes his neck. They both listen for a long minute looking at each other. "I don't--"

"Just shut the hell up," Jasmine says. Above them, on the mountain, they both hear something moving. For five minutes, they listen as the thing in the woods stomps above the ridge. It doesn't sound like a human walking through leaves.

Whatever it is, it sounds gigantic. Preston grabs the shotgun out of his tent, Jasmine gets the hatchet, and they move away from the fire to hide in the dark, each behind a tree. The crunching, dragging sound gets louder as it moves down the ridge toward the fire.

Just up the mountain, it growls, its gargling roar shaking the night.

"It's a bear," Preston whispers, trembling.

"*Raaaaaaaa!*" roars the seven-foot grizzly as it stomps into the firelight and grabs Preston's tent with its long razor-sharp teeth shaking, ripping it apart. Claws high in the air, the grizzly grabs Preston's backpack and begins to chew. Preston jumps from behind his tree pointing a shotgun at the bear.

"*Raaaaaaaa!*" the grizzly growls in rage, its unblinking glassy eyes looking to the horizon, its arms moving up and down like Godzilla. Preston fires both barrels of the shotgun's blanks at the grizzly as it runs toward Preston, its mouth wide open and extending a long, wriggling tongue. Jasmine jumps from behind her tree as the grizzly turns. She swings the hatchet and it strikes the animal in the mid-section. It seems not to notice as it lunges toward Preston.

"Hold it!" Preston yells. "Cut!" He ducks the swinging arm. Jasmine leaps onto the grizzly's back and grabs it by the head. Preston follows suit. The grizzly falls, its mechanical arms and mouth still moving.

"Here's a zipper," Jasmine says. She unzips the back of the bear suit as Preston pops off the grizzly's head.

"Nigel you asshole!" Preston yells tossing the bear head into a shrub.

"Please lady, no!" Nigel cries staring up at Jasmine, who looms above Preston. She's holding the hatchet over her head as if to strike, her eyes filled with murder.

"Didn't anybody tell you, Nigel, that there are no grizzlies in the Tallapoochee?" Preston yells with whiskey breath into Nigel's face. "*You fuckin' ninny!*"

"Don't do it!" Nigel shudders, still watching Jasmine.

"Get out of that suit," Preston says, trying to unzip it. "Stand up, Pisswilliam Bartholomew Frankie." Nigel stands with his hands in the air looking back and forth from Preston to Jasmine wearing a latex bodysuit and slippers. "Tell us what's happening at the compound."

"Pandemonium," Nigel says with both hands resting on his sweating head. "Mr. Price it's total and utter chaos. Mr. Godwin is holed up in the egg with Chef Annon Martiz and that Satanist blonde. They've got guns and won't let anybody else inside. Godwin is working with your people in Colorado to finish the show, but TBS keeps saying that it's no good. It's the eighth circle of hell, Mr. Price. The sous-chef is missing, and the Tallapoochee County Sheriff has the compound surrounded because of the murders. Suzie Baxter has taken hostages, and the police have a warrant for your arrest. The camera operators in the caves have been hunted down and interrogated. Conspiracies abound and everything's out-of-hand, Mr. Price. Just bonkers. And those rozzers in the black suits, the grounds crew, they left in vans the minute Suzie Baxter started shooting into the crowd."

"Amateurs," Preston hisses. "So Tick thinks he's going to save the show with a limey in a bear suit? And you up there with the camera behind that tree!" Preston screams. "Don't think we

262 | Ballad of Jasmine Wills

don't see you!" Preston spins, yelling to the top of his drunken lungs, "I see all of you *fucking mothafuckas!*"

"Look, Mr. Price, I just want my pay."

"You mean you want me to *pay* you?" Preston stops to glare. "I fired you, Nigel."

"I'm cool with that. I just want my pay."

"Look, Nigel. Tick Godwin hired you and *he* will pay you. *You* have been chasing *me* in a bear suit, so *I* don't pay you. I *sue* you. I suggest that you walk due east, over the mountain, and get yourself back to Liverpool or wherever you came from before you get yourself arrested for impersonating wildlife."

"That's bullshit," Nigel says.

"Get out of here!" Jasmine yells, brandishing the hatchet, and Nigel starts walking down the trail.

"This is some bullshit," Nigel utters once more over his shoulder.

Preston checks out the robotic bear's mouth and arms as Jasmine sits by the fire listening to Nigel's slippered feet crunching faintly in the distance.

"What's wrong with you people?" Jasmine says, her eyes heavy. "All this for some crappy show?"

"Quit preaching," Preston says, clutching his sleeping bag. "Nigel destroyed my tent. Is there any chance that I can bunk with you? I mean, it is going to get cold before morning." Preston coughs and holds his chest.

"Stay away from me," Jasmine says, zipping the tent in his face.

26

After days of hiking, their meager food stores long gone, Jasmine and Preston finally make it to the border between Tallapoochee National Forest and Sukhuce State Park. They stagger in silence by a yellow Smokey the Bear sign at the edge of the trail. After walking a few miles into the Sukhuce, Jasmine sees a clearing in the distance. Her canteen is filled with brown water from a mud hole, but she hasn't gotten up the nerve to drink it. She keeps hoping that around the next curve she will come across a clear branch or freshwater spring, but that hasn't happened in days. Preston's mind appears to have been poisoned by the sun because he's mumbling non-stop, and his GPS batteries are dead. They lurch from the narrow trail into a dry clearing, a flat acre of land covered with trimmed yellowing grass. There is a brown pavilion with picnic tables, a swing set, restrooms, and a gravel parking lot. There is only one vehicle in the lot, a white Sukhuce State Park truck. A man in a brown jumpsuit wearing orange earmuffs and eye protection goggles swings a leaf blower back and forth near the pavilion. They both look for a water fountain or a faucet but are gravely disappointed.

Even the bathrooms are glorified port-a-potties with no running water. The truck door slams and the government truck is gone leaving a trail of yellow dust.

Jasmine notices a garbage can at the trailhead and limps over to it. Scorched and sweating, Preston hobbles just behind her after getting his backpack caught in the swing set. Jasmine looks down into the garbage can, sees a half-empty bottle of soda, and turns it up feeling the sugar and caffeine course through her dehydrated body. Digging a little deeper, she finds a box of day-old fried chicken bones with a little meat on them. Preston walks up to the garbage can with a dirty face and hungry eyes. He looks for a minute at the box sitting on a pile of refuse, then grabs a breastbone. They gnaw at the white cartilage attached to chicken legs and suck bone marrow with animal intensity. Preston is filled with memories of San Francisco, those dumpster days, but tells himself as he licks the inside of a Styrofoam mashed potatoes and gravy container that this is different. Six more miles and they will be eating surf and turf specials at the Skyline Diner. Jasmine finds a pizza box with a few crusts and an unfinished bottle of hot Mello Yello to complete their meal.

"Stick this in your backpack," she says handing the last of the pizza crusts to Preston. They hear a car coming up the gravel road and turn from the garbage can. Without a word, they stagger up the hardwood trail and Preston is cheered to see the little wooden mile markers along the path. He figures that at their pace, he and Jasmine will only have to spend one more night in the woods before reaching the lodge on Sukhuce Mountain. *A camera crew will be needed for the press release*, Preston thinks, and then Manuelita will link in footage of Jaekel Sneade's murder that will exonerate him. He and Jasmine will have to spend the next couple of weeks flying here and there to give interviews. Then, perhaps, Maui.

In higher elevation, as the trail becomes a series of long rock cliffs and peaks, the pace slows. A lone helicopter circles overhead. Jasmine falls onto her side after stepping on a flat rock that slid beneath her feet. A half-mile further down the trail, Preston twists his right ankle. Flies and mosquitoes circle the reeking pair. Holding onto a high crevice in a craggy rock, Preston moves his foot up and down for a groove to push himself up. Standing on the firm ground below him, Jasmine clasps his foot in her hands so that he can pull himself up to the top of the rock formation. He then reaches down to take Jasmine's hand. The terrain gets more and more treacherous, and at one point the trail appears to split heading both south and east. Preston thinks, after an hour of walking, that they are lost. Jasmine takes her first drink of mud hole water and realizes that it's not that bad if you let the dirt settle and don't drink it all of the way to the bottom. Grit and little lumpy pieces of dirt get caught in Preston's throat and he dry heaves. They cross what might be an unmarked trail but decide to keep going east seeing the occasional circle of rocks from old campsites. A rusty overturned single-engine aircraft lies on its side, its broken wing stretched skyward like a warning. As they sit in the middle of the trail to rest, a Vandyke-bearded hipster wearing a Post Office shirt passes them without a word.

"Th-they're closing in," Preston utters.

"I hear water," Jasmine says pointing at a downhill slope off the trail. Groaning, they stand on rubbery legs and meander down the slope to see a large, deep pool behind a veritable screen of shortleaf pines.

"Look!" Jasmine whispers pointing at four deer that stand frozen next to the pool, their eyes and ears alert. One jumps away, its white tail darting up, and the others follow. In silence, Preston and Jasmine take off their shoes and dip their sore feet into the cold, clean water. The pool is a large bowl of flat yellow rocks. Preston sees little fish in the sandy beds at the far edge and the steady stream of water splashing off cyclopean stones in mossy falls. Despite himself, he begins to smile. Preston spies a small turtle at the water's edge and his heart opens unexpectedly like a Venus flytrap. He stares at the turtle as his eyes fill with tears. Preston slows his breath and meditates on the turtle, safe and happy in its hard little shell.

Jasmine stares down at her reflection, then pulls off her clothes too fatigued for modesty. She gets into the water and closes her eyes. Sitting up, the pool comes up to her neck and she rubs her face and body under the cool water. She drinks by putting her lips to the pool's surface then leans back to dip her hair. Preston sits on the water's edge, his face red and contorted, crying open-mouthed toward a blazing sun. As he looks to the sky, his nose runs, the full force of his broken heart pouring from him suddenly in a twisted stream.

"What the hell's wrong with you?" Jasmine says with a turn.

He shakes his head, crying harder.

"What, Preston? What?"

"The turtle," he says pointing at the little animal on a sunlit rock at the pool's edge.

"What? It's a turtle."

"My turtle," he says, his breath hitching, his hands and fingers splayed like tree limbs. He tries to talk between long bursts, but his body shakes uncontrollably. Jasmine realizes that he may have finally lost his mind. "I've tried to do all this," he waves his arms around. "I've lived my whole life in the shadow of a bunch of bohemian assholes but I'm not groovy!" he screams, shaking his head wildly, "I'm not groovy!" Preston's whole body shakes as Jasmine's arms surround him. He puts his face between her breasts and cries hard, his hands clamped to her shoulders. Looking at the little turtle at the edge of the pool, Jasmine's eyes grow serious, and she too breaks down. She moans open-mouthed looking through her tears at the strange, dirty man clutching her like a child. This sad little man with the mop-top wig and silly glasses, so strangely formed. Then Jasmine begins to cry. She cries for the babies who never came. She cries for Parrish and her Mama and Daddy. She cries for Don-Don selling four-door sedans and watching the world go by. She cries for her fat self and her skinny self and the crazy man in her lap. And there they are, Jasmine and Preston, blubbering in the middle of the woods with their arms around each other, pulling each other tight, holding on to keep from washing away, needing to wash away. For an instant, their lips touch, fingertips touching faces. Then they're kissing, at first gentle pecks, then tongues are darting into mouths. All of a sudden they're groping, reaching for places that tingle, touching kissing sucking breathing hard, crying, and moaning. Gear tossed, a sleeping bag stretched out at the water's edge, and they're thrusting, thrusting, their groans breaking over the sound of the waterfall. The turtle gets out of there. Jasmine moans, the hum of the low kazoo everywhere, in her body and in the robot on Mars and the Hubble Telescope, at the bank, at Big Time Pies, gilded pinwheels of light and color now upon her, in her, over her, and across hard pink skies. She clenches her fists over her head but not to strike, grabbing into the earth as she feels her hips rotating up and down against him, the feeling unstoppable.

And then it happens.

Holding Preston's hips tight like a vice, she pulls him into her with all her might shaking and shuddering with deep, deep whimpering groans. Looking up as the pleasure flows through her, Jasmine notices that Preston is groaning too, but in pain.

"My back! My back!" he screeches, rolling off of her. "Oh, Christ my back!"

"Not again!" Jasmine cries, covering her face with her hands.

"J-j-just wait a minute," Preston cringes, holding up his hands as Jasmine tries to pull him up. "Wait."

"Does it hurt?"

"No," Preston says, sitting upright. "It feels great." He stands up.

"Oh God, Preston," Jasmine gasps. "You ain't crooked."

"No," Preston smiles standing up and jogging in place. "I'm not."

A bush rattles behind them.

"Who's that?" Jasmine says pointing at a dense patch of trees behind Preston. He turns to see that someone has crept up on them and is now crouching behind a Mountain Laurel bush. A second figure applauds from behind a hickory tree.

"Come out from behind there!" Preston yells. "I see you!"

"You know," Tick chuckles from behind the bush, "I always knew the right woman would straighten you out." Pointing a camera at the naked lovers, Tick stands with strips of white bandages covering his hands and face. He looks just like the Invisible Man. Angelique emerges from behind the hickory aiming a semi-automatic rifle at Jasmine.

"What more do you want? You got what you want, right?" Preston whines standing next to Jasmine, both naked, with his hands raised in defeat. "If that's not a finale Godwin I don't know what is."

"I must say you've outdone yourself," Tick sighs, still filming, his eyes fixed on the camera's tiny digital screen. "It's true, an emotional love scene between captor and captive with spontaneous sexual healing just ices season one of *Diet Extreme*. It's a wrap. I guess you've found your 'love-self' after all. Bravo, Preston. Bravo."

"You and Preston were doing this *together*?" Jasmine gasps, trying to cover her body.

"No," Preston says. "Don't listen to a word he says."

"Jasmine, honey, don't let Price fool you." Tick grins like a Cheshire Cat to show off his missing teeth. "He always wants to play the victim, but he had to know we were out here filming his every move. Preston tricked you into hiking all this way for the show. Then he seduced you for the show. Down deep you have to know that. None of this is real. Preston isn't real. I mean how do you explain *this*?" Tick brandishes the Yoko Ono wig and raises it high like a pelt. "Do tell, Preston, what *were* your plans?"

"I don't do that anymore," Preston whispers.

"But you dream," Tick says, unscrewing a silver canteen.

"Please, Tim, no." Preston turns away as Tick waves the canteen under his nose.

"What is it?" Jasmine says as Angelique moves in behind her and puts the rifle to the back of her head.

"And I live your crooked dreams," Tick says, holding the canteen to Preston's lips.

"We're finished," Preston says, drinking the fizzing concoction.

"My lawyer will contact you later this week with a buyout proposal," Tick says. "Drink up, Jasmine!"

"Just go ahead and shoot me," Jasmine says naked with hands on hips. "I'm done being told what to do."

"Please drink it," Preston says. "Let's get this over with."

"I'm coming back from the dead and killing you all." Jasmine snatches the canteen and chug-a-lugs.

"*Something in the way she moves,*" Tick sings and stares at Jasmine's body. "*Attracts me like no other lover.*" He pulls two wooden contraptions from behind a boulder as Angelique points the gun.

"Let's sit down," Preston says taking Jasmine's hands as they sit at the edge of the pool. "In a few minutes, we're going to feel dizzy."

"Oh crap," Jasmine says as she closes her eyes, almost smiling. "I feel it already."

"*Oh Yo-o-oh-ko,*" Preston and Jasmine hear as they both fade out. "*Oh Yo-o-oh-ko--*"

Clunk. Clunk.

Preston wakes before sunrise, standing in a dreary haze, head pounding and stark naked, the Velcro straps around his neck and shoulders squeezing his body with bruising pain. It hurts to open his eyes, his head turned backward by the straps and harnesses, his right arm outstretched. Tick and Angelique are long gone. His body is in a strange pose, like he's looking around behind him. He feels Jasmine's fingers and looks to see her naked next to him in a similar position. They both wear wigs and are holding hands. The straps are tight and there will certainly be bruises. Preston finds himself unable to move.

"Jasmine?" Preston chokes, his mouth clamped by a harness. "Jasmine?"

"What?" Jasmine whispers, her eyes closed.

"I'm stuck," Preston says. "Can't move."

"No shit, Sherlock," Jasmine grunts. "Me too."

"Can you get your hand on any of the straps?"

"Preston, I feel like I've been molested or something."

"Me too."

"Pull the strap around my hand with your fingers. Can you get to it?"

"Yes."

Preston can use his index and middle finger to pull open one of Jasmine's hand straps. Trying to get loose, he freezes in an instant of awareness. From the rear, he and Jasmine are a perfect John and Yoko, positioned in a replica of the 1968 *Two Virgins* album cover. With this inspired gesture, Tick has outdone himself as well. With this final act, he has transformed the unlikely pair into a masterpiece of performance art.

Working methodically, Jasmine frees Preston's hand up to the elbow. Then, through a series of maneuvers, they release themselves from their postures.

"Here comes the sun," Preston groans, grabbing his slacks. "Let's climb."

27

Jasmine sits at the edge of the hotel bed changing channels with the remote control as reflections of her image flash across her face. She scratches her bug-bitten ankles, stands, stretches, and sits down again. This small room in the Sukhuce Lodge bothers her. A vacuum cleaner hums in the room below, and elderly people in hiking boots stomp above. Jasmine sees her face on almost every cable channel, her before/after profiles, the news reports, the frozen entrees, the compound rampage, the expanding media mystery.

On CNBC there's a split-screen of bandaged Tick in Atlanta and Isaiah Please in Boulder, the running captions "Price Compound Cult Rampage" and "Exercise Trainer Opens Fire on Cultists" ticking beneath the talking heads. The image changes to a grainy black-and-white surveillance shot of a hooded figure in black fatigues firing an AR-15 into a crowd of people holding cameras and iPhones. Jasmine sits at the edge of the bed shocked, watching a hand-held closeup of sous-chef Morris, his face bloodied and in handcuffs, as he runs bald and screaming behind a terrified crowd of UCLA production assistants toward the abandoned egg dome. Cut to webcam shots inside a cave, shaky flashlights pointing at a blood-spattered wall, and a hieroglyphic egg in silver spray paint.

"These images we're getting," the commentator says, "Mr. Godwin, can you tell us what we're seeing here?"

"You have to understand," Tick explains as he sits mummified in bandages and a blue Zegna suit, "these people have been on this isolated compound for many months cut off from everything, under the influence of the charismatic TV personality Preston Price. From all reports, Mr. Price simply lost control of his followers."

"Mr. Godwin," the commentator reports, "outside our studios here in New York the street is packed with people, mostly women, waiting for news of Jasmine Meadows. They are holding signs, wearing her popular t-shirts, and across the nation there have been candlelight vigils. What do you say to the thousands of Jasmine supporters who watch her show and wait for news of her rescue?"

Photos of Jasmine flash on the screen: holding her nose and glass of wine, doing jumping jacks at 248 pounds, close-up of a blank face, scowling at the Venus of Willendorf.

"Remember," Tick said, "Jasmine Meadows is resilient and resourceful. She will emerge from the mountain top. She may be confused, even traumatized, but I have no doubt she will return. And I think that if she were here now, she would say not to judge *Diet Extreme* or TBS too harshly. And though season two will feature a new abductee, perhaps even a male 'diet extremist,' Jasmine Meadows will always remain close to our hearts here at TBS."

"Next year," the commentator says, "will people remember Jasmine Meadows, or, as she is called by her adoring fans, J-ME?"

"Perhaps not," Tick says. "Glory fades in TV land and our social media memory is short. But today she has become more than a symbol. She has become a beacon of hope for the unschooled masses, for the overweight, the uncouth, and the angry out there. Jasmine Meadows, wherever you are, our hearts are with you."

"But you were out there, in the compound. How did this all happen?"

"To be perfectly frank," Tick says. "This was caused by the egotism and ineptitude of *Diet Extreme* co-creator Preston Price. He inadvertently caused this to happen. You had this high-profile show, everyone under surveillance, all these competing factions, and the intense secrecy on the set. The tension created by Price, this enigmatic and quite charismatic leader, caused the tragic domino effect that we've been seeing here today."

Photo images of Preston Price flash on screen: exercise video box, Liminoid press release, meditating in kimono, maniacal look inside the egg studio.

"Did he *tell* Suzie Baxter to open fire on the compound?"

"Of course not," Tick said. "That's absurd. Preston Price has not broken any law. It's true that he became mentally unstable during his protracted isolation in the dome and made some bizarre decisions. But this is the last thing he would want to happen to this popular show that, I might add, he helped me create."

"You were injured during your escape. What happened?"

"I was attacked by Suzie Baxter in a small pantry. I was terribly injured, and I will be disfigured my entire life. Unfortunately, there were no cameras there."

"Preston Price is at this hour still missing. What were the circumstances surrounding his escape? Do you have any idea where he might be?"

"All will be revealed," Tick smirks under his bandages. "When you watch the two-hour season finale."

"With us here today is noted bestselling self-help expert Dr. Isaiah Please. His most recent book, *The Six Pillars of Self-Admiration*, hits the shelves this week. Dr. Please has set up a Cult Victim Hotline for the victims and families of the Price Compound Rampage and he is here to talk about victims healing from what he calls 'astral molestation.' Dr. Please, you have to know that Preston Price is one of your most loyal followers. He attended many of your seminars and discussion groups. And, as I understand it, the two of you have also spoken on more than one occasion. He has said in interviews that your work is, in fact, the basis for his success."

"Preston Price," Isaiah Please says as he stares directly into the camera, "is a misguided lunatic."

Jasmine turns off the TV, walks to the window, and pulls back the curtain. From the fifth-floor balcony, she can see the mountains bursting with fall color. Tallapoochee Gap is one of the last little peaks along this range, but Jasmine is focused on the people standing on the sidewalk between the parking lot and the hotel. The women, weekend bird watchers, keep staring up at Jasmine's window. They have been there since Preston and Jasmine hobbled into the Sukhuce Lodge and checked into their suite. A portly gentleman wearing plaid slacks is looking up at Jasmine's room with a pair of binoculars. Another little man stares at Jasmine's window shielding his eyes from the sun like a saluting soldier. There are more people now, all looking up at the window, talking and texting, their faces frozen in anticipation. When Jasmine pulls back the curtain an inch, she sees them jump and point, one clutching her hat and spinning around in a circle. The growing mass of people cheers and applauds. Across the parking lot, orange oak leaves and plastic candy wrappers swirl like little flakes in a snow globe. Jasmine pulls the curtain closed and sits back down on the bed. She's starving, really starving. Preston thinks he will be picking up cheeseburgers for two at the Skyline Diner. She'll never get that burger.

There's a little red button on the hotel telephone, and the minute Preston left the room she picked up the phone and pushed it. She crouched over the receiver, hands atremble, her eyes on the door.

"Yes, this is an emergency. I've been kidnapped. A man has taken me hostage. He just left the room. Five-foot nine--used to be five-foot-two--round glasses, ugly hairpiece, twitching hands."

"My name?" She stares into the hotel mirror. "I'm Jasmine Meadows."

Hunger is a fine, strange sensation since most of her life she has put artificial food into her body to keep from feeling. But now she needs to feel, to feel this, as the sirens whine through windows of glass and the lights of the Sheriff's cars spin. Jasmine pulls the curtain back to see the County deputies dragging Preston across the windy lot, his arms and legs flailing, the news vans pulling in with their satellite dishes aimed at the heavens.

Jasmine can't hear Preston, but she can see his lips moving, repeating the chorus, even as they strap him into the back of the squad car, as his John Lennon wig drops and is swept across the lot with yellow and orange leaves, candy wrappers, and fast-food garbage. It's a pinwheel of color through kaleidascope eyes.

Beautiful Jasmine. Sweet Jasmine. You know why the fat lady sings.

THE END

ACKNOWLEDGMENTS

Key events in this book are based on an original story my father told me years ago, a tale that can also be found in his "Benton County" books. That story in Chapter 9 about Tick Godwin imitating a dwarf at dance clubs, that's also his. He recalls that as a child in the 1950s:

> On Saturday night we would go to Pensacola with other adults to clubs. They would dress me in my Sunday suit with bow tie. Mama would say if they ask you how old you are, tell them that you are a midget. I had a corncob pipe to enhance the effect. I got Shirley Temple drinks. I usually went to sleep in a booth listening to the band.

Uh, thanks dad! I am much obliged to Madison Jones, Adam Roberts, and Kimberly Wright for their diligent readings and re-readings of my work in our longstanding workshop. Thanks also to Addy Herron, Susan Martin, Steve Forrester and countless others who have helped me with this project. In this novel, you'll find numerous references, quotes, and mentions of art, music, cookbooks, and movies. Books quoted include *The Real Mother Goose* and Rena Salaman's *Healthy Mediterranean Cooking* with references to Titian's *Pastoral Concert*, Cezanne's *A Modern Olympia*, and the Venus of Willendorf. A lively pastiche of the "squeal like a pig" scene from the movie *Deliverance* is also included in these pages. Characters in this book sometimes break into song, including Preston's squeaky rendition of Lefty Frizzell's "The Long Black Veil" and Jasmine's brainwash-busting recitation of Lee Greenwood's "God Bless the USA." Lionel Richie's "Say You, Say Me" and "This Time Tomorrow" by the Kinks can be found here, as can riffs on Howlin' Wolf and the Oak Ridge Boys. Referenced occasionally are the songs and physiognomy of Elvis Presley as well as too many Beatles lyrics to count. Special thanks to my wife Kelly, daughter Lily, Cousin Charlie Franco, cover designer MaDora Frey, photographer Tonia Eden Mayton, and the cat.

AUTHOR BIO

A child of the Alabama backwoods, Lee Rozelle was often cared for by Miss Mamie, an old woman in a farm bonnet who shucked corn, shelled peas, used an outhouse, and chopped the heads off chickens without much ado. When Lee was school-age, his mother worked at a daycare facility for people with intellectual disabilities, and he spent time there, too. These experiences combined with Lee's ardent childhood desire to become a ventriloquist shaped his artistic vision. Lee is the author of nonfiction books *Zombiescapes & Phantom Zones* and *Ecosublime*. He has published stories in *Cosmic Horror Monthly*, *Southern Humanities Review*, HellBound Books' *Anthology of Bizarro*, *If I Die Before I Wake* vol. 3, *Shadowy Natures* by Dark Ink Books, *Steel Toe Review*, *Dark Dossier Magazine*, *Pattern Recognition* #5, and the *Scare You to Sleep* podcast.

leerozelle.com